I0767933

ALSO BY BEKKAH FRISCH

The Great Quiet

SHAPE OF OURSELVES

A NOVEL

BEKKAH FRISCH

Bombus Books, LLC
Fulton, NY: 2025

Bombus Books, LLC
P.O. Box 343
Fulton, NY 13069

ISBN: 979-8-9877421-3-6 (eBook); 979-8-9877421-2-9 (paperback)

Trigger Warnings

This book may be difficult for readers with specific past experiences to enjoy. Please be forewarned that there are descriptions of: grooming behavior, allusions to childhood sexual abuse and childhood physical abuse, descriptions and allusions to suicidal ideation and completion, as well as emotional abuse of a disabled character.

CONTENTS

*To every woman who has stepped into her power
with kindness and empathy.
To Gary, for encouraging me to step into mine.*

*Author's Note: The Yugambeh people use multiple
names for themselves and strongly believe that the
Western practice of only using one name simplifies
their complex nation's identity. To honor this, readers
will see the people referred to as both the Yugambeh
and the Minyangbal.*

Chapter 1: Memories from Another Life

"For the first time since the rating was introduced a decade ago, the Greater Sydney region has been declared at catastrophic fire danger. The news comes as bushfires rage across New South Wales—"

The grim details of the reporter's story are silenced when Pania hobbles over to turn off the TV. She stares at the blank screen, leaning heavily on her cane. Bushfires in the south. As if she wants to think about that. Her eyes flicker over the bird-shaped birthmark on her upper arm; how many species will breathe their last in the devastation?

Instead of dwelling on the news, Pania works a pair of sneakers onto her size 11 feet and begins the slow descent from her one-bedroom unit on the second floor to the streets of Coolangatta. Her trackie pants *swoosh* as she moves, and the sound brings the ghost of a smile to her full lips. She shakes her head in an attempt to rid herself of all these mental distractions. It's almost time for the meeting. Time to focus on the problems at hand.

\#

"You already had your turn," Pania says, putting up a hand to silence the new guy, some blondie with absolutely no clue. And the bar is set pretty low for that here. She has to make a conscious effort not to roll her eyes. The hospital cafeteria has hosted her along with a motley assortment of other folks with traumatic brain injuries every Tuesday for the past five years to "provide person-centered supports." In that time, plenty of clueless victims—*err, survivors*, she corrects herself— have sat in this circle of chairs.

"I did?" Blondie asks, genuinely confused. Sam, the neurology resident running the group, murmurs her confirmation from behind a laptop. "Oh," he says, deflated.

A lot of faces come and go, and Pania can already tell Mr. Memory Loss isn't going to be here long either. Hard to benefit from a group you can't remember anything about, even if Sam pretends her flurry of papers makes a difference.

"Lin, what were you saying about your son?" Pania asks, nudging the woman next to her gently.

But Lin appears to have lost her nerve. Instead of continuing her story, she lowers her gaze to Blondie's shoes and whispers something so quietly Pania doubts even Lin herself can hear it.

"Speak up, would ya? My ears aren't what they used to be," Pania prods. "Besides, poor Robert over there doesn't even know what's going on." She gestures to the older man in flannel sitting across from her, oxygen mask clicking out its two-step rhythm. Robert is the only one who's come to this group as long as she has. The two of them were among the first brain injury patients to start the TBI support group.

"I said he can go," Lin says, her voice trembling a bit.

At this, Blondie softens. "No, no, I want to hear about your son. Even if I won't remember it twenty minutes from now."

An uneasy silence falls over the circle, broken only by Robert's oxygen and the clanking of dishes somewhere behind the cafeteria counter.

"He keeps saying I'm not the same, even when I'm just running the vacuum or walking him to school," Lin finally admits weakly, delicate hands folded primly in her lap. "That's exactly what his father said before he left." She pauses and clears her throat. Her eyes are still on Blondie's shoes when she murmurs, "I don't want to lose him too."

Sam lets a moment of quiet pass before saying, "Thank you for sharing that about your son, Meiling. It's very common for family members to say TBI survivors are different after their injury. Has anyone else in the group experienced this?"

Blondie slowly raises his hand. "In case anyone forgot, I'm Tim. And, I mean, obviously people say I'm different. I don't even remember my girlfriend, and she complains about that all the time. But—" he cuts himself short. Sam quickly reminds him of his train of thought. "Thing is, I feel like I'm the same person and everyone else has changed. Sometimes, I think they're only pretending that I'm different."

"Lin, what's your take on that?" Pania asks.

The diminutive woman shakes her head slowly. Her bangs fall over her dark brown eyes.

"Does anyone have tips for dealing with this reaction from family members?" Sam asks.

Robert pulls back his oxygen mask. "Ask them what changes are bothering them. I stopped eating meat shortly after the accident. Something about it just tasted sour to me. But my partner took it personal, like it was his cooking or something."

"Did talking about it help?" Blondie (*Tim, call him Tim,* Pania reminds herself) asks.

"Oh sure. But it's easier to smooth over diet preferences than other things."

"That's very true," Sam says. "Before you talk to family members about differences in your personality or habits,

I'd suggest you mentally prepare yourself. Could be a really hard conversation."

"I'll say," Pania replies. "Sounds exhausting." She takes a moment to be grateful that's not something she'll ever have to worry about.

Of course, it wouldn't have been bad with Sal. They only knew hard times when they knew each other, and that didn't stop them from being close... until it did. Even now, thinking the name sends a shiver crawling across her neck, like a spider waiting to strike.

\#

Pania's favorite routine was their walk home from school, when they roasted their foster families or their classmates, or sometimes both. The school was really just a glorified shack on the edge of town with two teachers: one for the younger students and then Miss Altro for older students like themselves. Most people sent their kids out of the area for boarding school, so Pania's classmates were by and large fosters too.

"Photo time!" Sal exclaimed, pulling a disposable camera out of her bag before Pania could get started on the jokes.

"Ugh, again?" Despite giving her new girlfriend a hard time over it, Pania secretly loved the amount of photos Sal already amassed since they became official last week. The envelope of prints from the first camera they'd filled was still sticking out of Sal's bag. "How many photos of us do you need?" Pania asked after the camera had clicked and flashed enough to satisfy Sal.

"What can I say? I like looking at you and me together," Sal replied. Light and mischief shone in her eyes.

"Alright, alright," Pania said with a bashful smile. "Now. Chicken or egg question. You think Paul has a drinking problem because of Lizzy's bad moods, or you think Lizzy's bad moods are because of Paul's drinking problem?"

Sal snorted. "Dude, now that's what I call two people who were meant for each other—if only to save the rest of humanity from having to date them." Pania laughs in appreciation, then motions for Sal to go on. "Okay, um, meanwhile, my foster mom thinks I'm so dumb, I wouldn't think to add grape juice to her wine after I steal some... and you know, I'm kinda glad. Makes it a helluva lot easier to get toasty when my room gets cold in the winter. Or when Kevin gets in one of his bad moods and I don't wanna care anymore."

"Save some for me sometime, will ya?"

"Oh, you bet." Sal turned and looked around to see if they were alone, and then asked in a lowered voice, "Hey, by the way, how often does Lizzy take out her bad moods on you?"

"What are you, my new child protection officer?"

"Haha, very funny," she intoned. Her smile faded and she tugged at the bottom of her shirt uneasily. "Just curious, is all."

Pania thought back to their first kiss, just a few weeks before. How Sal had shrunk from her touch when she'd dared let her hands wander. How she kept her shoulders and arms covered at all times like some kind of nun, even when they headed to the creek to swim.

She squeezed her girlfriend's hand, hoping to communicate she understood. There were no more jokes to be shared on that particular walk.

#

Pania rubs her neck to scare away the goosebumps before anyone notices them, and Sam looks pointedly her way.

"Does anyone else want to share?"

Tim repeats the story of forgetting his girlfriend Jenny for the third time in a row. *Oh Blondie. How much is this really gonna help you?*

When Tim is finished, Sam hands out a few sheets filled with brain teasers, crossword puzzles, and even a few Sudoku. "For anyone struggling with memory, these types of activities can help improve short-term and working memory. Other activities that can help are listening to music you enjoy, socializing with friends, and, believe it or not, even dancing." Her smile is sly, as though she'd suggested they go smoke weed behind the hospital instead of simply move their bodies around to some beats.

"Dancing..." Tim mumbles something unintelligible to himself. Looking up from his paper, he asks, "Hey, can I borrow your pen? I like those suggestions."

Sam winks and points at the sheet on his lap. "They're already printed on the back."

"Sweet!"

The resident re-adjusts in her chair, as if to say, *Well that's settled.* Taking in the rest of the room, she dutifully asks again, "Anyone else want to share?"

The others shake their heads, so she continues, "Great work, everyone. I'll grab the rest of today's meeting notes from the printer and then we can break until next time."

Lin rushes through the open double doors of the cafeteria and then ducks into the ladies' room off the hallway, hand held protectively over her face. Pania hobbles behind her, cursing her unbalanced body for being so slow.

Muted sounds carry through the thick wooden door when she reaches it. Pania sighs and then opens it.

Her friend is nearly doubled over facing the line of stalls. But it quickly becomes clear that Lin isn't crying. Her shrieks are angry and the few words in her native Chinese. In Pania's surprise, her cane scrapes harshly against the gray tiles.

In seconds, Lin's demeanor is tightly controlled. She stands up straight. Runs a few fingers through her pin-straight hair. But the small smile she pastes on her lips doesn't quite extinguish the fire in her eyes.

"I didn't mean to startle you," Pania stammers. "Thought you might need a friend."

The smile wavers. "I'm fine," Lin responds. "Impulse control issues, you know?"

That's right. Part of Lin's injury, though something she doesn't like to talk about.

"Uh-huh." Pania rubs her thumb along her cane to calm her nerves. "Well, if you need anything..."

"I'm fine," she repeats. "I'm just so over hearing about Jenny and her—" she pauses to make air quotes, "*so not sexy* pajamas." Lin rolls her eyes at the detail the newbie had shared three times over the course of the meeting.

"As long as you're good," Pania replies with a half-smile.

"Right." Two final words from her friend reach her as she turns to go: "Thank you."

Chapter 2: Heartbreak by Post

Lin glances at the bedside clock. 3:12AM. She sighs. It's nearly impossible for her to sleep well now that she's sleeping alone. Though, truth be told, her circadian rhythm hasn't been normal since the accident.

The sheets are twisted from all the tossing and turning, so she kicks them off and heads downstairs for a glass of water.

She doesn't bother with lights, instead relying on moonlight. Despite her exhaustion, she still finds pleasure moving in the darkness. For two full years, her balance was too off-kilter to walk in moonlight or even the shadows of dusk and dawn. It may be a tiny victory, but it's one she clings to.

Her movement on the stairs startles something. Another house gecko, probably. A slender, dark body crawls along the wall and disappears behind a picture frame.

The picture might be shrouded in shadows, but it still gives her pause. It's a print from the last family vacation they all went on together: her, Jian, Huan. A mere three weeks before everything changed. They were visiting the Bell Tower of Xi'an, and Jian was holding her hand outside of the camera's view, behind their son's back. The pressure of his sticky hand on hers had reminded her of the old saying: hold hands with you, grow old with you.

Then again, maybe not too old, Lin thinks now. She steps heavily onto the living room floor and heads to the fridge, trying not to think about how rare those sweet gestures had been, even back then.

"Really?" she says to herself. The counter is littered with shredded cheese from what must have been Huan's midnight snack. "After all I do for him, this is what I get." Her voice is louder and sharper than she intends as she sweeps the cheese into her hand. "UGH!" A dob of vegemite sticks to the side of her palm.

Huan's mumble reaches her from the next room. "You okay, Mum?"

"Oh, I'm great," she snaps back, too tired to be polite. "Just great."

He shuffles into the kitchen and flips on the light. His blue pajamas are dotted with the same vegemite that she's aggressively scrubbing off her hand. The sight of it annoys her, but she tries to hold it in.

He sighs, then gathers himself with a deep breath. "Need me to get you anything?"

"A maid might be nice. They could follow you around and save me all sorts of trouble." She tries to make light of the moment, but he's too sleepy to play along. She gives him a good-natured poke with a soapy index finger.

"Mhm. Well, I'm going back to bed." He turns, muttering something under his breath. Her ears don't quite catch the words, but the tone is clear enough.

I can't even get a glass of water without bothering someone, she thinks, wondering what she did wrong this time. Next to the stairs, their idyllic family photo taunts her from underneath its cover of darkness.

#

The next morning, a knock on the door startles her out of the nap she'd unintentionally taken on the living room sofa. "Hold on," she hollers.

The stairs reach up and grab at her feet as she stumbles up to the bedroom for her housecoat.

Wrapping it tightly around her thin frame, she rushes back down to the door.

"Good morning, Mrs. Meiling. I have a package for you."

Lin looks over the postie on her doorstep. He looks barely older than Huan, though she knows he must be at least in his twenties. His motor bike is parked next to the neighbor's mail box, and she wonders how many tries it took him to get so perfectly parallel with the curb. If only he'd put half as much thought into identifying her surname. "Meiling is my first name, not my family name," she says coldly. "Do I have to sign for it?"

The boy reddens at her words and looks at the package again. "Sorry, Mrs. Lee. No, it just—just didn't fit in your mail box. Didn't want it getting lost."

A family law firm is listed in the return address. "Of course not," she mumbles as she takes the crumpled manila envelope. The weight of the papers inside presses against her palm with the heft of a shared lifetime. She sinks to the floor, dust from the threshold rubbing into her soft yellow lounge pants.

At her first sob, Huan stirs in his bedroom. "Mum, are you all right?"

The postie leaves the door open and backs down the sidewalk as though she's a wounded animal ready to strike. His shaky "g'day" doesn't reach Lin any more than Huan's questions. No one can reach her now.

#

They had met at university, where Meiling had gone for a better education than her hometown could provide. Jian was there following his father's wishes, studying economics. The two fell in love over a set of equations neither could solve.

The courtship had been wonderful. But as graduation drew closer, a knot grew in the deepest pits of her stomach. *What will Niáng think?* Her mother's marriage to Bàba had been arranged by the village matchmaker, and their parents' marriage before them. All of Niáng and Bàba's friends and their friends' children relied on the matchmaker too. *If they don't approve of Jian...*

She and Jian agreed that they had to avoid shocking her parents with their unsanctioned dating. Doing so would almost certainly doom their chance at a happy union. So, she returned home alone and Jian came separately a few weeks later to ask the matchmaker for her hand. Perhaps it had to do with the flashy gold watch on his wrist, but the elderly woman readily agreed to their match.

"I think the two of them will be perfect for each other," the matchmaker relayed to her parents the day after Jian's visit. "He sends his greatest respects to the people who raised Meiling, and gifts to thank you for the privilege of having schooled with her." Outside, several new appliances were stacked in her hand cart. An invitation for tea was dispatched immediately, and their marriage was agreed upon by the end of the week.

Not only had Meiling been able to follow her heart to university and an honest man she loved, she had done so without bruising her parents' sensitivities or raising too many eyebrows in the village. Her life felt like one series of victories after another.

#

But none of that matters now. Lin rolls her shoulders a couple of times from her spot on the couch, attempting to assuage the worry apparent on Huan's face.

"I'm fine, really." Lin tries to sound insistent, but her feeble voice betrays her.

"It's okay if you're not okay," he replies. He's kneeling in front of her, ever the respectful son.

She smiles. "Wise words, my child." Gesturing to the paperwork, she asks, "Did you know?"

"Yes and no," he replies uneasily. "I mean, he didn't say anything about it to me, but Dad hasn't been here in weeks. What did you expect to happen?"

Her hopes that Jian would return seem childish to her now. She sobs into her son's strong shoulders, glad she wasn't alone when the envelope arrived.

Just as she's wiping the tears on her housecoat sleeve, her cell phone rings up in the bedroom.

"I'll go grab it," Huan offers and lumbers up the stairs. When he returns, he hands her the phone without a word.

"Hello?"

It's the school.

"Oh, um, my apologies," she says. "I needed him to help me on some errands this morning and I forgot to send in a note. Yes, yes, we're finished now. He'll be there in time for his next class."

Her cheeks flush with the teensiest bit of pink. "The school."

"I know." His voice is toneless, flat. "That's the third time this month."

"You don't have to stay next time," she offers.

He keeps his tone neutral, but she can feel the annoyance behind his words. "Do you mean the next time you're crying in the doorway for the whole neighborhood to see, or the next time you throw things across the room because of a chatty maggie?"

Lin sighs and tucks a few strands of hair behind her ear. "Right."

"Make sure you go to group tonight," he says. "I can't help you, but maybe they can." With that, he disappears into his bedroom to get ready for school.

"No promises," she whispers, "But I'll try."

That night, the new kid is complaining about his girlfriend again. While Lin has no interest in opening up to the group about her love life, the words are out before she can stop them.

"At least she's trying to work with you. My husband of eighteen years served me papers this morning... he didn't even tell me himself that's what he wanted. He let the damn postie do it."

Tim winces. "I'm so sorry to hear that. What are you going to do?"

"Guess I'm getting a divorce."

Chapter 3: Dancing with the Lights Off

"Hey Tee, what kind of day are we having?" Jenny asks when Tim tumbles into the kitchen the next morning.

"What'd'ya mean?" Tim asks, cracking a smile. "Last night wasn't enough for ya?"

Jenny smiles into her coffee mug, her caramel brown eyes twinkling. "So, you remember me today? That's a good sign."

"Oh come on, Jenny. Why wouldn't I?"

She sighs. "Great."

"What?"

"It's almost funny. You forgot about your memory problems again, didn't you?"

"Is this a joke?"

"That accident was no joke."

"Wait, accident? Is Brian okay?" Instinctively, he pats himself down and looks for his phone to check on his best friend. They go just about everywhere together.

"Don't worry, Brian's fine," she reassures him. "Or at least, he was the last I heard. It was you who had the accident, showing off on one of those wild four-wheeler trails."

"Psh, I know what I'm doing on those trails." He feigns arrogance, hoping his smile comes off as natural instead of nervous. Instead of meeting her eyes, he takes in the coffee mug, the plates with sausage and scrambled eggs, the crumpled napkin. *Looks like every other morning, but sure doesn't feel that way.* "And what do you mean about Brian being fine last you heard? When was the last time we saw him?"

"It's..." She sighs. "It's been a while. He feels guilty or maybe freaked out about your accident, I think. These things take time to process."

14

"Oh." He runs a hand through his hair, a nervous tic he's had for years, and then takes a seat next to Jenny.

"Relax, Tee," she replies, patting his hand. "We've had this conversation at least a dozen times since the accident."

"We—we have?" His eyes flick back to meet her chocolate brown ones, to take in her freckled nose and slightly sunburnt cheeks.

"Mhm. And it's not a big deal if you're scared. Check the memory downloads on your notes app."

"Memory downloads?"

"Hey, you came up with the name." Jenny giggles.

"And how can I be sure of that?" he teases.

"Maybe it's in there somewhere, eh?"

"Only one way to find out," he replies, pulling his phone out of his athletic shorts.

"When you're done with your *download*—" Jenny air-quotes the word playfully, "let me know what you wanna do tonight. After all, it's Friday, and I'm playing hooky."

"Oh, I love it when you play hooky." He winks, trying to maintain this sense of normalcy before delving into whatever chaos awaits.

Jenny giggles. "Not another word until you're done. Now let me enjoy my coffee, wouldja?"

"Fine, but I already know what I wanna do tonight," he says with another grin.

"I'm gonna have to feed you to shut you up, aren't I?"

"You know it. Now pass me that sausage."

As Jenny slides the plate over the rickety wooden table, she smirks. "Not. One. Word."

"Wouldn't dream of it, babe." As he scarfs down his breakfast, he skims through his notes. *Oh god, where do I even start?* There must be dozens of items in there, with labels like *Forgot Jenny* and *Tuesdays are Group Night*. Out of curiosity, he opens one labeled *Forgot what Miriam did*. All it says is: *You lucky bastard.* He smiles to himself. *Gotta be the only win in here, so I'm gonna take it.*

Going back to the list, he sees one about forgetting the accident. He breathes a sigh of relief, but then his mood deflates as he uncovers the truth about his brain... and as he realizes how many times he must have already uncovered this truth, and how many more times he'll have to uncover it again.

"What a way to start the day, huh?" he jokes.

"Sorry," Jenny replies with a small shrug. "Last time you forgot the accident, you said that's how you wanted to handle it. Said you wanted to rip the bandage off and get on with it."

"If I could go back in time, I'd smack myself," he grumbles.

"If only you could," Jenny echoes. He's about to make a joke in response, but she's staring off into space. Following her eyes, he takes in the kitchen's familiar navy-blue walls and the worn faux wood cupboards. Wordlessly, he reaches for the carafe and refills his coffee cup.

The day may have gotten off to a somber start, but Tim refuses to let an accident that happened months ago ruin his weekend.

"I forget you sometimes, right?" he asks her as they wash up the dishes together.

"More often than I'd like, that's for sure," she replies, bumping her hip against his.

"Then let's do something fun tonight, you and me. To make up for all the date nights we've missed out on in the past year." He boops her nose to lighten the mood.

"What d'you have in mind?"

"Let's head to the club, go dancing. I'll get you one of those drinks with the little umbrella in it, your favorite ones—ugh, the name's on the tip of my tongue—and anyway, we can invite some couple friends if we still have those. It'll be great. Whatcha say?"

Her eyes light up as she sets clean forks in the strainer to dry. "Yeah, okay."

#

According to Jenny, they haven't gone dancing since before the accident, but Tim's finding that hard to believe. After all, they go to the Snake Den almost every weekend—or at least, they did up until his memories go blank. *How could he have become such a snooze fest?*

"My legs do still work, yanno," he yells through the flat as she's getting ready.

"Well yeah, but we've been cautious about the flashing lights in case you get seizures, Tee. Kinda takes the fun out of going to the club." She pokes her head around the corner into the living room where he's waiting. "Besides, you were super dizzy all the time for a while... couldn't even consider dancing until you sorted through your balance issues."

"That was then, this is now. How will we find out if the lights bother me if we don't even try? Can't go around avoiding everything forever."

"Now that your leg is out of the boot, your balance is back, and you're physically healthy again—other than that uncooperative brain of yours—I'm inclined to agree with you." She keeps her body hidden behind the corner. When she speaks again, she shakes a finger at him to emphasize her words. "But don't think I'm gonna let you drink. It makes your memory so much worse."

"Long as I get to dance with you, I don't care." He's dressed in his favorite khaki-colored pants and a loose-fitting blue Henley, the top two buttons left playfully undone. His favorite cologne fills the air with the scent of bergamot and vanilla. "I clean up good, right?"

She looks him up and down and winks. "Yeah, you do. Now give me five. Just need to finish setting this hair and put in my earrings."

He perches on the arm of the couch, scrolling through his social, amazed at how much his exes have changed in the past year. His finger slips and he hearts an old photo. *Oh shit, oh shit.* Jenny comes back out, and he closes the app as casually as he can. He'll have to un-heart it later.

When he looks up, he lets out a low whistle. Jenny's wearing a dazzling green dress that hugs her curves. Her curled hair has been teased into an artfully messy updo. "Let's go, sexy lady." He opens the door for her and gives an exaggerated bow. "After you."

At the club, it's as though a celebrity's risen from the dead. The bouncers high-five him on the way in, the bartender gives both of them free drinks, and it feels as though the entire crowd is staring at them. "We're back, baby," he yells, getting a cheer from the crowd of strangers.

Jenny clinks his glass of Coke. "You bet your ass we're back."

Tim might not recognize most of the songs the DJ's playing, but the beats are still the same. He tries to put the morning out of his mind and focus on Jenny, who's on fire on the dance floor. *She's fun, she's gorgeous, and she's going home with me. How crazy is that?*

He spends the rest of the night just trying to keep up.

Even when they get home, Jenny wants to keep dancing. So, they sway together in the dark of their bedroom until she finally collapses on the bed in exhaustion.

#

The next morning comes all too fast. Tim rolls over to face Jenny and he tucks some of her messy curls behind her ear. "How come I feel so shitty when I didn't even drink?"

She grins. "Two good memory days in a row? Be glad all it cost you is feeling a little hung-over."

"I definitely wouldn't wanna forget such an amazing night." He scooches closer and kisses her nose. "And hey, now we know that flashing lights aren't going to make me seize up. So, we can make this more of a habit again, right?"

"Maybe." Her voice is hopeful. "But it really depends on you, my dear. I'm not taking you anywhere on a bad memory day."

"Why not?" he asks, pretending to be indignant.

"Because if we get separated, I never know if you're gonna forget your own name or catch an Uber home."

He gives her his most charming half-smile. He can't think of a good comeback, so he turns to his phone's notes app to catch up on anything he might have forgotten. The note about Miriam gives him pause. What could be so bad that he's lucky to have forgotten? Other notes in her contact info give him a sense of how deep the betrayal runs. A knot in the pit of his stomach suggests visceral, emotional memory, even if the specifics elude him.

Before he can process what wounds are lying in his past, forgotten, his phone vibrates on the nightstand behind him.

"Yeah, hello?" He instantly regrets having answered before looking at the number when he hears his mother's voice.

"Tim, how are you today?" the woman gushes.

"Don't fuckin' call me. You know I'm not speaking to you."

"Do I? We caught up for over an hour on Tuesday. Besides, I'm your mother, I'll never give up on you." Her tone takes on a snippy edge. Based on some of the things he's read, Tim's mentally preparing himself for a volley of guilt trips.

Before she can get started, he interjects. "My accident is not a weakness for you to prey on. Guess you've been working on getting even more manipulative, huh, Miriam?"

She huffs. "Look, what happened was terrible but—"

"Don't you dare finish that sentence." He shouts into the phone, "Now go to hell!"

#

Mum was sitting in the kitchen and picking at the dead skin on her thumbs. Her lunch plate sat on the table next to her, littered with castoff crumbs and a dab of mayonnaise. "Hey, you know where the charging cord is for my 3DS?" Tim asked.

"No clue, kiddo," she said without looking up. "Bout time you took a break from that thing anyway. Why don't you go help Phil in the greenhouse for the afternoon?"

"What about my charger?"

She sighed. Her breath blew a piece of her curly brown hair off her nose. "Where'd you see it last?"

"I dunno." Tim shrugged. "Living room, I think."

"I'll take a look around for it," she said. She didn't move. "Now skedaddle."

"Fine." Phil was her latest, and longest-lasting boyfriend, since Dad ran off. Tim hated dealing with the plants, but at least Phil was cool. Didn't make him work too hard.

He wandered outside, screen door clacking behind him. The wind picked up, and he hurried across the yard to get out of the cold.

"Hey Phil. Mum kicked me outta the house. Whatcha got going on in here?"

Phil looked up from the pallet table, where he had a mound of dirt and a bunch of droopy little plants. He pushed on his glasses. A clump of dirt was stuck to his nose. "Just transplanting these tomatoes. Sure could use a hand."

"Yeah, okay," he replied as he shuffled over.

"Hey now, don't sound so glum. Tomatoes are a lot harder to kill than the strawberries you were helping me with last week."

Tim rolled his eyes. "Sure, whatever."

Phil talked him through the steps, cheerily divvying up the homeless tomatoes and the planting trays spread out over the table.

"Seems like a waste of time," Tim remarked once they'd gotten into a rhythm. "Why not just plant 'em in the bigger trays to begin with?"

Phil leaned in and pointed at the tiny roots on the plant Tim was holding up. "Every time you transplant tomatoes, you bury 'em a little deeper and the root system'll expand, start coming out of the bottom of the stem." The man's fingers brushed over the stem as he talked, alighting briefly on Tim's knuckles. "Helps keep the plants from tipping over once they're loaded with fruit."

"Huh."

They worked in silence for an hour or two more, and then Tim's stomach started grumbling, much to Phil's amusement. "Sure are a growing boy," he said with a laugh. Then, conspiratorially, he whispered, "Hey, can you keep a secret?"

Tim barely ever did anything worth hiding to know for sure, but he wanted to impress Phil. "I'm fifteen. Duh, dude."

The older man cracked a smile and slide out a box from under the table. "Don't tell a soul. Especially not your mum." Underneath some baggies of dried herbs, there were boxes of Tim Tams and bags of Cheezels.

"Yeeessssss! Wait, why wouldn't I..."

"That's not oregano, buddy."

Oh. OH. "I'll keep your secret, but I'm gonna need some of those biscuits."

He pulled out an open box and slid it across the table towards the boy. "Deal."

The only bummer was not being able to lick the chocolate off his fingers without getting a bit of dirt to go with it. *"Puh!* Remind me to wear gloves next time so I don't ruin my hands for Tim Tams."

"Ha! Will do," Phil responded.

Tim wiped his hands aggressively against his cargo shorts. "Now pass me a bag of those Cheezels."

"You got it."

Chapter 4: Casual but not Cool

Pania heads to the bistro for an early dinner with Auntie Elaine. Just as Pania suspects, they spend most of the meal talking about the community garden they help care for, which is eternally short on volunteers.

"I found half a dozen tomatoes rotting right on the vine this morning," Elaine says with a groan. "That never would've happened when Margo and Joe were here. They'd have found someone who could've used them."

Of course, anyone can just grab a tomato straight off the plant anytime they need one. Still, this is one of Elaine's favorite gripes and not one she wants to bicker over now, so she holds her tongue. The point still stands, after all. Even before Margo and Joe left on their trip through the hinterland, it was a struggle to keep up. Between keeping weeds at bay, thinning out the overcrowded squash, harvesting and re-staking the tomato plants, and a host of other tasks, it's quite a commitment to keep the gardens and park a refuge for the community—and it requires time most of the Minyangbal people in Pania's circle simply don't have.

Pania leans heavily on her cane as she makes her way out of the restaurant, a poignant reminder of how unreliable her own ability to care for the gardens can be. It's still early to go to group, but she doesn't want balance issues to make her late. Her body has been unpredictable today.

"Thank you," Pania says to the bikini-clad young woman holding the door for her.

"Whatever," she replies with a roll of her eyes.

"Excuse me?"

The woman's eyes flick over her cane. "I saw you walk in here without it."

"It's not that simple, I—"

"Sure, it isn't." The woman winks and then struts off down the street, as if daring Pania to chase after her.

Pania sighs. Maybe she should just go home. Left to the hospital, or right to go back to the unit... After a long pause, her feet move left.

Lin needs support, and Pania's not sure the woman will be able to get what she needs from Timmy boy or the ever-clinical Sam. They don't have the inside scoop on unexpected losses. Not the way Pania does.

That night, Robert was absent from the circle of chairs. "Has anyone heard from him?" Sam asks the group. "He didn't mention having family in, and I know he lives alone."

"Don't worry about him," Pania says, "he never goes anywhere on Boxing Day. He'll be back next week."

"What's so bad about Boxing Day?" asks Timmy, knocking frantically on the faux wood of the cafeteria tabletop as though it could save him.

"It's a personal thing, and I don't know that Robert would like us all talking about him while he's not here."

"Oh, of course," Timmy replies. As Sam rifles through her notes from last time, he asks, "Hey, where's the guy in the oxygen mask?"

Lin snaps, "It's the anniversary of when his partner died. Give the poor man some space."

Sam's professional smile gives way to a professional frown. "That's terrible. I didn't know."

"Well, if you'd been here when it happened, trust me when I say you'd never forget."

#

The day had been brutally hot, and all of the group's regulars and not-so-regulars seemed to show up early to take advantage of the air-conditioned cafeteria free of in-laws and over-stimulated children. At first, the young resident running the group had been ecstatic to see so many faces on a holiday week, but it quickly became clear none of them were there to talk beyond a murmur of vague *"mhms"* in response to his well-planned conversation starters.

When the oldest person in the group had to answer his ringing phone, the annoyance was clear on the resident's face. He was too busy grumbling under his breath to notice as the man's calm demeanor was replaced with anguish, his wrinkled face taking on a terrible gray hue.

He rushed to leave, but his foot caught on one of the folding chairs and sent him reeling onto the floor. The resident snapped into action to help him up and called for a nurse to take him down to emergency to check on his bleeding nose.

The man accepted the help, insisting as he left that she takes him directly to his partner, who had just been admitted with a suspected heat stroke.

"I'm coming, Michael." His words echoed down the hallway, back to the group, whose members fell more silent than ever.

#

The next week, Robert is back in the group's small circle of chairs, almost as though nothing had happened. He nods sympathetically, shaggy white hair falling over his eyes, as the others discuss both the big and small challenges of invisible disability. His pale wrinkled hand rests comfortingly on Tim's knee as the boy recounts the harassment that he received the first time he and his girlfriend parked in a disability spot. "We've all been there," Robert says. "Luckily they don't bother me now that I'm older and always on the tank." He pats the tinny oxygen tank parked next to his chair.

Across from him, Pania chimes in, "Wonder when I'll get my turn. I think being First Nations adds another ten years before people accept I've earned the accommodations I use. I don't drive, but you should see the stares I get on the bus."

In the sympathetic silence that follows, Sam says softly, "It is very difficult, isn't it? I'm sorry you go through that, Pania."

"Thanks," Pania replies. *And you're welcome for the education.* Sam wouldn't know a thing about the trouble with racism in this country if Pania wasn't there to tell her.

Lin begins her turn with a sigh and a wet twinkle in her eye. Robert leans forward and gives her his full attention.

"Huan's such a great kid," Lin says. Her chair scrapes along the linoleum as she shifts away from Pania, towards the empty chair on her left. "I wish he understood how hard I work to show him that. He deserves better than what I can give him."

"Every parent feels like that sometimes," Sam replies in her best reassuring voice from her spot across the circle. "That just means you care about him. You're a good mum." She makes a note of something on her laptop.

Probably about how helpful she's being. Pania struggles not to roll her deep brown eyes at just how clueless the privileged young resident could be about... well, everything.

"It's not normal parent guilt. You don't understand." Lin pauses for a second. "You don't have children, do you Sam?"

"Well, no," Sam replies uneasily.

The look on Lin's face says, *Gotcha.*

"And you don't have a neurological disorder affecting impulse control?"

Sam sighs. "No."

"Then you can't pretend this is normal parent guilt, okay?" Lin's face changes after her snapback. It's almost as though she's trying to hold her breath after being underwater too long.

Lin's forehead wrinkles as she says, "I just did it again, didn't I? Was that too mean?" Before anyone can answer, she says, "This is exactly what I do to Huan! And I never mean it but it keeps happening." Her eyes fill with tears.

Tim is quick to speak up. "Before I forget, I wanna tell you I understand. I've been accidentally doing stuff like this to my mum all the time too." He barely pauses to breathe, rushing to stay ahead of his fading memory, eyes on his phone instead of the group. "Apparently, we had some huge falling out, and some days I remember and some days I don't. My girlfriend keeps warning me not to call her, and I have notes all over my phone and her contact info... but you know how it is. When you want to talk to your mum, you just call your mum."

"Sounds like you didn't have much a relationship to ruin, at least," Lin says sarcastically.

"It sure doesn't feel that way on the days I don't remember. When she picks up and all she does is cry because she misses hearing my voice. You have any idea how shitty that makes me feel?"

Lin face palms her forehead, looking frustrated that she snapped. Sam focuses intently on the interaction, but she lets the group navigate the conversation on their own.

"What about the days when you do remember?" Robert asks.

Tim looks back down at his phone. "Apparently those are worse, cuz what she did makes me feel even shittier than those phone calls."

"I'm sorry to hear that," Lin says meekly. "And I'm sorry I wasn't a little more sensitive. Sounds like a lose-lose situation."

"You ain't kidding. But wait, how did we get on this conversation?"

Sam pipes up. "We were talking about Lin's son, Huan. And for the record, Lin, you don't need to worry about being too mean to me and hurting my feelings. It's an injury, and it's not your fault."

"Yeah, your son," Tim interjects, slapping his hands against his worn jeans. "You should do something together, reconnect over his hobbies."

"Good idea," Robert says. "What kinds of things is he into? Robotics club? Maths? Maybe you could tour a few universities together."

Lin puts her hands on her thighs and leans towards Robert, her demeanor alone enough to shut Robert down. "Are you saying those things because I'm Chinese? He's a typical teenager." She rolls her eyes. "He likes playing squash and watching cricket, heading to the beach with his mates. Who knows, he might even like girls, but he'd never tell me."

"Why don't you think he'd tell you?" Sam asks, laptop humming as she types.

This time, Pania speaks up. "Did you tell your parents when you had the hots for somebody?"

Sam blushes a bit. "Point taken. Still, do you think he's able to confide in you when he needs advice or a listening ear?"

"It was better before the accident," Lin says. "But I can't say I blame him if he doesn't trust me now. I don't exactly keep my mouth shut the way I used to."

"Right," Sam murmurs. "What if you headed to a cricket match together?"

"Maybe," she replies uneasily. "It's true that I don't care much about the sport, so the risks of me making a scene are low." Then, she sighs. "But never zero. He wouldn't forgive me if I ruined cricket for him."

Tim looks up from his phone. "Cricket *is* life."

Lin's eyes turn to fire but somehow she keeps her anger contained. It takes all of Pania's restraint not to smack him upside the head.

#

Lin dashes out of the cafeteria, not waiting for Sam to print and distribute her notes. Tim catches up to her while she's waiting for the elevator and asks her for a minute.

"Look, I don't know what I did back there but—" he holds up his phone. His notes app is open, and at the top in all caps is written: BOY YOU FUCKED UP. APOLOGIZE TO THE ASIAN LADY. "I'm real sorry. Is there anything I can write down that will help me be better next time?"

"First off, you can learn to shut your mouth," Lin replies sharply.

Tim's eyes widen, but instead of getting defensive, he says, "I'm sure I deserve that. I'm sorry."

Her demeanor softens in turn. "We're all just trying to do our best for the people we love. No shame in that. I know your memory is a real challenge, and we haven't done much to support you in that either."

He types something in his notes. "My doctor told me this group was life-changing for people that're fucked in the head." He points a finger at his temple. "But I don't think I fit in here."

The tightness in Lin's cheeks eases and she puts a well-meaning hand on Tim's arm. "Give it time. How long has it been since your accident?"

"Around eight months, I think."

"It's still early days. Trust me. I'm on year four, and I'm still having things come back to me." She pauses. Sighs. "But, so far, not my impulse control. So I'm sorry if I've been rotten to you."

"You're good." he says, waving off her apology. "Can't exactly blame you for your injury. I still don't fit in though." In a stage whisper, he adds, "It's cuz the angry Abo lady hates me, isn't it?"

"As long as you're writing stuff in your phone, put down that you'll never use that term again."

"What, Abo? It's just short for Aboriginal."

"It's much more complicated than that." She smashes the elevator call button, trying to contain her frustration. "It's just as bad as calling me the Asian lady."

"What's wrong with that? You are Asian, aren't you?"

"I have a name. Lin. Use it." Maybe her poor impulse control isn't so horrible after all, because her message seems to get through.

"Okay, okay," he says, holding his hands up defensively. As he types, he mumbles, "No more Abos. Asian lady is Lin."

#

Pania is shuffling down the hallway when she hears Blondie tell Lin, "No more Abos."

Lin's response isn't audible from a distance but the woman doesn't appear shocked or upset. The woman just nods and then they share an elevator. Pania slumps down onto the hospital floor, not caring how filthy the tiles are or whether she'll be able to get back up.

She just needs a minute.

A walker scraping against the tile floor draws her back to the present. "Do you need some help?" Robert asks. "I uh, probly can't give it to you, but I can go get someone."

"Don't need help, thanks." She keeps her eyes on her shoes.

"Then how about a distraction from whatever's got you down... literally and figuratively?"

Even though Pania hasn't lifted her eyes, there are giggles hiding behind his words. "Depends. How many bad puns are in the story, hm?"

"Well, well, I can always tone it down if you're gonna be a grump about it." His wrists are a bit shaky, and the walker squeaks against the floor.

She crooks her head to make sure the silly old man isn't about to fall over. Satisfied, she nods. "Alright. Lay it on me." A pause while a smile sneaks its way onto her face. "Figuratively, not literally, please."

The little *hee* Robert allows himself tells her that she's hit the mark—and that she might be here a while.

"So, you've heard plenty about how I got my injury, but have I told you why I cared so much about diving in the first place?"

That's right. The old bogan didn't stop complaining about that accident for at least a goddamn year. It had been a cave dive gone wrong, off the coast of Malaysia. He'd smashed his head on a rock somehow or other, and his partner Michael had also gotten hurt in the process of rescuing him.

"Fine then, talk to me about your favorite dive."

"Not my favorite. The one that changed my life." Her involuntary groan gives him pause. "No, not that one. The one that changed my life for the better."

Phew. She doesn't need to hear the thousandth version of the cave-diving story.

"It was a Christmas gift to myself. I booked a trip to see the southern end of the GBR instead of sitting around and moping that my family wouldn't talk to me."

"Oh, so this was when you were young, huh?"

"Yep." He taps his tank, as though scolding his younger self. "Before I realized I didn't need anyone who couldn't accept me as I am."

"This before you met Michael, then?" Her back is starting to hurt, so she stretches a bit to one side in an attempt to ward off the knots that are surely already forming under her shoulder blades.

"I'm getting to that," Robert responds with a quick *tsk, tsk.* "Just be patient."

Pania holds up her hands in surrender. *Here's to hoping I can get off this floor by the time he's done.*

"Diving the reef is always incredible. I'd taken a couple trips up north already, so I thought I knew what to expect. Well," he pauses to draw a breath, "that's the thing about the ocean. It never ceases to surprise ya.

"So here I was, paired up with some stranger for a dive buddy because I had no friends, and couldn't get out of my own head long enough to even remember his name. Anyway, so we all get down there and of course, it's absolutely gorgeous. Really took my mind off of all the family trouble I was having, ya know?" He leans against his walker and stares off into space.

Pania grunts. "Yeah, yeah. There any point to this story, or are you just going to moan and groan about missing the ocean again?"

"I told you. Be patient!" He smiles. "But yes, I have a point. Promise."

She makes a circular motion with her fingers. "I'm too tired to be patient. Move it along."

"The details *are* the story." He huffs. "But I hear you. So anyway, where was I... that's right. So we got down there, and the guide is pointing out various kinds of fish hiding in the reef. Well, me and my dive buddy were towards the back of the group, being pokey. And the next thing you know, the entire group is out of sight. And all we could see was the empty coral reef. Most of the fish had scattered because of our group.

"And like I said, I was kind of stuck in my head at the time, so I was starting to panic, thinking our group was going to leave us behind. The guy next to me could see it, so he grabs my hand and points off to one side. And there, floating next to the reef, was this enormous loggerhead turtle. December's their nesting season, you know, so they were returning to where they'd been born. And this old fella was looking at us curious, like, hey, I don't remember seeing you here before. He raised a flipper and it was just like he was waving us over."

"Mhmm," Pania murmurs. "And did you follow him?"

Robert smiles. "My partner did, so naturally I did too." He pauses, lost in the memory.

"And...?" Pania asks.

"Right. And there over the ridge was a whole group of 'em, all hovering above the coral with their flippers folded underneath their shells. Looked all prim and proper, like they were—like they were having a meeting or attending church. When we swam into view, every single one of 'em looked at us and then looked at the turtle that had waved us in. It was the most surreal experience I've ever had."

"Sounds nice," Pania replies blandly.

"But it changed my life because that night, my dive partner and I took to chatting about turtle hierarchy and social life at the bar. Turns out, he wasn't straight like I'd assumed. And I finally got his name through my thick skull. Michael."

"Aw," Pania says with a bit more interest. "I didn't know that was how you two met. How sweet."

"Best day of my life," Robert adds, his voice full of daydreams. "He was the one who taught me to stand up for myself, to stop getting bothered by people who didn't give a damn about me and only wanted to turn me into something I'm not."

Pania nods. "Glad it worked out for ya. Now if you don't mind, my back is in knots. I'm ready for that help up now."

"Right then. I may not be able to do anything for you, but I'll go find someone who can," he says, whipping his walker around and moving quicker than she'd seen him move since that fateful group meeting on Boxing Day long ago.

The next day, Pania struggles through her balance exercises. She hasn't bothered to go to therapy in years—whether occupational, physical, or their fancier balance-focused cousin, vestibular therapy. The amount of progress she makes on her balance is painstakingly slow, so she won't go back until the exercises she does on her own all become too easy.

The path of recovery has never been linear for her, even if she has, indeed, made plenty of progress. The first few months after the accident were a dizzy blur. How embarrassing it had been for her to fall out of her chair as the new kid in school, to feel the stares of her peers and the barely restrained giggles of the bullies. Every fall made recovery feel further away, especially on days when her head connected with her desk or her chair or god knows what else on her way down. The other students hadn't known what she'd been through. The not-so-subtle glances at the cast on her wrist, the rude questions and ruder jokes forming on their lips, made it that much harder to break the silence.

Back in the present, Pania shudders. Her decisions right after the accident, after leaving Sal as good as dead, have haunted her and will surely continue to haunt her until the end of her natural life.

Best not to think of those things at all, much less while marching in place all alone in her apartment. A few years ago, she'd slipped doing an exercise alone and hit her head on the table's edge. It happened to be the very table she was instructed by her previous therapist to use as a stability support. *That really worked out,* she thinks sarcastically. Luckily, a conference call she was meant to lead was due to start just a few minutes later. Half an hour later, the ambo guys showed up to do a welfare check. Their grumbling vanished when they saw the blood.

Not only had that incident taken her recovery at least seven steps back, she'd had to pay to replace the living room carpet. The blood refused to wash out.

No, best not to think of any of her past while working on her balance. She pushes the blood-stained carpet out of her mind as her feet practice the familiar (if still difficult) routine of taking a single step forward, followed by a single, controlled step back. This particular exercise is maddening in its simplicity. And yet, after just two or three repetitions, her arms fly out to her sides to keep herself from tumbling to the floor.

If only she'd been that quick to react a few months back at the movie theater. But she'd had other priorities then; she'd wanted to save the popcorn she was carrying. Thank goodness Auntie Elaine had been paying attention. The popcorn may have ended up a lost cause, but she'd avoided a twisted or broken ankle. They'd even managed to see the movie. Though far more theatrics happened before the screen fired up than Pania preferred.

And... done! Her arms rest at her sides, exercises finished for the moment. Her toes sink into the lush new carpet she'd chosen for the living room, a cozy and yet persistent reminder of the importance of pacing herself.

A few minutes of practice, a few times a day, seemed to give Pania's body the best results. Run herself ragged and she'd lose all of her gains with a week in bed after a fall or an illness that got the best of her exhausted state. Slow and steady wins the race.

Though after thirty years, her recovery could hardly be considered a race. *At least I can sit in a damn chair now.*

Chapter 5: Crick, Crack

"Hi Bàba, hi Niáng," Lin says in Mandarin over the Facetime call. She's hoping her parents don't notice how empty the house is, or that she has nothing better to do on a Saturday night than call home. "How are you?"

"Doing fine, Meiling, but where is your husband? Your son?" Niáng's tone is sharp, accusatory. What she's really saying is, *Why aren't you with them?*

"They're having a boy's night," Lin replies. *I mean, it's not really a lie.*

"Tell them both we say hello and we miss them." Her father's words are gentle. It strikes her how well her parents balance each other out, how they make each other whole.

"Of course, of course," Lin says. "And how was your evening with the Zhangs last night? I do hope you sent my regards."

They engage in their small talk rituals. Then, her father informs her the government has extended the spring holiday again to slow down the spread of coronavirus. Her parents may live remotely in rural China, but Lin's unnerved by their proximity to this new disease. "Don't worry, my dear," Bàba says to calm her fears. "You know I work the fields alone and we sat outside at the Zhangs'. And, after all, none of us have gone anywhere near the City of Wuhan—have you forgotten how far away that is from us, simply because you are living abroad?"

"No, no, of course not," she replies, her head down to communicate meekness and respect for his words. "But it is a daughter's duty to care for her parents, and talking about the risks of this thing are all I can do from here. I just want you to be safe." Her father smiles softly, as if to say, *Message received. We love you too, daughter.*

The conversation moves on again, but Lin can tell her mother is still stuck on Lin's family life; she hasn't bought the boys' night excuse. Finally, the woman asks, "Meiling, my dear, what are you doing on the wall back there?"

Lin turns as if she hadn't noticed the blank spots where Jian and Huan's father-son photos used to hang. "Oh, nothing really. Huan was doing a report on family for school, and he wanted to bring in a photo of Jian to go with his report. And you know boys, hah—it's been two weeks and he still hasn't put them back yet! I'll have to get on him before he loses track of them." She rambles on a bit, making up details about Huan's supposed report on his father, his pride in Jian's professional accomplishments at the airline, how proud of his family the boy is. The more she talks, the less her mother seems to believe, but neither woman is willing to let go of the façade of Lin's comfortable life abroad. To face the uncomfortable truth.

Her father remains relatively quiet through the call aside from current events, as is his habit. But when Lin's mother goes to hang up, he stays her hand. "I'd like to talk to Meiling a bit longer, father to daughter. You go on and I'll be right in."

After her mother leaves the room, her father's eyes are sad. Matter-of-factly, he asks, "It's over then, isn't it?"

"What?"

"All the dancing you and your mother did around the subject and you're going to make me say it out loud?" He points behind her, and while it's not clear from the camera angle, she knows he's looking at the empty spots on the wall. He's trying to say it without saying it, so she doesn't lose face.

Lin's eyes fall to her lap before she whispers, "No. You don't have to."

"I only bring it up so directly because I want you to know you always have a place here with us if you need it. Or even simply want it. Your cousins would love to see you back home and, at least for now, you can still come to us."

"Much appreciated, Father." She takes a long, deep breath. "But my life, my son, is here now. Even if my husband isn't."

"I understand. *Jiayou,* my daughter."

She nods slowly. "I am trying to stay strong."

Her father looks like he is going to cry. He absolutely hates divorce, and Lin knows her situation has to be killing him. "You should have family around while you go through this, Meiling. We can get down there sometime this fall, keep you company through the winter. As soon as your new country will let us in, if you need us sooner."

"And what," she snaps, "have you looking at me with puppy dog eyes because I'm a failure and a divorcée?" She sucks in her breath. "I'm sorry, I didn't mean to say that out loud. The accident, you know?" Lin taps her temple, hoping for just a little more forgiveness for how often she has broken *xiao*, the understood commitment to show piety and respect to one's parents.

Aside from a huff, Bàba doesn't acknowledge her outburst. Lin stumbles on. "I—I welcome you to come if you are worried about the coronavirus, about protecting your health, but otherwise? Otherwise, I think it would be best for the two of you to stay home."

"Should you change your mind, just say the word and we'll be there as soon as possible. For you and for Huan."

"Thank you, Bàba. Stay safe." Lin's too tired to search for anything else that will help her save face, so she leaves their conversation at that.

"Talk again soon, daughter."

"Talk soon," she echoes as she switches the video call off.

#

Saying something always seems to get her in trouble, so Lin doesn't want to use words on this particular Monday morning. Instead, she just leaves the pair of tickets on the kitchen table for Huan to find. This is her opportunity to start fresh.

"Hey Mum," Huan calls around a mouthful of cereal. "Where'd these come from?"

The morning is magically normal. She wants to keep it that way, so instead of speaking, she points at herself, then points at her son.

"Aw, sweet! Dave's been after me to go to a game with him. We'll have an awesome time, thanks Mum."

Her happiness crumples, the magic broken. "I uh, thought we'd go together. You and me."

"Oh." He takes in her face, then hurriedly adds, "Oh, that sounds like fun too! Dave has plans this weekend anyway, I wasn't even thinking. Of course we'll go."

"You won't be embarrassed of your crazy old mum?" Her smile contains more sadness than happiness, more fear than triumph.

"No more embarrassed than any other teenager spending Saturday night with his mum." His lopsided smile brings Lin back to the old times, when her family could still pretend it was whole.

"I'll take it."

#

The young woman's resume is well-formatted and her uni grades are stellar, but Pania knows it won't be enough. The woman sitting at the dully painted metal table across from her is strong, strong enough to hear hard truths.

"Do you want to get an interview, or do you want to get rejected without a second thought?" The wind shuffles the paper, so Pania pins it down with her pointer finger.

"I hear you, but what do you mean specifically?" The woman's beautifully braided blonde hair shines warm in the morning sun, shadows from the park's ironbark trees only magnifying her inner light.

The older woman points at the heading in the upper right corner, where it says "Naretha Taumata." "I know this is standard practice, but they don't need your first name. In fact, I'd say you need them to not have your first name. You might get laughed out of a couple of interviews once they discover that you're First Nations, but at least you'll get in the door first."

"How did you do it? Find such a great job, I mean." She rests her chin in her hand as if to say, *I'm listening*.

"Didn't give up. I got laughed out of more than one interview, myself. It helps that I have a white-sounding last name. Phone interviews are going to be your friend."

"Right, but won't they still have my full name by the end of it?"

"HR will, sure, but nobody else has to. I asked everyone to call me Ms. Kelly at first. When they got curious, I said I prefer to go by my last name. You could also give 'em a white-sounding nickname."

"Other than, you know, having my name on it—" here the woman pauses to sigh dramatically— "what do you think of my resume?"

"It's a great start. You have a pen?"

When she shakes her head, the many pins on her blouse flutter in the breeze. One in particular catches Pania's eye. The words "Australia Day" are crossed off with a red X, and underneath it says, "Day of Mourning."

"Wrong. You always have a pen. Be more helpful than the next guy. Let them think you'll be easier to work with." She gestures towards the pins. "Don't have anything like those on your shirt, your bag, or anywhere else an interviewer might see or you'll get labeled too political and a poor team player."

"You're asking me to give up the things that make me who I am just so I can get a job." She huffs.

"Listen Naretha, you can do whatever you want, but this is how you get in the door. Once you're in, you go right back to being you." Pania pulls a pen out of her bag and starts crossing off line items under the resume's education heading. "In the meantime, don't go bragging about your First Nations club, and cover up your chin tattoo with concealer when you interview in person. Trust me." Her own tattoo-less face is somber. Discouraging the woman is the last thing on her mind, which is why she holds in her other piece of advice. *You never know who you can trust. So trust nobody.*

#

"Way to go, Mum, this is a great game!"

A bunch of nobs getting into it over a ball might not do anything for Lin, but seeing Huan enjoy the game and enjoy it with her is worth every bit of the hassle with public transit and bumping into strangers and overpriced tickets.

"Oh, good thing," she responds. "Tickets cost the same whether or not it's a bust. Selfie?" The camera is already activated on her phone, so Huan leans in. His natural smile turns stilted in front of the camera. It's the awkwardness of every teenage boy being forced to take pictures with his mum, and Lin loves the normalcy of it. She snaps an extra under protest from Huan, hoping to capture as much of the experience as she can.

He playfully swats the phone down, and the device flies free of her loose grip to land on the seat of the people in front of them. "Sorry Mum," her son says sheepishly.

"No worries, I've got it." She reaches for it and shouts over the noise from the loudspeaker. "Pardon me, just reaching for my phone!"

The man turns at the exact moment Lin is leaning into their row, and their heads collide.

"Sorry," Lin says instinctively.

"Just keep your Wu Flu hands out of my way and we won't have a problem," the man growls.

"Excuse me?"

"I said keep your Wu Flu-infested ass and your spawn out of my way."

Lin isn't sure what happens next. The rage is blinding, and her body surges with its energy.

When the burst finally ebbs, she is standing outside the club facing a locked gate. Her purse is gone, where is her purse? Her head whips around, and that's when she spots Huan, shoulders slumped on a bench facing the parking lot. Relief calms her heart rate when she recognizes the shape of her purse on the bench next to him.

"Do I even want to know what happened in there?" she asks, now that she can think about something other than her purse.

"Once we're able to find you a mirror, you'll know plenty enough," he replies sullenly. "Oh, by the way, the teams are tied and going into overtime. Not that we'll get to see it anyway, so we might as well go. Beat the crowd before we end up beating more spectators."

Oh. "I'm so sorry, Huan, I didn't know what I was doing. I just wanted to defend you from such a racist son of a—"

"I heard what that stupid Brisso said. But what you did had nothing to do with defending me, and we both know it. Stop pretending, okay? And let's go home."

"Right," she whispers, too ashamed to reprimand him for his disrespectful tone. She lets Huan take her hand and lead her home, like a puppy being punished for playing too rough. The ride home is silent, and her son buries himself in his computer the moment they get in the house.

After taking in her bruised hands and the shiner brewing on her left eye, she orders takeout for dinner. When their meals arrive, Huan grabs a burger and heads straight back to his room. Staring at his closed door, she starts to wonder if he'll ever speak to her again.

#

"So, how is the new support group going?" Tim's neurologist asks at his next appointment. Something about her bright smile and perfect hair irritate him.

He shrugs. "Let me check my notes." The appointment hardly seems like it's for him, with how much he has to reference his phone to answer any of the doctor's questions. He scans the few lines of notes he has about the TBI support group that this doctor had apparently recommended to him. "Fine, I guess. I dunno, there's not much context here."

"Give it time," she reassures him. "Speaking of time, can you draw an analog clock for me? Your support group meets at 19:00 hours, so make that the time on the clock if you could."

Weird request, but okay. "Yeah, sure," he mumbles as he takes the pen and paper she pushes towards him.

The doctor continues talking while Tim draws. "The support group is really helpful over the long term, because it gives you a direct connection to people who get what you're going through and who have their own ways of dealing with their brain injuries. The resident who runs it is really bright; she worked with my office during some of her clinical rotations. Her tips and expertise, along with ideas from the other members of the group, can help you cope better with day-to-day life in between appointments."

"Blah, blah, blah," Tim says. He looks up, then blushes. "Sorry, didn't mean to say that out loud."

She cracks a smile. "You're not going to offend me, so don't worry about that. But if you still have trouble coping with your day-to-day stuff in, say, two or three weeks, plan on going back to that support group, alright? Figuring out what coping mechanisms you need to function normally can be life-changing."

"Got it." He types out in his support group note, *Go back in a few weeks if you haven't figured your shit out yet.* Then, he slides the paper with the messed-up clock on it back to the doctor and asks, "Anything else we need to cover? When's our next appointment?"

#

The next few Tuesdays at group are too quiet, and it isn't simply because of Tim's absence. With Australia Day coming and then going, and the air quality worse and worse from the bushfires down south, Pania doesn't have the energy or, frankly, the compassion to spare for Lin's family drama. *Anybody who wants me to care probably shouldn't be racist where I can hear them,* she thinks bitterly. Pania stays silent while the woman cries over her impending divorce proceedings and her family troubles, instead letting Robert and the others take the lead.

"Maybe you could try connecting with your son over something he isn't quite as invested in," Robert suggests when she mentions that the cricket game was a fiasco. "Snorkeling off of the beach is always a good time. Michael and I used to go every Friday right around lunchtime. It's an easy way to see fish and other wildlife without diving, and you can go when there's not as many people in the water scaring things away. I'm sure a teenager would love playing hooky from school for a day."

"Well, the less I have to be around people, the better, that's for sure," Lin says. When she goes into the story about the Wu Flu cricket fan, Pania can't stop a heavily sarcastic huff.

"What's on your mind, Pania?" Sam asks.

"Nothing you would understand," she replies.

Lin's eyes narrow. "I'm sorry that it's not as bad as the stuff you face, but it still hurts. Racism is racism."

"That's rich," Pania replies with an acerbic laugh. "Feels a bit different when you're on the receiving end, does it?"

"What are you talking about?" Lin asks, voice rising in anger. "This isn't some sort of oppression Olympics. We can—"

Sam interjects, "What's going on?"

"Look, I can turn a blind eye to plenty of things, but I really don't need to put up with this shit." Pania pushes herself off the chair and walks off as quickly as her unbalanced legs will let her.

"I'm really confused," Lin yells towards her.

"No energy for hypocrisy," she calls back without turning around.

In the elevator, Pania sighs. *Why are people like this?* Her cane has just hit the sidewalk when Lin's voice reaches her.

"Please, let me get you a coffee. Help me understand."

Pania turns. It's hard to discount the confusion in the woman's face, knowing how biologically difficult it is for her to fake her emotions. But how much time does she want to invest in a woman who isn't bothered by an out-right racist saying out-right racist things?

"Look, you might not think it's a big deal, but I heard what Tim said to you the last time he was here." She continues hobbling along, not waiting for the other woman to catch up.

"What Tim said to me..." Lin trails off as she searches her memory. Her pace slows, matching Pania's gait.

"He said, 'No more Abos,' and you just agreed and got on the elevator with him. I mean, what the hell?"

"I told him off for calling you an angry Abo lady and made him make a note not to use that *word* anymore. I figured it wasn't as important to tone police him in that second as it was to get him to stop the rest of the time."

Relief rushes through Pania's body. Her stiff shoulders loosen and she unclenches her jaw. "Oh. Thank you." Her free hand dares to brush Lin's, then points loosely towards the tiny café across the street. "And sorry for jumping to conclusions. Still up for that coffee?"

Lin smiles. "Of course. And you're welcome."

They meander over and order coffee and pastries. They settle into a table on the sidewalk next to a flowering olive tea-tree. Lin rubs a few of its leaves between her fingers and breathes in deeply, savoring the lemony scent, before taking a bite of her pastry.

Pania breaks the silence. "So, tell me about you."

"Well, you already know plenty." She sets down her raspberry tart and starts ticking off items on her fingers. "Getting a divorce, have a teenager who hates me, oh, and I can't control my emotions or even what comes out of my mouth most the time."

"None of those things are you," Pania replies, locking eyes with her. "Those are all just things that are happening to you." She takes a sip of her iced coffee, but doesn't break eye contact. "So, tell me about you."

Lin redirects her gaze to her plate, fingers anxiously picking at each other. "What else is there to know?"

"Oh, come on." Pania pulls on a loose piece of hair, freeing it from her braid. "Do you like gardening? Most people wouldn't think to rub the leaves of a tea tree."

Lin shrugs. "Meh, I just love lemon. Can't keep plants alive myself anymore so I enjoy them while I'm out. I mostly spend my spare time trying not to have a meltdown. Might catch a soap opera here or there. I'm boring, I guess."

"Somehow, I doubt that. Boring people don't have so much fire in their eyes."

"I can't control that, remember?"

"Still..." Pania replies, rubbing her hands against her drink. "Maybe you just need to get out a little more, find some adventures of your own."

"I can't exactly go places alone. I'll probably blow up at the first person who looks at me cross-eyed." Her words come faster and faster as her emotions rise. "And who would go with me? Huh? My husband who's divorcing me? My son who isn't talking to me? My parents who live in northern China and are literally barred from entering the country?"

Pania holds up her hand to stop Lin's spiral. "Hey, I'm not afraid of a temper, and I could get out more myself. Let's plan something, you and me, huh?"

The deep wrinkles in Lin's brow relax. "You sure?"

"Yeah, I feel like I owe you one." Pania doesn't mention how much she likes to watch as Lin's worries fade into a smile, or how much she likes being the reason behind that smile. "So, what sounds fun?"

Chapter 6: Runaway Train

Tim wakes up with the feeling that he's forgetting something. Not exactly an uncommon thing for a guy with a memory problem, but it's been nagging at him a lot more than usual.

To cope with the fact that his days slip away like they were written in water, he's started keeping a journal. After breakfast every morning, Jenny reminds him about it. The last half a dozen entries all start the same way. "I got this weird feeling I'm forgetting something important."

So this is what Groundhog Day feels like, he thinks. If only he were Bill Murray and could figure out how to break this curse. But he's not, so for the sake of tomorrow, he documents the feeling again.

The nagging feeling isn't about Jenny, though he was surprised to wake up next to such a hottie this morning. His phone calendar is chock full of dates like birthdays and anniversaries, support group meetings and therapy exercise reminders and doctor's appointments, and all of the other day-to-day details of his life, so he's sure it's nothing like that either. *Wouldn't the feeling go away if I saw the thing I need to remember again?* He doesn't know, but he tells himself that must be the way that works. After all, the feeling refuses to be denied.

Seems like the memory isn't going to resurface any time soon though, so he closes the journal and puts on his favorite gym shorts. His calendar has Power Walk scheduled in for the top of the hour, but there's no reason to wait.

He grabs his headphones before heading out the door so he can blast some EDM, with an alarm set for when he needs to turn around and go home. A recent anecdote in his journal prompted him to label the alarm with his address. He can see and almost feel the panic emanating from his shaky handwriting, even if Jenny never found out about that particular incident. She has enough to worry about. Handling the rent by herself couldn't be easy, even if her real estate agent grandma had gotten them a great deal when they moved in a few years back.

On the quiet sidewalk, his strides are purposeful to bely the fact that he has nowhere to go and no one to see until his girlfriend comes back from work. The last thing he needs is to have all the retirees around here thinking he's some kind of burglar and calling the cops on him.

The entire place is serene. *Least the old chooks know how to keep a garden.* Freesia, lavender, and carnations alternately fill the air with their perfume and dot the plain brown houses with explosions of color. His favorite spot on this particular street is the line of spotted gum trees. He walks over, careful to check for nosey oldies before breaking off some of the loose, peeling bark. *Not like I'm going to hurt it.* He runs a hand over the smooth trunk underneath, relishing in its sharp, fresh scent and its mid-morning coolness. His eyes close, taking in the moment.

The current song on his playlist ends, and the sound of a tussle across the street breaks him out of his reverie. Two kookaburras are flipping and pushing each other on the sidewalk, no doubt fighting over the lovely lady perched on a nearby hydrangea blossom with a twig hanging from her mouth.

The birds lock beaks, feathers raised and wings flapping as they try to intimidate each other into submission. The smaller one flies off, but instead of it being an act of defeat like Tim had initially thought, it's a new attack... on its reflection in a nearby window. Tim palms his forehead. *Stupid bird.* He's about to continue on when the bird's original nemesis speeds over. Its beak hits the smaller bird right in its neck, knocking it to the ground in an eruption of feathers. The smaller bird's neck snaps, and it lays bent at an unnatural angle. There will be no more lovely ladies for him.

His phone dings, reminding him to head back. He drops the smooth, spongey bark on the ground and wipes his hand against his shorts. His finger hovers over the alarm's stop button when he remembers the panicky journal entry he'd left for himself last week. He hits snooze instead and starts the journey home, careful to skirt the angry kook and its bloodied, unmoving victim.

#

Elaine's kitchen has always made Pania feel at peace. The cozy wooden cabinets, the intimate table, the big window over the sink: the space gives her a sense of being wanted, of being seen. Though Pania knows it isn't really about the space at all. It's about the woman behind it.

"You seem distracted," Elaine says. "Everything okay?"

Pania smiles and picks up her fork. "Don't worry, I'm still going to eat, Auntie. Just thinking about how much I love this kitchen."

"Really?" the older woman asks, a hint of skepticism in her voice. "These cabinets are still exactly the same as when you lived here."

"Before that, actually. I think that's why I like them." Elaine had taken Pania in not long after the accident, after running away from her last foster home. This unchanged kitchen is where Pania felt her life start to stabilize, instead of continuing to spiral beyond her control.

"Well, when I decide to change them, I'll save one for you." Elaine pushes the last of the breaded prawns towards Pania's plate. "Finish that up, would you?"

"Always with the food!" Pania pushes the pot back to Elaine. "I can't manage another bite, seriously. Put it in the fridge."

The two women clean up. Pania's happy to stand at the sink and let the citrus scent of dish soap replace the ever-present smell of smoke from the bushfires in the south, even if only for a little while. As she scrubs the plates, Pania's thoughts turn towards Lin: how quick she'd been to misjudge her. Elaine had given Pania grace when she'd needed it without so much as a second thought. *Still trying and failing to live up to Auntie's example.* Luckily, this particular misunderstanding had been cleared up without causing too much trouble.

Pania ponders the relief that flooded her when she realized her mistake, when she'd realized Lin was actually looking out for her behind her back. That fuzzy, electric feeling that made Pania want to touch her.

The museum they've decided to visit together might be too close to Pania's teenaged haunts for her comfort, but something tells her it's going to be worth the trouble.

#

While there were a couple of poor white kids among their ranks, most of Pania's secondary school classmates were Aboriginal kids. Rumor had it Miss Altro was a former nun who used to teach in one of the mission schools out bush. Some days, Miss Altro tried to keep them in line and drill math facts into their heads, but there were many more times when she gave up seemingly before she even started.

Their morning catechism always started with a recital of the Lord's prayer. The school wasn't run by nuns or by church people. Most days, Pania felt it wasn't really run by anybody. Anybody except Miss Altro, that is, and she insisted on the Lord's prayer. Her obsession with that stupid prayer is probably how the rumor of her being a nun got started.

Pania and Sal had started a game where they swapped out one word of the prayer each day. The entire class had bets going on how long it would take Miss Altro to notice, but the condition for most of the bets was that only the two of them could participate.

"Obviously it would be unfair if the whole class did it," Mallory had complained. Of course, she'd wagered a stolen joy ride in her foster dad's Mustang and the ten bucks he kept in the glove box that they could change the whole thing. The bruises her foster dad regularly left on her arms and abdomen may have given Mallory plenty of reason to make the offer, but they also suggested the price of getting caught making that offer.

So, the rest of the class recited the prayer dutifully and eagerly listened for the day's changed line. Those who didn't sit close enough to hear it for themselves waited in agony until the notes started circulating.

The adjusted line started getting tough to keep a straight face through just a week or so into the game.

"Feed Altro to the bitch on Fourth, as we eat those who trespass against us."

They'd spent all of lunch period yesterday trying to decide if matching the number of words or the number of syllables was more important. Eventually, syllables had won out. If Miss Altro could get over the subject matter (and the blasphemy), she might be impressed at how closely they examined the rhythm and sound of the traditional prayer before deciding how best to butcher it. Of course, she'd be less impressed at the range of profanities they planned to insert the following week.

Miss Altro wasn't in a particularly forgiving mood that day, and she strode down the aisle with a ruler in her hand after their unenthusiastic amens. "What's going on over here, hm?" She eyed the students sitting closest to Pania and Sal, who were struggling not to burst out laughing—another condition of several bets that the girls in front of Pania and Sal had going. "Is the Lord's prayer a joke to you?"

The teacher's voice was harsh, like bullets charging towards a target. The ruler came down hard on several desks at random as she walked by. On her way back up to the front of the classroom, she quizzed them on when Australia was "discovered"—normally a topic of intense eye-rolling. But that day, everyone played nice and gave her the 1788 date that they knew she wanted.

Great job, you people found the land that we'd already lived off of for generations, Pania thought sarcastically. But she sucked in her breath at the reminder that she would never know how to live off the land the way her family had. Her family... they were nothing more than a few hazy memories. A group of people laughing on a porch, her mother holding back tears and telling her it would be okay, that she would come get her from the nice man as soon as she could. The seemingly eternal car ride he took her on to reach the foster family willing to take her in. The terror of not knowing where home was, where her family was. *Not a nice man if you ask me.*

January 26, 1788 may not have marked a discovery, but it was certainly a day that demanded to be remembered.

#

Back at the flat, the dishes piled in the sink remind Tim of Jenny. *She works too hard to have to deal with these too.* He scrubs them up quickly by hand. He couldn't find the dishwasher detergent, but there was dish soap sitting next to the sink. Besides, the movements were calming, and he thought it might help jog his memory about the important thing that's been lost inside his head for the past week. After the last cup is stacked precariously next to the sink, he goes for his phone.

Instead of booting up his FIFA game, his fingers pop open Instagram to check his notifications. He's got a message... from his ex, Mel? *Hey Tee, just wondering what you've been up to lately. Would love to get a drink and catch up if you're interested.*

And just like that, the forgotten task bursts to the surface. Un-heart Mel's photo. Too late for that now. While he may not remember most of his relationship with Jenny today, it's crystal clear to him that he doesn't deserve her, and that she's a million times better than Mel. So, he sits at the table and hmphs and harumphs through what he can say that will squash this the fastest.

After several iterations, he hits send on: *Hey Mel, just doing my thing, recovering from an ATV accident. My girl Jenny's been the best through the whole thing, might even propose soon, idk. Hope you're doing well. -Tim.* Mel tended to run when things got too tough or too serious, so he figures both at once oughta do it.

He doesn't stop to think about whether he really intends to propose. Being able to afford a ring on a disability pension, with no job prospects, is more than a bit questionable. He jots down the idea in his journal anyway as a question for a good memory day.

That done, he flops onto the couch and opens up his FIFA game. Time to go back to being a baller.

His virtual team has just won their championship when Jenny comes in the door. "Hey, bit early for you, isn't it?"

She hangs her purse on the back of the door. "Nah, it's actually a bit late. Accident on the M1, and you know how that goes." He watches as her rush-hour frustrations are slowly replaced by bone-deep exhaustion. Her caramel eyes are devoid of the brightness and mischief he sees in all of their Instagram photos together.

"Ah, I must've lost track of time," he replies, noticing how thick and dry his tongue is in his mouth.

"When was the last time you got off the couch?" she asks, a slight edge of annoyance seeping into her words as she kicks off her shoes.

"Uh, I only sat down for a minute to update my game after my walk." He gestures to his phone. "Just won the championship!"

"Okay," she replies. "So you haven't eaten or drank anything all day?"

"Uh... oops?" He cracks an apologetic grin.

"You're going to need to add some lunch alarms into your daily batch if this keeps up," Jenny says as she turns towards their room to change.

"I saw in my notes that I get some sort of support funding. Maybe I should use that to have someone come in and check on me, you know, midday."

"Maybe..." Reluctance creeps into her voice. "I just hate sacrificing our privacy like that, you know? Like, what if they come in and find our—" she clears her throat— "our box?"

"I mean, can't we have someone just drop in and remind me to get off the couch to eat, maybe check that I haven't done anything stupid like leave the burner on in the kitchen after brekkie again?"

"Hard to say, Tee." Her eyes fill with worry. "They get to decide the rules, not us."

"That doesn't sound right," he replies.

"It isn't," she responds firmly. "So just add a few more alarms into your daily batch, okay?"

He nods.

"By the way, did you remember to pull the chicken out of the freezer?"

His eyes widen. Before he can formulate a response, she says, "Whatever, I'll just order some Chinese."

"Um, okay," he says. "I did do the dishes though!"

She makes the OK sign with her thumb and pointer finger. Under her breath as she walks away, she adds sarcastically, "Gold star."

Later that night, he hears her walk into the bedroom and sigh heavily. "Everything okay?" he calls from the kitchen, where he's loading a round of dishes into the dishwasher.

"You left shit all over the bed again, Tee," she calls back, sounding exhausted more than annoyed. "Where do you want me to put all this stuff, anyway?"

"Hold on, be right there," he yells. "I don't remember what's there to put away." When he speed-walks in, he sucks in his breath. Jenny's holding his half-open journal, and a flash of his earlier entry parades across his mind. *Please don't be on that page, please don't be on that page.*

"Where do you keep this?" she asks, pages of the journal ruffling back and forth in her loose grip. "I didn't want to lose it on you."

"Um, right, just right there." He points next to the bed, willing himself to act casual.

"You okay?" She raises an eyebrow. "You act like you've seen a ghost."

"Um, yeah, I'm good. No different than normal, yanno? Memories coming and going like a runaway train." He gives a little *heh, heh* so she knows everything's all right.

"Kay." She tosses a dirty t-shirt and an empty box at him. "I'm heading into the shower, so better have the rest of this crap organized before I'm out. I need like fifty hours of sleep in the next eight hours if I want any hope of being functional in the morning."

He taps his temple with a sarcastic grin. "And you think I'm the one with the brain problems."

"You know what I mean," she snaps as she walks past him. "Just don't leave the room 'til it's done, uh? Don't want you forgetting on me."

"Right." Alone in the room, he deposits his journal just under the bed on his side. He breathes out in relief and checks his phone. A new message... from Mel?

I'm not looking for anything serious. Just need to blow off a little steam, if you still know what that means.
Ah yes—their old euphemism for sex.
He leaves her on read.

Chapter 7: History Lesson

Pania's suggestion to go out together couldn't have come at a better time for Lin. Huan has been staying with Jian since the cricket incident. When he texted her that he wanted to stay with his father all weekend too, it had come as a punch to the gut. Having plans for Saturday, at least, has given her a much-needed distraction.

The two women had spent over an hour at the café, batting ideas back and forth, before deciding to visit a museum up in Southport. "A museum?" Pania exclaimed when Lin first suggested it. "Why not look for a concert, a festival, an art installation? You know, something a little more... adventurous?"

"There are far fewer people to piss me off at a museum." Lin made fists and held them up for Pania to see raised scabs and yellowing bruises. "Gotta start small. Besides, I moved to the Gold Coast as an adult. It's a bit embarrassing, how little I know about its past."

"All good points," Pania had conceded. "Museum it is." They'd quickly organized the details and exchanged phone numbers before heading home in opposite directions.

Now, Lin sits on the bench next to the bus stop they'd chosen to meet at, fiddling nervously with her thumbs. She'd taken her time this morning, styling her bob until every strand of hair was in its proper place, pulling out makeup she hasn't touched in months, and even spraying her favorite perfume. But somehow, she still got to the meeting point first. It takes all of her willpower to avoid texting Pania. *I'm only five minutes late.* A single bus delay could put her back more than that.

The seconds tick by. Lin's fingers find her phone, pulling up apps just to close them again. The fidgeting takes her mind off of all the things that could go wrong when she's taking up space by herself in public. *Going to group doesn't make me this nervous, and I always go there alone. Get it together, Lee!*

One shaky breath follows another. Her nerves are finally settling when Pania's voice carries across the street. "Hey Lin, you ready for that adventure?"

She smiles and stands up, looking for the source of the other woman's voice. "I got us an Uber!" Pania yells. That's when Lin spots her friend's hand waving from the back window of a green SUV, loose skin under Pania's arm shaking in tandem. Even across the street, her friend's bird-shaped birthmark looks like it's flying to meet her.

#

The tension in Lin's face dissipates with the click of her seatbelt. "You know, you're so lucky to have such a cool birthmark," she says. "People have gotten tackier tattoos on purpose."

A rush of electricity charges through Pania's body as the woman settles in next to her, lightly touches the birthmark as she talks. Seeing Lin finally able to relax because of her gives Pania no small amount of satisfaction. She tries to play it cool as she says, "Yeah, got lucky with that one. Anyway, didn't want to press our luck on public transit. Too many creeps, racists, and people with no manners to speak of." She gestures towards the front seat. "But Tanya's cool."

"Aw, thanks!" The white woman's tight curls bounce and she breaks into a smile. "Now, where we heading?"

Once they get the driver oriented, a lump settles in the pit of Pania's stomach despite her best efforts to stay focused on Lin. While this museum is only half an hour away by car, it's still the closest to the hinterland she's allowed herself to get since leaving her old town—and Sal—behind forever.

She needs a distraction. Lin starts humming along with the tune on the radio. The song ends, and Pania starts up a conversation about music genres, which leads to the local music scene and Lin's insistence that she "can't handle that kind of thing anymore," which leads to the topic of life before their injuries.

"I was just a kid. I didn't appreciate what I had," Pania says. "Life wasn't always good to me, but at least my body behaved."

"How old were you when it happened?"

"The accident? Barely sixteen."

"Mmm," Lin murmurs, "Least you had your youth to help you recover."

"More like I lost my youth to recovery."

"Fair."

"So, what about your injury?" Pania asks, hand resting lightly—she hopes casually—on the seat between them.

"Ugh, I hate talking about it because it was so stupid. It was only..." Lin pauses, fingers counting backwards. "Just about four years ago now."

"For brain injuries, that's not very long at all," Pania says, attempting to sound reassuring. "Things will keep getting better as long as you keep trying."

"I'm just... I'm not the same person anymore, you know? I feel the same, but outwardly, everything I do is different. You ever feel that way?"

"I mean, I was sixteen..." Pania trails off, thinking of all her life encompassed before the accident. How much of it she'd wanted to escape, and how much she hadn't realized she had that she could lose. "I was never going to stay that person, so I don't dwell on it too much. But I do want to know more about pre-injury Lin."

"I dunno. I was more controlled, more rational. I've never felt so ruled by my emotions."

"Sounds like old Lin had a stick up her ass." Pania laughs.

"Hey!" Lin says, playfully tapping Pania's arm. Then, she adds, "Well, maybe. But it came in handy plenty of times!"

"Name one time."

"Fine." Lin draws herself up to the challenge, a grin already teasing the edges of her thin lips, which are coated in a playful shade of red. "Huan was three years old. Our house was under renovations—so, not particularly toddler-proof—and he managed to find a permanent marker one of the contractors had left hanging around."

"I smell trouble already!" Pania let herself go in another big belly laugh and briefly wonders what Lin's lips might taste like. "Anyway, what did he use it on?"

"His arms and legs, the walls, his stomach, the new appliances in the kitchen." Lin rolls her eyes and smiles at the memory of the mess. "But the worst part was what he drew." Pania arches an eyebrow in curiosity. "They were flowers and dragonflies according to Huan, but..." Her cheeks go red.

"But what?"

Lin draws the shape of Huan's flowers in the air. "They unfortunately looked much more like male anatomy than they did flowers and dragonflies."

"Let me get this straight. Your three-year-old covered your new kitchen in dicks."

"Yes! And I couldn't laugh or get too mad."

"Ohhh lord," Pania says with a chuckle. "What did you do?"

"After getting the marker away from him, plenty of bathing and scrubbing and bathing and scrubbing. Oh, and I went through every inch of the house and found four more markers before Huan could. The next day, I also made sure to give the contractors an earful, not that they cared."

When Tanya parks the car, the conversation is still flowing comfortably, a river of words drifting lazily towards the sea.

Once the green SUV drives off, however, Pania's shoulders tighten into knots. The car's departure leaves a small cloud of dust in the gravel parking lot, and she coughs a bit into her elbow.

"Come on," Lin says, gaily looping arms and steadying her without a fuss. The muscles in Pania's jaw relax back into a smile. *Maybe this trip was an even better idea than I thought.*

Even with the dust from the parking lot swirling through the air, her lungs are happy. Weeks have passed with the acrid taste of smoke in her mouth from the bushfires not so far away in the south. Here, she can almost forget that the country is still burning.

They head inside the small house-turned-museum, which is neatly hidden behind native plants and a painted fence that has seen better days.

"Hello?" Lin calls.

The foyer is stuffed to the brim with knickknacks and photos. A few antique tools hang on the wall behind a cluttered counter, but there's no one in sight. She turns to Pania. "It is open today, right?"

"Yes, from 8 until 16:00 hours." Pania glances at her watch, though it's just past 10 in the morning. "I know they have some really nice gardens here, but I'd rather talk to someone before we head out there, make sure they're not going to be too much for me, what with all the rain we've been having."

"There is quite a lot to see in here, too, isn't there?" Lin replies. She wanders around the room, taking everything in.

There's a coffee table loaded with photo albums, so Pania settles into a recliner next to it and grabs one to thumb through. The dust on the cover sends her into a sneezing fit.

"Bless you!" Lin calls from across the room after the first two sneezes. After the third, she giggles. "Okay, okay, I get it!" She approaches her friend.

"Get what?"

Lin's hand alights over Pania's shoulder. "You want me to stick a little closer, huh?" She winks.

Pania brushes the woman's hand off, but the memory of her touch lingers on Pania's skin. "Just need to figure out if we can get out of this musty old place before my brains fly straight outta my nose."

After Lin walks away, Pania turns back to the photos in her lap. She instantly regrets it. The album is filled with smiling faces, all white, all on beaches. Annoyed, she swaps it out for a smaller album. This one features all the native plants grown on the grounds, along with a few photos of the volunteers who help maintain it.

"Hello there!" A friendly male voice disrupts her train of thought. "How can I help you?" A well-dressed man with glasses and a smart beard emerges from a door at the far end of the room.

Lin moves towards the man, her words smooth and measured. "Good morning! Do you offer guided tours or is it all more of a self-led experience?"

He holds up his hands, signaling the otherwise empty room. "I'm available if you'd like, or you can browse on your own. Is there anything in particular you were looking to see today?"

"Actually, I was hoping you could give me a bit of a history lesson."

"You've certainly come to the right place for that," the man replies before holding out his hand. "I'm John. And you are...?"

The conversation continues, and he walks Lin through some of the antiques littered around the room and some of the stories behind them. "Does your friend want to join us?" he asks Lin.

Pania points at her cane and waves them both off. "I'm good here," she says before turning back to the photo albums. The next one she grabs is a bit dusty, eliciting another delicate sneeze.

"Bless you!" John calls from across the room.

"Thanks, mate."

She looks up and Lin catches her attention. There's mischief in her eyes. Lin uses the index and middle fingers on her right hand to suggest legs walking on her left hand, wordlessly asking if she needs to come closer. Pania grins and shakes her head before turning back to the book in her lap.

The album itself is old, the binding damaged from years of wear. The first image is of an old shack. At first glance, it could be the building she's sitting in, but the environment is wrong. This thing is in the middle of nowhere. There's a small wooden sign above the door.

Boys. She flips through the album, heart rate rising with every page. The miserable faces of children whose smiles don't reach their eyes, whose emaciated limbs are hidden behind over-sized clothing... she can practically hear the threats that elucidated those sorts of smiles.

She hasn't been paying any attention to them, but there are neat captions beneath each photograph. An image showing an empty classroom is described as an "opportunity for Aboriginal children to gain a traditional education." *What utter horse shit.*

She wonders where the kids in the photo album in front of her are now. *Dead, probably.* Not too many escaped unscathed from missions, whether the wounds were physical or hidden deeper beneath the surface. Even dear old Elaine, who managed to maintain her family ties during those years, has her scars. Pania considers herself incredibly lucky to be too young to have gone through mission life.

Lin startles her out of her thoughts. "Hey, did you want to try roaming the gardens? John says they're not too swampy if you're up for it."

"Yeah, let's have a go." Pania slams the album shut. "I've had enough history for one day."

John comes outside with them, prattling on about ribbonwood trees and out-of-season flowers as they wander. The grounds are damp, but Pania doesn't have any trouble finding her footing on the well-kept dirt path.

Lin points to a shock of tiny orange blossoms growing up a boulder. "Beautiful, aren't they?"

Pania comes closer and leans against Lin as she follows her friend's gaze. "Absolutely fiery," Pania agrees. "What are they called?"

"Wallflowers."

"Nothing forgettable about them."

Lin smiles. "Not all wallflowers fade into the background."

"Thank goodness for that." She winks, but Lin is still looking at the flowers and doesn't notice.

At least a half-dozen meters ahead of them, John calls out, "Do watch out for that dead branch hanging over the path! We haven't had a chance to prune it back yet."

Lin turns towards him and hollers, "You gonna let us enjoy these gardens, or are you just gonna keep rushing us through?" Once the words are out, she turns back with a look of horror. "Oh no, I can't believe I—"

But Pania's deep brown eyes are dancing with laughter. "Good on ya. He needed to hear it. If I hear one more word about how the hibiscus look in July..." She makes a loose fist and shakes it at the sky before the two women break into a fit of laughter, Pania still half-leaning on Lin for support.

By the time they're done giggling, the guide is back by their side. "Sorry, I can get so wrapped up in the details that I forget to stop and enjoy how lovely it is out here." He makes a show of taking a deep breath. "There's nothing better than the way the gardens smell after a nice rain."

"No worries, mate," Pania responds, dropping her hand from Lin's shoulder. "We'll let you know if we need anything."

The realization dawns on her that she's standing too close to Lin, so her feet quickly find new places to go. "Wait for me!" Lin springs down the path after her. "You sure can move when you want to!"

"Oh, I, uh—" Pania looks around for something to say. "I just wanted to check out the markings on this tree."

She runs a hand over the jagged edges where the bark has been damaged.

"Every scar tells a story," John pipes up. "If you'd like to hear it…"

"We're good," Lin replies, waving him off. She runs her fingers over the tree. "I'd love to hear this story though." Her fingers tap a jagged scar on Pania's hand.

Lin's words cut like lightning, cracking open wounds in her soul that have never fully healed. Pania yanks her hand away and heads back down the path towards the museum. "Some stories aren't meant to be told." Pania registers Lin's voice calling after her, but it doesn't matter. All that matters is getting away from intrusive memories of those last weeks with Sal.

#

The Lord's prayer game went on for another month before they got caught, though Miss Altro certainly suspected something was going on long before she figured it out. The woman may not have been particularly energetic when it came to their math or history classes, but their class quickly discovered how much she cared about that silly prayer.

Girls in secondary school weren't supposed to get canings, but Miss Altro said the circumstances were exceptional enough to warrant one anyway. That Friday after school, she caned them both six times across their hands. "You're lucky I don't have the strength to do it as hard as this blasphemy deserves," she'd spat in Pania's ear before she got started.

Yup, definitely used to be a nun, Pania decided as the cane flayed open her hands. Nuns were some of the only people who could hurt you that deeply while trying to convince you that you deserved so much worse. And end it all with some shit about the glory being God's.

I don't need a God that can find glory in this.

#

What did I do now? Lin wonders. She calls after Pania, glad that her latest misstep didn't involve a fistfight. Somehow though, this particular mistake feels worse. They'd planned this trip to be foolproof. Pania had specifically said she wasn't afraid.

"Look, Pania, please—" Lin catches up to her and puts a hand on her arm. Pania pulls her arm away forcefully, stepping off the path to get further away from Lin. Before Lin or John, who is seemingly paralyzed, can react, Pania's crashing to the ground enveloped in a cloud of dust.

"Are you okay?" John hurries over now that he knows what he can do. "I should have warned you, there are quite a few wombat burrows around here. Let me grab an icepack from inside. And a chair. I'll be right back." He scurries off, leaving the women alone.

"Are you hurt?" Lin asks.

"Think I sprained my ankle. It'll be fine."

"I'm not sure what I did," Lin continues meekly, "but I'm sorry. I didn't mean to upset you."

Pania sighs. "Look, it's not your fault. Let's just drop it, okay?"

Lin focuses her eyes on the ground. "Okay."

Later that night, her eyes blur as she watches a livestream of the Lantern Festival. The festivities could be taking place anywhere—although Lin knows it isn't China, thanks to all of their coronavirus-related restrictions. But where the celebration is happening doesn't matter. She has no one to go with her and no hope to bring to this new year. Her parents are alone and under new restrictions from the government, her mother only able to leave the house every other day to go to the shops and her father only able to leave to work their fields alone. As a testament to Lin's failures and loneliness, even the *yuanxiao* she'd ordered in is falling apart. Not a single one of the walnut-filled treats retains that circular shape supposed to symbolize familial harmony and happiness.

Chapter 8: Like a Weed

"I was thinking," Sam says at their next meeting, "it might be nice to do a group activity—"

Next to Lin, Tim put his hands over the rips in his jeans. He leans forward as he cuts the resident off. "Isn't that what this is?"

"I was thinking of something outside the hospital cafeteria." She shrugs. "Especially if this coronavirus thing becomes a problem here, it may become necessary to meet outdoors."

Lin's insides start to quake, and the cafeteria lights suddenly seem blinding. She hopes against reason that she'll be able to hide her fear of public places, or at least that Sam will be kind enough to ignore it. Not to mention fear of the virus itself—her family in China may not be able to say much when they video chat, but she's picked up on many of the subtle and not-so-subtle ways the virus is upending their lives. As casually as she can manage, she asks, "What would you want to do?"

"Well," Sam replies, shifting in her chair and smoothing an imaginary wrinkle in her lab coat. "There's some new research that suggests gardening and working with the soil can help TBI patients. I was thinking we could meet at Bilinga Beach next week and help clean up the flower beds. Make a positive impact on the community, you know?"

"None of us drive, but some of y'all might come with someone who does," Pania pipes up. "And there is never any parking over there. It's a regular nightmare."

Lin breathes a sigh of relief. Most of them take public transit, of course, but she would have to stay away from anywhere too busy regardless. She gives Pania a grateful smile. Sam notices and she pounces like a teacher spotting kids passing notes. "Do you know of any good places that we could help out, Lin?"

"I don't have the slightest clue who even takes care of public garden beds."

"Volunteers, mostly," Sam responds. "Which makes it a wonderful opportunity for us to get more involved in the community. So, anyone know of a community garden that could use some extra love but isn't as popular as the beach?"

The group falls silent aside from Robert's oxygen mask as they all ponder the question or ignore it, as the case may be.

Pania groans, as though the information is being forced out of her. "Fine, I know a place."

Sam asks Pania to put her into touch with the park's carers so they can determine what needs to be done. Pania recites a woman named Elaine's phone number through gritted teeth.

#

Elaine texts Pania the very next morning. *You said the doctor running your support group was some clueless white lady. Didn't realize that was a warning.*

Pania puts her piece of toast down, careful not to get jam all over her fingers, and sighs. *We both know there haven't been enough volunteers since Margo and Joe left. And your knees can't handle weeding like you used to. Figured we could use the help.*

It isn't long before her phone vibrates against the dull white of her kitchen table. *Fair enough. Better hope the rest of your group behaves.*

For a split second, she finds herself hoping that Lin, at least, might be inclined to misbehave... But the woman is in the middle of an emotional divorce; surely exploring a new flirtation is the last thing on her mind. *Especially after that scene you made at the museum last weekend.* Her lips curl into a frown at the memory.

To Elaine, she just texts back an emoji of a Black woman shrugging. The last few minutes she has before logging into work are spent looking for hope in the retro yellow kitchen walls.

#

Over a week passed before Pania was truly out of the hinterland. Luckily, the accident hadn't broken anything worse than her left wrist, so she walked and then stuck her right thumb out roadside once she was far enough from town. Her balance was off and she kept having these blinding headaches, but she pressed on.

There was no going back now. Her foster parents never seemed to care whether she was around or not, and they certainly wouldn't be eager to bring a car thief home. Then there was Mallory's dad to contend with, and how could she ever face Sal? When push had come to shove, Pania ran to escape the lights and sirens, leaving Sal unconscious in the passenger seat, blood still flowing from a gash in her forehead.

"Where do you want me to drop you?" the lady she was hitching with had asked when they reached the coast. The lady was elderly, her all-white hair in a short perm. Cheap perfume permeated every inch of the woman's ancient station wagon.

Don't give this lady any reason to snitch on you, Pania told herself. Her eyes were focused on the world outside the window, so she pretended she hadn't heard her while her mind searched for something safe to say.

"Honey, where did you want to get out?" she asked again, her thin voice a bit louder.

"What?" Pania did her best to look startled. "Oh, yeah, you can just drop me at a payphone so I can call my friend. That way, we can figure out where to meet."

"Mm, if you say so," the lady said without an ounce of conviction. At the next corner, she put her blinker on. "There's one just over there. Do you want me to wait for you?"

"Nope, I'm good," Pania responded, grabbing her bag and hoisting herself out of the car. "Thanks for the ride!"

The Ford Falcon lingered after Pania closed the door, so she headed towards the payphone and started digging for change. The booth was empty, so she walked in and made a show of waving goodbye to the old woman. The station wagon still didn't move, so Pania muttered a curse under her breath and dropped a couple of coins in the slot. *Better hope this thing doesn't eat my money.* She faked a phone call, putting on a cheery face. She only pushed the button to get her change back after the ancient yellow boat finally faded into the distance.

Now to figure out what she was actually going to do next.

The ten bucks she'd lifted from Mallory's dad's Mustang and the twenty she'd stolen from her foster mum's purse were going fast, but she needed to buy herself some time. And some lunch. So, she spent as long as possible savoring a cheap burger and free refills at a local chain. When the staff started giving her the side eye, she headed to the beach in search of a safe spot to stash herself for the night.

Around dusk, a cop confronted her as she wandered. "Have you been drinking?" he asked. When she shook her head no, he came closer, until he could smell her breath. "Sure looks like you have." He pointed behind her. She turned. Before she could take in the uneven footprints she'd left behind, her balance betrayed her and she fell into the piping hot sand.

"Ow, ow, ow!" she cried. The cop bent over. He might've been offering his hand, but he was also mumbling something offensive about drunk Aboriginal kids that Pania only half-understood. Pania shrank back.

"Ah, there you are, cousin!" Pania didn't realize the woman was talking to her until she was being tapped on the shoulder. "Are you okay, cousin?"

"Auntie?" Pania whispered, wondering who on Earth might recognize her as kin.

"Thanks, officer, I'll take it from here," the woman said. Her voice turned stern as she continued. "Where did you think you were going on your own? You know your medication makes you dizzy!"

The cop backed off, much to Pania's relief.

"Are you all right?" the woman's voice turned to concern. Pania found it hard to focus on her features in the fading light, but she could tell the woman was Aboriginal. That alone made her feel safe enough to confess the truth.

"No."

#

One of the conversations Pania and Lin had had leading up to their ill-fated museum trip has been circling in Lin's head for days. Or, rather, for nights, as she's lying in bed struggling with sleep. She'd given Pania some of the facts of her life, and the woman had shaken her head as if they didn't matter. *None of those things are you. Tell me about you.* How she'd answered Pania escapes her now; more than likely, she'd dodged the query to the best of her ability.

Ducking that question was nearly second nature, but in the silence of her own head, it's much harder to get away. And in her head, she knows that the real answers to her identity are as out of reach now as they were back in that café. *Maybe I'll try something new tomorrow, figure out at least something about whoever I am now.*

Tim's mentioned that he goes for power walks every morning. Maybe she should give those a try. But when morning comes and she finally sees Huan out the door for school, the idea of going on a walk makes her squirm. The neighbors here are too friendly, and if someone tries to start up a conversation with her, she's afraid she'll bite their head off. Figuratively, obviously. She lets herself have a little giggle at how ridiculous she's become, that it even crosses her mind that the metaphor might be too close to the truth.

The morning goes by as quickly as the internet tutorials on different topics fly across her tablet screen. Drawing videos are satisfying to watch, but her hands are too unsteady and her patience too thin for drawing to bring her any joy. The energetic young women in the dance workout videos Lin tries only annoy her until she's shouting at the screen. "Wait until your husband leaves you for an empty flat. We'll see how happy you are with your tight glutes then, Kelly!" By lunch, she's also ruled out hobbies ranging from painting and sculpting to writing and doing yoga.

Her mind wanders as she munches on a sad lunch of tuna on crackers. *Do hobbies even matter? They don't tell me what kind of person I am.* Having given the question of her identity enough attention to make herself feel uncomfortable, she rewards herself with an afternoon catching up on soaps until Huan arrives home. Her heart aches at the way her son shrinks to avoid attracting her attention, curling his shoulders down and hiding in his room under the pretense of homework. *There's my identity right there,* she thinks, *and it wants nothing to do with me.* She longs for the days when she could still be the motherly type. When her patience flowed as strong as the Yangtze.

She swallows the emptiness of the afternoon, along with her prescriptions, as dutifully as she can manage.

Sam calls the next morning. Lin gives a firm warning to the overly chatty magpie outside the living room window before taking the call.

The resident explains that the group is going to meet at the park during their normal group time next week.

"Is this..." Lin struggles to find the words. "Is this really necessary?" The thought of being out in public for extended periods of time still makes Lin flinch.

"If you're not ready for it, I understand if you need to stay home," Sam replies gently. "But growth tends to be painful."

"Fuck, I must be growing like a weed then." The words fly out accidentally.

On the other end of the line, Sam chuckles. "Like I said, I understand if you're not up to it. But there are a lot of cognitive benefits to both gardening and giving back. Do you garden at home?"

"Not really. Maybe I'll pick up a few potted plants, stick some herbs in the kitchen or something."

"That would be a great start," Sam replies.

"Maybe, maybe not. About six years ago, Huan gave me a daisy he'd grown in school. It was dead inside of a week. I'd probly chuck it across the room if I killed one that quickly now."

"The community gardens would be a great place to learn some skills to help you succeed."

Lin sighs, running a finger up and down a streak on the window. "Yeah, I know."

"Just think about it, okay?"

"Right."

Sam makes her take down the carer Elaine's phone number in case she does decide to come and can't locate the park, or the group. Lin wonders if this is some sort of trick Sam thinks will make her more likely to go, but she adds the number to her phone all the same.

She hangs up and slumps against the wall, taking in the unmatched socks she'd thrown around the living room that morning in frustration, the pile of dishes rising above the kitchen sink that she's still waiting for the patience to tackle. *It could be a good hobby, and the heavens above know I need a hobby.*

The midmorning light catches on some cobwebs taking over a collection of Huan's childhood photos. She focuses on the middle picture. Huan was in kindergarten when she'd taken it. His goofy grin had felt like her whole world. He'd picked out the frame himself. Its bold, primary colors have grown on her over the years. Now it serves as a reminder of easier, happier times.

The hairline crack in the glass isn't visible from her spot on the living room floor, but the mere reminder that it's there—and that she put it there—splinters her thoughts.

Sam's right. I've got to fix this brain. And if I pick up a hobby along the way, so much the better.

She steels herself against the dread over being out in public as much as she can, and makes a mental note to bring some sandwich fixings. People are much more willing to forgive and forget if you feed them.

#

Pania brings the grocery bags up slowly on her wheeled cart, so thankful that Robert's building has an elevator. She would've had to stop helping with his groceries ages ago otherwise, even though the poor guy doesn't have anyone else. She's acutely aware that she's one of the reasons he hasn't been pushed into an assisted living flat empty of memories of Michael, so she continues on.

Even if the old bogan can be a bit much sometimes. The pair have discussed his assumptions about Lin's son and his interests several times. As a gay man whose family avoided him in the early '80s, he gets how harmful stereotypes can be. But decades of conditioning can be hard to unlearn.

"Panny!" he calls, waving happily when she opens the door. Between halting breaths, he continues, "You remembered the mango and the ice cream?"

"First things on my list," she says with a smile as she sets the bags on the small kitchen table. "But where is your blender, hm?"

She notices his finger's a bit shaky when he points towards the counter. "The nurse left it next to the coffee pot."

"Oh, good. You know I don't have the balance to get it off the top of the fridge—not on these legs." *Or this shitty ankle.* But she avoids mentioning that to him, because the last thing she wants is to have to go into the trouble she ran into at the museum last weekend.

She bustles about, fixing their smoothies and putting away his groceries for the week. Pania has the tact to keep it to herself, but it's after 14:00 hours and this is certainly Robert's first meal of the day. Michael never would have let that happen.

"You run out of protein shakes a bit early this time?" she asks casually.

"Yes," he says with a sigh. "The night nurse is pregnant, and the poor thing was having a hard time so I forced her to have one. Her boyfriend isn't good to her, I think. She always comes in hungry."

"This the Wednesday and Friday nurse?"

"Yeah, Sheila."

"Want me to pick up granola or something, keep some easy things in the house for her? We can't have you running out of your stuff any more than we can have a pregnant working woman going hungry."

"Yes, just something simple, that would be fantastic."

"You got it."

The two share the rest of their milkshakes in companionable silence.

"Are you planning to try the gardening thing next week?" she asks.

"Oh no," he replies, wiping his chin with a napkin. "What help could I possible be to them?"

"More about what help the garden can be to you, you know." She scrapes the bottom of the glass with her spoon, avoiding his gaze.

"And what help will it be, huh? It'll exhaust me and then poor Mary will have to be at attention all night while

I suffer." He waves the idea away like it's a fly buzzing around his head. "No, I would be absolutely useless in a garden. Anyway, how much do I owe you for this week's haul?"

Pania pulls out the receipt. "Guess you've got a point there. Just shy of $120."

He pulls a few bills out of his wallet and pushes them towards her. "Thank you, as always. You're the only one who comes by and makes me feel like I'm not just a useless old man waiting to die."

She slips the grocery money in her purse. "You are absolutely not a useless old man, my friend," she chides.

"Doesn't always feel that way."

"You give a lot of great advice in group. Don't discount how much your experience is worth, especially in there."

"Still, I take more than I'm worth." He turns towards the hand cart she uses every week to haul his groceries.

Now it's her turn to wave him off. "Don't worry about that. I figure I pay it forward for you, maybe someday, someone will do the same for me."

"I know they will."

She stands and puts a hand on his shoulder. He pats it affectionately. "Remember," she says, "you're far from useless. And I'll see you next Saturday afternoon."

"Of course, my friend."

#

It's the dead of night, and Huan is crying, as though he's just a child again. Lin runs through the house, trying to find him. But his room is empty: no clothing, no furniture. Even the retro Frogger curtains he'd insisted on in grade 5 and loved ever since are gone. And yet still, his cries reach her ears.

"Where are you?" she yells in Mandarin, forgetting that Huan has always been more comfortable speaking English. "Huan!" She nearly trips over a dead duck, and one of its bloodied feathers sticks to her foot.

The crying intensifies and she hears her son's tiny, pre-school-age voice whisper, "Oh no, she's coming! Run!"

When she awakens, tears are streaming down her own cheeks, and she listens carefully for any signs the dream was real. Of course, the house is silent. Huan didn't come back from his father's on Monday. Said he wasn't ready yet.

The emptiness of the house only reinforces the truth behind her nightmare. She doesn't need to consult her mother's tattered copy of *The Book of Dreams* to tell her what that meant.

She texts Huan a quick "thinking of you," hoping the damage can be mended. That her house won't be loveless and empty forever.

The morning comes and then bleeds into afternoon. Her nerves are strung tighter and tighter. Huan still hasn't answered her text, and she's terrified to send too many messages. To seem desperate.

And yet, the silent house mocks her. She has to do something about it, but what? The takeout order for one screams of her loneliness. A news report on the problems with housing people still displaced from the bushfires gives her an idea, and within the hour, she's advertising the never-used guest bedroom for "preferably a single woman" on one of the official hosting sites for people impacted by the fires.

"Starlight shines far," she mutters. "Time to do something good and show Huan I'm not some kind of monster after all." *And get my baby home.*

#

The listing is only live for a few days before someone named Rosaline M. takes her up on her offer. With no one to discuss the event with, she spent the morning of the woman's arrival pacing and explaining her fears to the magpie out the living room window. *Sure beats trying to shut the damn bird up.* "You know, you're not so bad," she says out loud. "We could probably stop fighting if you just let me sleep past 6."

The bird doesn't respond, just pecks at something in the grass.

"Figures you'd ignore that."

A knock at the door gives her a quick start. She quickly pats her hair and smooths out her t-shirt. When she opens the door, her little worries about fly-aways and wrinkles evaporate. This is a woman who has seen things. Her bag is patched and even several feet away, Lin's eyes water from the scent of wildfire smoke.

"Hi, I'm Rosie," the woman says. "Are you Meiling Lee?"

"Yes, yes, come on in," Lin says. "And please, call me Lin."

"Of course." Rosie steps inside. "I hate to intrude on your hospitality so quickly, but is there any way I can use your shower? Haven't had a proper one in a week."

Lin's not about to argue with that. "Go ahead. Were there other bags on the porch that I can grab?"

The woman's smile is softened by sadness. "Nope. Just this."

"Okay." Lin hesitates, concentrating on every word and gesture in an effort to avoid offending her guest. "I'm going to order some dinner. Does Thai sound good?"

When Lin is alone again, she sinks into the couch, so drained from the brief interaction that she forgets to put in their takeout order.

Chapter 9: Roots

The day the group is meeting at the park comes fast, and Pania makes rookie mistakes in her code all through the workday. "You know how it is when you stare at something familiar for so long that it becomes indecipherable?" she asks a colleague on her last call of the day. "That's what today's been like for me."

"Ugh, sorry to hear Kel," the man replies. "Have a beer or two after hours, loosen up a little. It'd do you good."

"You know I can't drink," she says. "I'm unbalanced enough as it is." Pania sighs into the phone.

"True, and you stumble when you walk too!"

"Very funny, Tom." He can't see her, but Pania rolls her eyes at her coworker anyway. "Jokes aside, how are the app patches coming for Linders?"

The two go through the list of feature de-bugging they still need to do, flurries of emails going back and forth in tandem with their conversation. When Pania finally gets off the phone, she has to rush to get to the community gardens on time.

Her fingers shake as she locks her apartment. *Trying to be everybody's hero is gonna bite me in the ass sooner or later. Just please, not today.*

Elaine and the other Yugambeh elders who care for the gardens have been struggling to find volunteers who have the time—and the non-arthritic knees—necessary to keep up the gardens. But it's an unspoken rule that it's a garden by Yugambeh people, for Yugambeh people.

Normally, Pania's days here are relaxing—tending the plants in one of the four raised beds on her good days, workshopping resumes with women about to enter (or re-enter) the job market... but today, she just wants to hide behind her sweating purple water bottle and disappear.

Leading the group here feels like a betrayal, especially given that Pania isn't Yugambeh. The local Clan took her in when she showed up in Coolangatta as a homeless teenager with nothing to her name except trauma and a broken wrist, but she's still conscious that she and her family belong to other land. Though to what land she does belong, she cannot say.

Too many of the Minyangbal people Pania would ask for help were already working two jobs or losing the battle to deal with their own traumatic pasts. The Yugambeh people she did ask all turned her down.

So when she spots Sam and Elaine by the overflowing trash cans with Tim and possibly his girlfriend trailing uncertainly behind, Pania instinctively turns away. In doing so, she nearly runs straight into Lin.

#

The first night she'd spent in Elaine's house had been strange in that familiar way: the unfamiliar sounds and smells, the terror of not knowing what would happen in the morning—or if she would even be left alone through the night. Pania had gone through enough foster homes to know she had to try burying the fear, and to know that she couldn't.

Beyond the fear, there was her disappointment in herself, the way she'd left Sal behind to take the fall. The chaos in her mind made it impossible to fall asleep. By morning, she'd found every loose cobweb in the hastily swept room and run through every possible variation of how that morning's breakfast might play out.

Turns out, Pania needn't have worried so much. "Made eggs and toast," Elaine announced casually when Pania walked into the kitchen. "Help yourself, then tell me about yourself."

Keeping her head down, she'd nodded in silent agreement. After downing a single egg and single slice of toast, she said meekly, "So, what do you want to know?"

"No," Elaine had responded flatly. When Pania dared to look up and meet her eyes, the older woman smiled. "You aren't done with breakfast yet. Have some more."

So Pania ate until Elaine was satisfied that she'd had her fill. Afterwards, Pania walked her plate to the sink on unsteady legs and started washing the dishes. A weathered hand the same deep copper color as the kitchen's cozy cabinetry stayed Pania's arm. "Sit down. We don't want you having another dizzy spell, do we? Besides, I want you to tell me about yourself, not turn into my maid because I gave you a place to sleep last night."

"Oh." Pania moved back into the chair. "Right." Her throat was thick with emotion at this gentle display of caring. "What did you want to know?"

The older woman spent the morning chipping away at Pania's discomfort. Gradually, the words flowed a bit easier, but there was still one thing Elaine hadn't asked about and it had Pania on edge: why she was on the streets in the first place.

Rather than bring it up, Pania waited until she felt Elaine's curiosity about the other parts of her past had been sated. Then, her own questions bubbled to the surface. "Why'd you tell that cop you were my kin?"

"You might as well be." Elaine shrugged her delicate shoulders. "I grew up on a mission and while I still know who my family is, there's enough of us that don't. Looked like you might be in that camp."

The lines of Pania's mouth settled into a frown. "Well yeah, but like... why?"

Elaine rolled her eyes. "If you're worried I want something from you, put that out of your head this very minute. Too many Aboriginal people have gotten lost because White Australia tries so hard to erase our culture, and I'm tired of sitting by and letting it happen." Her eyes gazed intently into Pania's. "So, I stood up and put a stop to it, at least once."

"Oh."

"Now, your bag was awfully small for holding everything you own. I was thinking we'd head down to the op shop and pick up a few things for you." Pania's features lit up, so Elaine added quickly, "Now mind you, I'm not made of money. So don't expect the moon."

Pania's eyes had to betray her excitement, but her voice was as level as she could keep it. "I won't. Thank you."

"We can talk about some of the ways of my Clan on the drive over. After all, you're going to be part of my Clan too."

The thrill of hope that chased down Pania's spine made her temporarily forget about all she had left behind.

#

Back in the garden, Lin bursts out, "Jeezus, you scared me!" Her cheeks flush and she tucks a stray strand of her hair behind her ear. "I mean, uh, hi Pania. Thanks for suggesting this place."

"Sorry for startling you. Need me to...?" she makes a stick figure with her fingers and walks it away from Lin.

"No, no, I'm good," she says, a quick grin crossing her face at the motion. "No worries. This whole thing's just got me a bit more on edge than normal." She gestures towards the tote bag on her shoulder. "Got some sandwich fixings to help smooth over any trouble I cause."

Pania pats her friend's hand. "Everything's gonna be fine. I'm actually one of the carers here. We won't bite. Except for those sandwiches. They're gonna be in trouble."

Lin's frown softens. "You didn't mention you volunteer here. Show me the ropes?"

"Of course." She leads Lin towards the bed that's most overgrown, breathing a little easier once Elaine and Sam are out of sight behind the weeds. "Alright, this bed is full of squash plants. You able to recognize those?" She takes a seat on a bench across from the squash bed and motions for Lin's bag.

After setting the tote next to her friend, Lin points to a few of the enormous leaves along the ground. "These, yeah?"

"Exactly. So everything over yay high—" she gestures towards her calves— "needs to go, roots and all. But, if you catch a few of the squash, that's okay too. This damn bed was way too overcrowded even before the weeds took over."

"Got it." Lin grabs one of the tallest weeds and gives it a yank. The stem breaks, but the roots stay firmly in the ground. "These suckers are in here good."

"Yeah. Best way to get 'em out is to get mad at 'em."

"What?"

It's Pania's turn to grin. "You heard me. I know you've got a temper in there somewhere, so let's put it to work."

Lin drops the weed she'd pulled onto the grass. "You've gotta be fuckin' kidding me." Her hands brush the legs of her jeans, then she picks at the bit of green already lodged under a fingernail. "I'm not doing that on purpose."

"Oh, come on. Got to let it out somehow or other. It'll feel good."

Her voice trembles when she responds. "I resent that. Besides, that's not the kind of help I was looking for from this group."

"You can just twist 'em instead," Pania says, propping her chin against her hand. "Do you really think that group's helpful? I mean, it's got its moments, but lately feels like it's gone downhill."

"Then why do you go?" Lin asks.

"Sam might be out of touch, but I figure her residency's almost over and then we'll get somebody worth their salt in there."

"So, I say again, why bother? Sam's residency isn't up for another six months, and there's no guarantee she won't keep on afterwards. Aren't there other support groups around that you could join?"

"Haven't looked, but even if there was, I wouldn't switch. Couldn't do that to the group."

The other woman grabs more weeds, this time twisting as she pulls them up. "What, think we can't live without you or something?" She makes a show of dropping them on the ground, and dirt scatters across the asphalt.

"Look, me and Robert have been there for years. Between the two of us, we have a lot of good tips for living with TBIs and a decent bond, even if he is a bit of a bogan sometimes. Not trying to be cocky, just stating the facts. Sam barely knows her head from her ass most days."

"Mhm," Lin murmurs. "Sounds to me like you need us more than we need you."

"What?"

"Oh, you get so much validation from that group."

"I suppose so," Pania replies slowly, voice betraying her discomfort. "I also happen to enjoy the people in our group. Is that a crime?"

"Of course not. But don't pretend you don't need us when you do."

Pania finds herself feeling grateful when Elaine rounds the corner of the path, her bright green hat a striking contrast to her thick, dark braids. "Getting started on your own, huh? I should've guessed."

"Helps that I know what needs the most attention," Pania says, pointing at the mound of weeds Lin's already pulled.

"Looks like a big job. Can we help?" asks the young woman Pania spotted earlier. She's following Elaine and leading Tim by the arm. Her faded, stained gardening gloves and ready-to-work pony tail make Pania smile.

"You the famous Jenny?" Pania asks.

"Uh-oh, famous?" She turns to Tim and grins. "What've you been telling them, eh?"

"Oh, I uh, don't remember," he says with a playful wink.

"Very funny," she replies. To Lin, she asks, "Mind if we join you?"

"Go for it," Lin says. The pair settle in on the opposite end of the bed. "I didn't even think about bringing someone with me. Coulda, woulda, shoulda."

"Well, Tee was having a bad memory day and he wasn't sure he'd recognize you all. Figured if there was two of us, at least he wouldn't forget where he was going or why."

The three of them are working out how to tackle the bed when Elaine nudges Pania's elbow. "They've got this handled. Come on, let's go put the others to work."

#

Lin's anxiety about making a scene in public fades when Tim and Jenny start working on the other end of the squash bed. Tim doesn't seem interested in saying a single word, which makes him much easier to get along with—even if she notes the timidity as odd for him. The couple make quick work of the weeds, and the young woman is in an infectiously good mood.

"Whoah, look at this monster," Jenny says. She yanks up a coral berry bush that had taken root in a corner of the bed. Once it breaks free, its tangled roots fling clumps of dirt towards Lin. A few of the bright pink berries fall on the girl's scuffed sneakers.

"Hey, keep your dirt to yourselves!" Lin tosses a clod back towards the girl with a laugh.

"Yeah, really Jenny," Tim says uncomfortably. "Not cool."

"Oh, no, I was just joking. All good Tim," Lin says. She's still smiling, but she can see that this type of therapy isn't really up his alley. "Not much of a gardener, eh?"

"Um, no, I know what I'm doing, just don't much like it."

Lin gestures towards the ever-growing pile of weeds on the grass next to the bed. "It's a lot of work, but don't you find it satisfying?"

He shudders.

"If it helps, you can use my gardening gloves," Jenny offers quietly.

"Yeah, then you'll be able to enjoy the sandwiches I brought afterwards without having a side of dirt to go with it!" Lin adds.

But the mood has changed, and Tim steps out of the bed. "Nope. I'm done. No gloves, no sandwiches."

"You sure, Tee?" his girlfriend asks.

He nods and sits on the ground, head in his hands.

Wait, is he crying? Lin takes a few deep breaths. *Not my fault. No way is this my fault. That's not my fault, is it?* She thinks over her words again, trying to figure out if she'd said anything offensive or mean. She decides to toss out an olive branch, just in case. "I'm sorry if I upset you," she says, wiping her hands on her jeans. "You don't have to have one of the sandwiches if you don't want."

He looks up, wiping at his nose and snorting. "What? No, no, this isn't about anything you did. You're fine." His eyes flick over to Jenny's for confirmation. "Right, Jenny?"

"Exactly," she says. "Lin, why don't you and me finish up this bed while Tee takes a quick break. Maybe take a quick stroll around, see the rest of the place, Tee."

With a shake of his head, Tim says, "I'm already forgetting why I sat down in the first place. Damn this brain!" He smacks his forehead in frustration.

To Lin, she whispers, "Be right back," and then she hops out of the garden bed and starts talking to Tim in hushed tones.

Lin's amazed at how clearly the two love each other. And more than a little jealous. How can these young kids have such a sweet relationship? Hard times certainly didn't bring her and Jian together.

\#

Jian wasn't supposed to come back from field work until the end of the week. On their evening phone call, Huan had mentioned to his father that they were using tissues in the bathroom because she'd forgotten to buy toilet paper over the weekend.

After that comment, Lin couldn't get Jian off the phone fast enough. She was as red as a poinciana from holding in her emotions. The moment she heard the dial tone, she chucked her phone across the room, straight at Huan's picture on the wall. "Why would you tell him that?" she wailed. "You want him to think I can't take care of you? That I'm a bad mother?"

Huan covered his head with his hands and whimpered an excuse. "I just thought it was funny."

Her heart softened. His eleven-year-old frame was still small enough for her to pick up, so she scooped him up into her lap. "Oh, honey, don't be sad. I'm sorry, it's really not that big a deal. I'm just embarrassed, that's all."

The boy squealed and wiggled his way out of her arms before running into his room and locking the door.

A newly minted crack in the glass over Huan's picture made her breath catch in her throat. She slid down to the carpeted floor and sobbed, not noticing that her phone was nowhere to be found.

Jian arrived the next morning after she'd dropped off Huan at school. He wheeled his luggage into the entryway, then leaned on the handle as if for strength.

"You're home early," she said.

"Huan called me back last night."

Every muscle in her body tensed, like a criminal caught in the act. "I... I..." Her fingers began folding over themselves like a pair of knitting needles. "I'm trying," she finished lamely. "He understands that it's my injury, it's not his fault."

"He's terrified of you, Meiling." His voice was calm and stone-cold. It would be easier if he yelled at her, but Jian never let himself be ruled by his emotions. She no longer had that luxury.

"I'm doing all of those tricks from my therapist, but literally none of them work," Lin whined. "When my temper starts, I can't hold back no matter what I try."

Her husband took his hand off the luggage he'd rolled into the entryway long enough to gesture towards their son's empty room. "Regardless of your injuries, Huan can't keep living like this, Meiling. I know your recovery has been tough, and I've been doing as much as I can to be there for you both, but throwing things? Screaming at a child?"

Her eyes found the floor and she wished desperately for an escape. "I was louder than I intended, but screaming's a bit of a stretch."

"What if the next time you throw things, you're not aiming at a picture frame?" He kept the luggage between the two of them.

"I'm trying the best I can." Despite her best resolve, the tears began falling. "I know it's not enough, but I don't know what else to do."

"Let's hire a nanny, someone to be here with you two whenever I'm not around."

She wiped her nose. "Can we afford that?"

He sidestepped the luggage to put his hand lightly on her arm. "Huan's safety is worth any price."

Lin took a shaky breath in an attempt to keep control over her emotions. *He thinks I could hurt my own son.* But before her anger could wreak more havoc, it turned to grief. *I can't even guarantee that he's wrong.*

#

Tim watches Jenny and the Asian lady—*no, her name is... ugh, what is her name?*—quickly tackle the rest of the raised bed from his spot on the grass. He's still too rattled to make conversation, so he pushes himself up and motions wordlessly to Jenny that he's going to wander around the park. She gives an approving nod, then bends back towards the dirt.

His hands are still shaking, and he knows he needs to get away from the organized gardens. It's overwhelming, memories assaulting him everywhere he turns, from the scent of fresh peppers to the sight of the tangled tomato plants. *Why can't my damn brain remember that lady's name, but it can serve up this shit whenever it wants?*

Tears fill his eyes, and he wipes at them with the back of his hand. He's walking too fast, not paying enough attention to where he's going, and he smacks straight into a familiar-looking Black lady with a cane. Luckily, she doesn't fall. She turns and looks like she's about to tell him off when something in her face changes.

"You okay?" she asks skeptically.

"Uhh, yeah, just allergies." He tries to play it off, knowing a lecture would be easier to handle than a stranger probing for the truth. Especially if it's a stranger who actually knows him, and he just can't remember. "Forgot I had 'em, yanno? Heh, heh. Damn tomatoes."

There's no way she believes him. Her fingers brush against his and he's back in that greenhouse in his mind, Phil casually chatting him up and planting seeds for more than just some doomed strawberries. He whips his hand away, triggering a half-healed sprain in his wrist that he had, reliably, forgotten about.

"I have to go."

Her eyes soften and she backs up a few steps. She's about to speak, but he can't handle any questions so he cuts her off. "No, no, no, I'm fine, I'm fine, I'm fine. I just... I just need a minute. I'm fine. I'm fine. I'm fine." Eyes carefully on the ground, he sidesteps her and her cane before continuing further away from the goddamn gardens, no energy left to fake a sense of calm. *Why in the world did I think I could come here? How could I have thought this would be a good idea?*

He runs until he reaches the sidewalk outside of the park and the run-of-the-mill smells of super-heated trash and asphalt. It doesn't matter that the bench is burning from sitting in the sun. His fingers are shaking, he can barely breathe, and honestly the fire on the backs of his thighs is bringing his mind out of that memory hellhole and scorching it back towards the present. "How did I use to deal with this shit?" he asks himself out loud, just to hear his own voice. "I'm here, none of them can really do anything to me anymore."

But his panic has reached too high a state to just talk himself out of it. The stress builds up until it spills out of his eyes, and he lets himself go in it. A few minutes pass, and the feeling starts to subside. He wipes snot on the bottom of his t-shirt and stretches his legs out.

"Hey," comes the warm voice of the familiar stranger. She sits next to him on the bench, careful not to touch him. "I know that look. Is there anything I can do to help, Timmy boy?"

"Oh, so you do know me," he says in reply.

"Sorry?"

"Bad memory day. Every face looks familiar but I can never place any of 'em. Even Jenny was a stranger when I woke up this morning."

"Oh. I'm sorry." She fiddles with her cane but keeps silent, letting him take the lead.

"Sorry if I've asked this before, but what's on the top of your cane? Is that a shifter knob?"

She smiles. "It is, and no, you haven't asked me that before."

"You like cars then?"

"No." She shakes her head. "Stole one once."

This lady does *not* look like your average car thief. She's tall and thin, but a little flabby, like maybe she's sick and lost a bunch of weight. Her thick black hair is loosely braided with a yellow ribbon like a goddamn *Anne of Green Gables* character, though he's pretty sure none of them were Black. Her pale pastel dress has this stiff white collar that would've been too old-fashioned even for his grandma.

"That's dope."

"Bout as dope as whatever riled you up in that garden." The sarcasm is so matter-of-factly delivered, it barely even registers.

"I'm not talking about that."

"Don't then."

"You gonna tell me more about that car? And remind me of your name?"

"Pania. And hey, still got the shifter." She smiles to herself, gently rubbing the top of her cane with her thumb. "Taking it mighta saved my life, but that didn't stop the nightmares. I had to deal with those for years."

He can feel his pulse slowing to a normal rhythm once more. "Distractions help you deal at all?" he asks in a whisper.

"Wish they did. Hard to find a good distraction when everything reminds me of her, good or bad. Even harder to escape from your dreams."

"What reminds you of who?"

Pania shakes her head. "It doesn't matter anymore."

"It matters to me."

"Needing a distraction to get yourself off the edge doesn't mean that she matters."

He winces. *Fair enough.* "The assholes who turned me into this bumbling mess still matter to me, even if it's just because I care that they're still paying for what happened."

"In my case, she wasn't the problem," Pania replies, leaning on her cane to stand back up. "Everything else was."

"Oh." He ponders that over in his mind, focusing on the details of her story in an effort to crowd out his own memories, the beginning of this encounter already fuzzy around the edges. "I'm sorry for whatever happened."

"Me too. And same to you."

"No, I'm fi—" he stops himself when he sees her knowing smile. "Right. Yeah, thanks."

His next journal entry, which he drafts in his phone notes after Pania walks away, focuses on Miriam. After the panic from the flashback passed, he'd started thinking about why he told Pania that Miriam and Phil still mattered. *They shouldn't,* he types, *but I told the truth when I said they do.*

This bothers him. Normally, he'd just push the feelings back down and go for a walk, get a change of scenery to distract himself from it. But fear of the garden, where he'll have to return to find Jenny so they can get out of here, keeps him in his seat. Not only will he need to find her, but he'll need to explain why they have to leave. Another task that seems impossible right now. So, he keeps typing.

It doesn't matter that she's wrong. Or that she's a piece of work, or a shit mother, or that I'm better off without her. All that really matters is that she's my mother, and that she betrayed me. Everything I've done to rebuild my life on my own (twice now, thanks to some stupid accident), none of it has done anything about how much that hurts. He sighs, looks up from his phone, takes in the lame little coffee shop across the street that Pania disappeared into. *Maybe nothing will.*

Chapter 10: Troubled Waters

Well, gardening went better than I expected, Pania thought as she crossed the street to grab an iced coffee. Though she purposefully left without saying goodbye to Elaine or Sam and Tim certainly did not have a good time, so what did she really know?

Tim had caught her off-guard, that much was certain. There was no trace of the cocky attitude he normally approached the group with. In the gardens, it became clear how messed up the kid really is. That frantic look in his eyes, the terror guiding his steps... her heart aches with how familiar it all feels. She sends him a mental apology for how harshly she'd judged him. *Thirty years ago, maybe I wasn't all that different.* She certainly feels different now. Her fingers rub the top of her cane. It'd taken years of practice, but her own triggers have finally been tamed.

As though summoned by her thoughts, Sal is standing by a corner table waiting for her order.

Or, at least, what Pania figures a grown-up version of her would look like. Right down to the flowy summer dress and the elaborate brown plaits threaded through with wildflowers.

A self-appointed hinterland princess.

Pania nearly drops her cane and somehow bumps into both the person ahead of her and the person behind her in line. "Sorry, sorry," she mumbles distractedly as she regains her footing, her sore ankle throbbing in protest.

The woman glances over at the commotion, but Pania can't bear to meet her eyes. All of her energy goes into dashing out of the shop, breathing hard and deciding that maybe she doesn't need caffeine so late in the day anyway.

There's no way that was her. No way. Sal's biggest dream had been to "go bush," as she used to say, to live in the mountains and try to track down her family. So why in the hell would she be here, of all places? But despite her growing determination that it wasn't Sal—that it couldn't have been Sal, that Sal must have been dead for years by now, that Sal probably never walked away from the accident—Pania doesn't turn back. *So what if that makes me a coward?* Some questions are just best left unanswered.

The scare does make it easier to face whatever Elaine's thoughts were of the day's activities. Pania pulls out her phone. Four new messages. All from Elaine. She sucks in a deep breath and opens her texts.

Not too shabby. That girl might be clueless, but at least she's a quick study. The next message, sent seconds after the first: *At least, when it comes to vegetables.* The message is punctuated by an emoji of a face sticking its tongue out. The next messages were sent a bit later. *Not that anything bad happened.* The final message: *You seemed on edge though. You okay?*

Pania's fingers pause. Five or ten minutes ago, she might have known how to answer that question. Now?

Just a long day. She hits send. Three bubbles immediately appear as Elaine begins typing back.

Want to talk about it?

"And say what?" Pania wonders aloud. To Elaine, she types back, *Not really. Planning an early night.* The encounter with—she stops herself from even thinking the woman's name—has Pania's emotions swirling in confusion. How strong and courageous is she, if one glimpse of her past sends her scurrying like a frightened mouse in the opposite direction? How different is she from Tim, really?

The only thing that seems to be separating them is the privilege of his skin color, of him not knowing what it's like to be Aboriginal in this country. After all the weeks she's spent quietly scorning him from a distance, their mutual instinct to run from the past, from their memories, is somehow just as disorienting as the sudden reappearance of that past.

Still, we're nothing alike. Her mind fumbles over itself trying to excuse her and Tim's similarities, trying to remember how different they are. After all, he was the ignorant kid calling her an Abo not that long ago.

As if that even compares to what I did to Sal. Maybe just admit he's not so bad, she tells herself. *Just struggling to survive his own shit like I've struggled to survive mine.* Her sleep that night is plagued by nightmares of nuns and punishments and Sal. She awakens even more tired and unsure of herself than when she'd nodded off.

#

"Why on earth didn't you talk me out of that?" Tim hisses the minute the door to their flat is closed. "You said I agreed on a day I didn't remember what happened. So for god's sake, why didn't you remind me what we were doing tonight before we left for a fuckin' garden?"

He'd hoped the words would shame her into apologizing, but the minute they fly out, he knows his tone is wrong.

She crosses her arms. "Is that really my job?"

"It's part of my injury. Seriously, just keep me out of my own damn way!"

"It was in the calendar," Jenny huffs. "And look, when I do warn you about stuff, you just tell me you're an adult and you don't need my help. You never listen to me, so why should I even bother? Just look at the calendar."

"There's a difference between reminding me about stupid shit and—and—" he sputters, unwilling to say the words out loud.

"And what, Tee? How is this worse than you calling your mom every single time you forget you aren't speaking? How is this worse than the time you got lost coming home from the goddamn ice cream stand around the corner?"

"Because *that*—" he raises his voice and points back at the door— "that's where all of it started."

"How the hell can I know that, when you never even told me what happened in the first place?"

He's taken aback. "Wait, what?"

"You've never told me what happened."

"Wait, really? But you know—you know what he did to me."

Jenny's arms drop from their defensive stance and she reaches for his hand. "I know what he went to jail for, but I didn't know that gardening had anything to do with it. Is that the park where he..." she trails off.

He gives Jenny a look. "You know I'm not from around here. How would that make any sense?" He rolls his eyes but he sees the way her eyes are begging him for answers, and feels her desperate pressure on his hand. So, he adds, "It was the greenhouse at my dad's house. After Dad left, nobody used it until... him."

"Oh," she says softly. "I'm sorry, I didn't know."

"Not exactly a proud moment for me," he replies uneasily. "Didn't feel the need to go into all the details."

"Hey, what he did to you isn't your fault."

He yanks his hand away. "It's not that black and white. Not to me." He heads to the bedroom and shuts the door behind him. "I'm going to bed early. I'll, uh, I'll talk to you in the morning."

#

It'd been Phil's idea for Tim to get a job instead of loafing around all weekend, and of course Mum had been all over it. Tim resisted until he realized that Sophie—the girl he'd crushed on all through English class last year—had a cashier job at the burger joint in town. Her golden blonde hair and dazzling green eyes had half the boys in his class drooling after her. Her freckles and unassuming laugh had most of the girls under her spell too. So, off he went with a million-dollar smile and a sob story about his deadbeat dad to charm the manager into hiring him.

When he got home that first night, Mum immediately ordered him to "get that disgusting apron out of my house." It reeked of hamburgers and fryer oil, even after it went through the wash, so he started hanging it just inside the greenhouse. Phil was usually in there tending to the plants, so they'd gotten into the habit of chatting about his shift when he got in from work.

Tim let it slip that he was taking Sophie out on a date after getting a couple of paychecks in the bank. "Figured I'd take her somewhere nice, that way her parents won't worry so much about what we're gonna do in the park on the way home," he'd said with a grin, though he'd only ever kissed one girl before and didn't plan on much more than that with Sophie. "Still can't believe she said yes!"

The older man offered to help Tim get ready ahead of his date. "You wanna make sure she says yes to a second date, right?"

"Yeah, duh," he'd replied.

If only he'd realized what Phil had in mind.

#

Jian texts her to explain his ideas for dividing their assets. *I want you to keep the house. And obviously you can't work anymore, so I'll make sure you don't have to.* Lin lets out a sigh of relief, blowing a loose strand of hair out of her face.

Her lawyer has told her a thousand times to expect the worst during these negotiations, especially as their court date nears, but he's been more than generous. Jian left everything except his clothing, heirlooms from his side of the family, and some father-son photos. He didn't even take her old sedan, though Lin hasn't been able to drive it in years. *I just wish he would've warned me about his intentions before sending paperwork through the damn mail.*

Instead of morphing into some kind of greedy monster, he's been true to himself through the whole process. Never ruled by his emotions. Always logical and fair. *I think it's only fair for Huan to choose where he lives full-time,* he texted when they were discussing custody arrangements, *but either way, let's keep him in the same school to avoid disrupting his social life.*

If only Jian would turn into a monster, so she could find it in herself to hate him. Instead, she has to watch as the man she was supposed to love and cherish forever instead slips slowly and predictably away, with no one to blame except herself.

Even the notice she understands. After all, he was very cautious of her newfound temper. It was why he left in the first place. And as much as she wants to believe she wouldn't have taken it poorly, Lin can't find it in herself to pretend she would've been okay.

If only I'd asked for help that day. The accident just keeps finding new ways to ruin her life. Even if he'd always been a bit too detached, even if sometimes she had felt a bit insecure, he had always been there for her to count on. And now he's gone.

#

Tim spends the morning after their fight going through his journal entries, starting from the beginning. There are only a few weeks' worth of entries, but already he's able to see patterns he wouldn't have been able to spot before. On his bad memory days, he complains about feeling unworthy of Jenny: her patience, her work ethic, her beauty. On his good memory days, there's anger at the way she lets his past and present get so mixed up, how she chooses not to remind him of things like his fight with Miriam or the fact that he signed up to do *goddamn gardening*.

After he catches up, he writes through the confusion in his head. Or, at least, he tries. His lunch alarm goes off and he still hasn't figured out how to deal with the conflicting emotions that have, up until now, been neatly cordoned off to "bad memory days" or "good memory days." All of them together are overwhelming.

He munches on a ham sandwich and notes the irony that Jenny was the one who suggested he keep a journal in the first place. He's not sure if he's grateful for the situational clarity or angry at her for the internal chaos that the journaling has unveiled, that he now has to deal with.

Time for a power walk. At least this neighborhood helps clear his head. No one around here has had a meltdown worse than a midlife crisis in decades, and all that tended to yield was a motorcycle. Tim's own problems always seem so temporary after immersing himself in such boring surroundings.

His headphones are blasting EDM, per usual, when he walks out the door. Before stepping onto the sidewalk, he resets the alarm with his address to go off in half an hour. *You can never be too careful.*

The eucalyptus trees are looking fantastic given the time of year, and their sharp forest scent is like balm to his emotional wounds. He takes several deep, restorative breaths before moving on. The song in his ears is too high-strung for his mood, so he pulls his phone out to switch it up and then checks his Instagram notifications.

He's got a new message from Brian, but it's just a meme. Scrolling back, it saddens him how infrequently they talk. In his text messages, he has to scroll to find the last message from Brian: an "hbd" casually thrown at him for his birthday a few months back.

He goes back to Instagram, curious to see what his best friend—former best friend?—has been up to these days. Not a single four-wheeler photo, but plenty in the club, on dirt bikes, and with girls. Tim rolls his eyes. *Guy's not exactly drowning in guilt.*

The phone goes back into his pocket, and he keeps moving. But there's no peace in the neighborhood for him today.

Chapter 11: Teeter, Totter

Pania's conversation with Tim and then her encounter with what she quickly began thinking of as "the ghost of Sal" have left her shaken. Nightmares wake her up in a cold sweat three nights in a row.

Last night's dream had been a twisted version of her first full day with Elaine. The day she'd ended up at the hospital instead of the op shop, though Elaine did come through with a few goodies for her on discharge the next day. Instead of the empty hospital room she'd had as a teenager, the nightmare has her rooming with Sal's mangled, dead body.

Flies buzzed around the room, landing in Pania's hair. One landed on her arm. Its wings and legs were covered in blood. Pania screamed, and then a nun walked into the room. "This is just a fraction of what you deserve," the woman said, tapping a ruler against the doorframe. "Be grateful, you little murderer."

She'd awoken that morning screaming her denials, long before her alarm was set to go off.

Despite having voluntarily submitted documentation about her disability as part of her accommodation request to work from home—or perhaps because of it—it's not in her nature to take time off without advanced notice. But after such a rough start to her Friday morning, the email about needing a sick day practically writes itself.

Once her day has been cleared, Pania's not sure what to do with it. Books aren't holding her interest, and the community garden feels too dangerous, too close to Tuesday's encounter. She tries sitting in silence for a while, but being alone does nothing to push away the memories of her disturbing dreams. Or the memories that had inspired them.

"Let's see what the old bogan is up to," she says to herself and texts Robert. He'd given up talking on the phone a few years ago because of the oxygen tank, but the old guy could only type a word a minute on his phone. So, after sending a casual *Want some company?* text, she takes a hot shower to help clear her head.

"I'm sure he's had enough time to text back by now," she mumbles as she pulls a t-shirt over her head. Rather than a text, her phone shows a missed call and a voicemail from Robert's number. *Ha! Hard to break old habits, after all.*

Instead of Robert, the voicemail was left by one of his day nurses. "Um, I don't know how to say this over the phone but Robert's not going to be taking company today. Feel free to call me back or stop over to the flat for details."

Poor guy. Must be back in the hospital. The distraction is just what she needs, and she's already thinking about how to convince Sam to host the TBI group in his room next week when she figures she ought to run the idea past Robert first. "And of course he doesn't have his phone with him." She sighs and dials the hospital. The receptionist has no record of him being in either the ER or a room, so Pania calls the day nurse back.

"Hello?" the woman's voice is timid, uncertain.

"Hi, this is Pania, you left a message on my phone about Robert being out of commission today. Which hospital did he go to?"

There's a sniffle on the other end of the line and it sets Pania's senses tingling. "Is... is he okay?"

"Robert's gone. I called the cops but I dunno what happened, he just disappeared."

Pania's eyes practically bug out of her head. "He what now? The man can barely move!"

"He asked me to wash up the dishes in the sink before I left." Another sniffle. "But there was no sponge, so he had me digging through his spare room closet for extras. Haha, the man doesn't know how to organize a thing."

"But wait, where on earth could he have gone? I just can't see him disappearing for no reason."

"I wouldn't have thought he would—or could—do this either, but we lost him just outside of the complex. He must have grabbed a cab."

"Are you sure he wasn't... I don't know, elder-napped or something?" She runs a hand through her hair, agitated by this turn of events.

"The cops are treating it like a suicide attempt because of the note."

"Back up." The words come out more demanding than she'd intended, but she's not going to waste time apologizing. "There's a note?"

"He left it on the kitchen table. Most of it I can't make out, but it's addressed to me. Said something about being sorry, and, uh, how tired he is of being a—useless, maybe?—old man."

"Ooh, Robert..." Pania moans. "The cops are out looking for him?"

"Yes, but there were only two of them so they aren't going to get very far on their own. Do you have any idea where he might go?"

"No, no... wait. Today's Friday? What time did he go missing?"

"I'd just finished making his lunch, so maybe noon or 12:30."

Pania feels the blood drain from her face. "Have them check the beaches. He used to snorkel with his partner around this time every week."

"God, you don't think he would...?" the nurse trails off.

"Let's just hope he had the sense to stay out of the water."

"Yeah, I've gotta pass this information along to the cops. Thank you." The line goes dead.

In the silence of her apartment, Pania asks, "Robert, what have you done?"

#

Tim doesn't want to do anything rash about Jenny, so he takes the rest of the week to go through the journal and write out his reactions and thoughts to it each day. *I'm writin' essays like a goddamn school boy.* Eleven-year-old Tim never would've believed it.

It's Friday, and sometimes Jenny leaves the office early, so he decides to take his journal down to the park so he can think in peace. He sets the phone alarm for an hour before he walks out the door.

Journal and pen in hand help him remember what he's doing out today, so he does double time to the park and quickly finds a bench in the shade. He rereads the entries so that they're fresh in his mind, swatting the occasional bug out of his hair.

He talks as he writes. "Okay, it's not Jenny's fault if I never told her specifics. Now that I'm not mad about it, I can see that. But I'm still struggling with the idea that she lets my past and present get so confused. Like... what if I built a chart to make it easier to tell what my

116

hard lines are? Might be clunky, might be worth it. At least I'll be able to see if she respects it. I can write half of it on a good memory day and half on a bad memory day." He continues, writing out some of his ideas and frustrations and trying to be fair based on what he's written already. Bad Memory Tim always thinks she's basically a martyr for him, but he doesn't see that in the entries of Good Memory Tim, whose entries are fewer and farther between. And well, he woke up this morning without knowing who Jenny was, so he's struggling with some of the bitterness he's reading in the entries where he remembers.

Why do you make me feel like this, Jenny? He scratches out some questions for himself to answer on a good memory day. Jenny was a bit irritable this morning—but, he reminds himself, the woman is under a lot of stress. Judging their entire lives together based on one morning feels icky to him.

His phone alarm is pinging before he's ready. Luckily, muscle memory never seems to leave him, so he resets it with barely a glance and keeps going. When it goes off again, he sighs and closes the book. *Might as well save some pages for Good Memory Tim. Gotta figure out why that guy's so angry.*

He sets the journal and pen down to check his phone before heading home. Nothing from Jenny yet, thankfully, but there is a new message for him on Instagram. It's from Mel.

You always were a great screw.

Tim rolls his eyes, but a grin slips onto his face. *Good to know I'm still more than a charity case to somebody.*

#

Pania doesn't want to wait for Robert's nurse to play telephone with the police if her friend is in trouble. *Don't need more ghosts haunting me.* Though her bones feel like lead and her body complains at every move, she manages her shoes and takes a cab to the beach.

Thankfully, Robert's year of complaining about his accident included quite a few days bemoaning the disruption and eventual loss of his and Michael's snorkeling routine, so she knows which beach she's heading to. Her arrival seems to be ahead of the police, so Pania hobbles as quickly as she can towards the water.

The sand proves difficult, at best, for her balance. After a few stumbles, she decides to stay on the sidewalk until she sees something worth investigating.

"Watch out, lady!" yells a teenaged skateboarder as he *whooshes* by. His thick dark hair whips in the wind, mimicking the nearby ocean waves.

"You watch out!" she snaps back. *That old bogan better be sitting on one of these benches so I can get out of here before somebody runs me over.*

Her irritation fades, replaced with nerves bundled tight in her throat, when she spots an odd silhouette beyond the swimming area near Snapper Rocks. On closer inspection, it's the red flag marking dangerous waters. But there's something else behind it.

A walker.

Fuck.

Running isn't something Pania has tried to do in a very long time, but she gives it a good try now. *Please be there. Please be there.*

"Are you okay, ma'am?"

The voice sounds young and feminine. And nervous.

"Not really," Pania hollers without stopping. "Looking for someone."

"Can I help?" The woman comes up on her right, matching her pace without so much as breathing hard. Pania catches the woman's playfully nerdy glasses and teased blonde hair in her peripheral vision.

"Can you run?"

"Yes."

"Oh thank goodness." Pania huffs and lets herself stop. Between breaths, she points across the beach towards the walker. "My friend. He's missing. Please. Make sure he didn't go in the water."

The woman nods and darts off. A few meters away, she stops and yells, "What's his name?" Pania uses all of her energy to shout Robert's name. Then she collapses onto the sidewalk. She chants in her head like a prayer, *Not in the water. Not in the water. Not in the water.*

Her breathing is still ragged when swinging arms on the horizon catch her attention. It's the blonde.

She's upset.

#

The court date set for the divorce hearing sneaks up on Lin. She hadn't needed to attend the day's hearing; the divorce was uncontested, and both asset division and care for Huan were being sorted separately. Indeed, most of it already was. But Lin felt it a sacrilege not to attend, not to see Jian one last time before their marriage fell in the eyes of the law.

She doesn't need to utter a word during the proceedings, simply sit and wait while a judge formalizes the decision her husband has thrust on her. Her eyes focus on her almost-ex-husband, how he's got his hair slicked back like some heaven-sent hotshot. Her fingers dig into her thigh to help control her anger. No need for the judge to see firsthand how she's earned this divorce.

Jian only looks her way once, his dark eyes shining. *Is he... crying?* But no, it's merely a trick of the light. The moment their hearing is officially over, he makes a beeline for the door. She lets him go. After all, she's not here for a confrontation. Simply to observe the death of their life together, together.

Once she's sure that he's safely on his way, Lin makes for the door. With every step, she can feel the air leaching energy, purpose, from her body. *The fuck am I supposed to do now?* There are no answers for her at the courthouse. She heads home in a fog, wondering if this feeling is worth a call to her therapist.

She'd nearly forgotten about the boarder staying in the guest bedroom. When the delicious aromas of soy sauce and vinegar greet her at the door, the thought that Jian beat her home involuntarily crosses her mind. But then, Rosie's singing drifts in Lin's direction, breaking the illusion. Her lilting melody carries a quiet joy within it. But its notes, and the reminders they bring of Lin's new life, offer only despair to her soul.

Her knees buckle and she sinks to the floor, simultaneously overcome with grief and annoyed at herself for being so damn dramatic. If only she had better managed emotions, none of this would be happening to her. *If only I'd been dealt a different hand.*

Rosie comes in with a bowl of steaming noodles, her flowing skirt seeming to dance with her every movement. When she spots Lin, she sits on the floor next to her and hands her some chopsticks. "I knew this was going to be hard for you, so I made Biang Biang noodles. Thought you might need a taste of home. Wikipedia said these come from your hometown."

Lin nods and silently takes the bowl. Though she's not sure she's hungry, she slurps down several of the surprisingly decent noodles to be polite. The *mm*s and *hmm*s seem to satisfy Rosie, who pats her knee and looks at her with concern.

"Thank you," Lin murmurs, "for making me feel less alone."

"Just returning the favor," Rosie replies. With that, she stands and heads back to the kitchen.

At least that's one thing I haven't managed to mess up, Lin thinks wryly.

#

The nanny lasted two weeks before the young woman stood between Lin and Huan. "I can't let you hit him," she had said. Her lip quivered. "It's not only wrong, it's illegal!"

"This isn't a school, Jasmine," Lin pointed out in a strained voice. "And it's standard practice in our culture. It's just a little slap on the wrist. Relax."

Huan was cowering behind her, playing up his fear of the very same punishment Lin had meted out on occasion before the accident. The girl turned around and motioned for him to go into his room. It was a suggestion she didn't need to make twice.

"Why am I here, Lin?" she hissed once Huan's door was safely closed. "It's time to let that practice go."

Words failed Lin in that moment. The punishment itself may not have been unheard of in her home before the accident... but she'd never had to worry about her self-control before the accident, either. Deep down, she knew the girl was right, even if she was coming at it from a fundamentally different place than Lin.

Her rage returned, that this nobody could be so wrong and yet still end up being right. Her jaw tightened and her hands burst with the need to move. Without thinking, she grabbed the empty coffee cup on the counter next to her and hurled it in Jasmine's direction. A shriek and the smash of porcelain against a cupboard were followed by a devastating silence. The girl's eyes shifted from panic to studying, as if she was trying to determine if Lin was still a threat or if the danger was over. Behind her, a solitary drip of coffee oozed down from the site of the impact.

Oh no.

The girl followed Huan to his room. When the cops arrived, they escorted her and Huan to the front door. "My baby, please, don't take my baby," Lin had pleaded.

They refused to leave until Jian came home. The rest of the night was a blur, filled with crying and lecturing and pleading and apologies and then, once again, with silence. "I just don't know who you are anymore, Lin," Jian said as she sank into the couch.

She whispered back, so quiet she didn't know if he heard. "Me neither."

Her parents were on the next flight to Brisbane. They spent the next six months living in the guest room.

#

Tim's ready with his plan when Jenny walks in the door. "Listen, I think this could really help us. I can build out a chart with some things I always want a warning about, and then if I give you shit for it on a day where I don't remember, you can just point to the chart. Better yet, I'll take a picture and keep it in my daily download notes."

"Um, okay," she says uncertainly. "If you really think it'll help."

"Great. Problem solved. Let's head down to Bunnings so we can grab the supplies I need to make it."

"Right now?"

"Bad memory day, means no time like the present."

"Look, can we just... not do this right now? We don't even have a spot to put it. I'm just too exhausted, Tee."

"But you say that every day."

"So? It's always true. I've got a lot on my shoulders, being the only one with an income."

"Wait... are you guilt tripping me right now? It's not my fault my brain is a disaster zone."

"Puh-lease," she snaps back, "you were beyond reckless. Sure, Brian never should've dared you to do it, but those trails were closed for a reason. Shoulda thought of that before you went on your little joyride. Maybe then you wouldn't be messaging your ex behind my back."

Tim's eyes widen. Jenny's demeanor changes. "Oh my god, I'm sorry, I shouldn't have said that." Her words spill out quickly, ahead of her tears. For a split second, he wonders if they're crocodile tears. "Please, don't be mad, it's just, it's been such a long day and I am so tired."

"You snoop in my phone now?"

"I didn't mean to, I was just checking when your next doctor's appointment was in your calendar and then it popped up, and—"

He holds up a hand to stop her. "I... I need some space." He grabs his journal and heads to the bedroom. There are no words for how he feels, but at least he can capture what was said so he can figure it out later. He rushes to get the words out before the encounter has a chance to fade, but he needn't have worried. The blaming and the betrayal sting long after he deposits the book back in its place underneath the bed. When Jenny comes in, he pretends to be asleep. For the first time since the accident, he finds himself hoping tomorrow is a bad memory day.

Chapter 12: Hanging by a Thread

The blonde refuses to go into the water, but she points towards the edge of the rocky outcropping, at a pair of clunky white sneakers that scream *old man*. "Are these your friend's?" she asks nervously.

The blood drains from Pania's face. "Shit. Call the cops." She leans against Robert's walker for support. "Tell them we know where Robert Buckley went."

Before she gets on the phone, the girl has the presence of mind to flag down the several dozen surfers out riding the waves. She orders them to fan out and begin a preliminary search of the water and then dials the emergency number.

It takes less than an hour for police, lifeguards, rescue divers, and ambulance crews to swarm the outcropping. The day nurse arrives and breaks down in tears at the sight of his walker. She clings to Pania, who is too busy disassociating to either cry or disentangle herself from the woman's grip.

Eventually, the blonde woman brings sandwiches around and tells Pania and the day nurse to keep their strength up. Pania takes one wordlessly and obeys, not noticing whether she's hungry or whether the sandwich tastes decent or whether she's sat there for three hours or three days. It's all the same to her until the jet skis come back with news about a body. Her stomach churns, and she knows she doesn't have the nerve to identify her friend.

"I've gotta go," she says to the day nurse. "I can't see him like that."

The woman sniffles and waves her off. "I understand. I need to see this through to the bitter end."

The blonde woman appears out of nowhere and offers a steadying hand until Pania can find a cab. "Thank you—I'm so sorry, what is your name?"

"Jan. It's no problem. I'm the one who's sorry. What happened to your friend was awful."

After she settles in the cab, Pania pats the younger woman's hand. "I really appreciated you today, Jan." The door closes and she gives the driver her address. Though her body arrives home just ten minutes later, her heart spends the night battered by the breaking waves at Snapper Rocks.

#

According to his journal, moon-eyed Bad Memory Day Tim has been waiting for a good memory day to figure out why he's so mad at Jenny all the time. *Ugh, I really have no fuckin' clue when my brain's misbehaving.* The last entry was only yesterday morning, but he can clearly see the same patterns of blame and martyrdom that he'd noticed even before the accident.

Okay, fine, you want a clue, might-propose-sometime-Tim? I spent two full years trying to get rid of Miriam and stop her from harassing me, stop her from finding things out about where I live, where I work, and alllll that shit. He might be mad, but he still takes a moment to enjoy swirling the pen to form a few extra l's. And to breathe in the delicious scent of the fried food from the Boliano's food truck just twenty feet away on the curb.

If he'd only remembered to bring his wallet, he could've grabbed a bacon and egg burger, made this chore a little less awful. But unsurprisingly, he forgot it, and now he has to get back to thinking through the mess his life has always been and figure out how to keep moving forward.

He looks back over the recent entries again and sighs. Thinking about how Miriam betrayed him, continues to betray him every day, is something he actively avoids. But obviously letting his bad memory days be a vacation from, well, his bad memories, isn't working out.

Miriam turned a blind eye when Phil started abusing me. Nothin ever would've changed if it weren't for the goddamn gym teacher asking about a bruise. <u>Miriam</u>— here he paused writing to viciously underline her name, ripping the paper a bit in the process—*just pretended a girl gave it to me. As if that would've made it normal. Besides, Sophie was so freakin delicate, I don't even think both of her hands together could've made a bruise that size... much less that nasty. And before you start excusing <u>Miriam</u>, it gets worse.* His anger is rising, and he's starting to forget why he wanted to write this out in the first place.

To stay focused on what his point even is, he knows he has to calm down. Tilting his head back, he inhales deeply, pretending on the exhale that he's back on the four-wheel trails with Brian, blowing smoke rings into the trees when the heat becomes too much to bear in the sun. Man, those were the good old days, when he wasn't constantly being surprised by his past. When it was just a casual buzz in the background, a live wire he knew how to avoid.

Anyway. Jenny knows all about why Miriam and I don't talk, will never talk. She knows the sorts of things Miriam ignored for the sake of "having a man around the house," though I see she's trying to convince you otherwise. She knows about the no-contact order I've got in place. But when Miriam calls, Jenny doesn't try to stop me from talking to her or even remind me that it's literally against the law. And now? We're gonna need to find a new place to live at the rate we're going. Miriam's gonna figure out where I live and start showing up at the flat, screaming at the door until the neighbors call the cops, maybe even try to get me into her car and adult-nap me or whatever and then get the no-contact order thrown out.

And if we have to move (again) to keep Miriam out of our lives, Jenny will no doubt remind me how much it costs literally anywhere else in this neighborhood and pull a guilt trip because I can't fuckin work until this brain stops its bullshit. The best part is she'll do it to you, Bad Memory Boy. And you'll act like she's a martyr for it instead of fighting back about the limits she swore to help you enforce. They are there for good fuckin reasons. Jenny keeps giving that woman hope that she can break back into my life, and one of these days, you're gonna pay for that carelessness. In more ways than one.

He pauses and takes another deep breath. *Maybe instead of thinking about proposing, you should think about getting independent enough to break up.*

#

"Hey Mum," Tim called as he walked into the house. Thursdays were Tim's day off from the dog groomers so he usually wandered over for lunch and stayed until dinner to stretch his grocery budget. They didn't have the best of relationships since Phil's conviction, and he'd moved into a tiny flat before he could really afford it, just days after graduating high school. Both his budget and his relationship with Mum were still strained almost two years later, but things were getting easier. They just needed more time.

"Mum?" he called again, a little louder. He doublechecked his phone. Nearly 12:30. "Whatever," he mumbled as he busied himself with sandwich fixings.

While he munched, he glanced at the clutter on the table. Some junk mail, a box of stale biscuits. An envelope with a handwritten address on it caught his eye. *There's no way.* The return address was in Maryborough. He took a quick peek inside the envelope, but it was empty.

The screen door behind him clattered shut. He jumped, but it was just Mum.

"Oh jeezus, you scared me!" she cried out. "Is it Thursday already?"

"Yeah, it is." He shook the envelope in her face. "Now, what the hell is this?"

The color drained from her face, but she recovered and retorted, "What, is it a crime to get the mail?"

Tim's eyes narrowed. "You really want to talk about crime?"

She huffed. "I'm just saying. It's not like I'm writing back."

"What did it say?" After the words were out of his mouth, he realized he probably didn't want to know.

Mum sat heavily down at the table and pulled the letter out of her bra. "He's just whining that they're transferring him up north." She tapped the paper on the table to emphasize her next words. "Far. Away." Her eyes met his, and there was a brief glimmer of... love? Sadness? Tim couldn't tell. "You're safe."

#

It's the end of Huan's first weekend back in the house since the divorce, and both mother and son are trying too hard to tiptoe around each other. "Just give him time," her mother had said on their weekly video call. "It's a big adjustment now that you're living in a broken home."

"Niáng!" Lin burst out angrily.

"What?" she'd asked, pushing up on the rounded ends of her freshly done bob. "It's ugly, but it's the truth."

Their video call had ended not long after that. Despite her anger, the truth behind her mother's cruel words stung, still stings. She thinks of them whenever she and Huan make stilted conversation, as if they're both navigating invisible fissures in their cozy two-story colonial.

"Sorry, I didn't mean to startle you," Lin says on Monday morning when she nearly bumps into him in the hallway between the bathroom and the kitchen.

"You're fine," he replies, keeping his eyes trained on her toes. "Sorry to get in your way."

Rosie's a natural bridge between them. Her flowing skirts and incredible knack at putting them both at ease make the days much more tolerable than they otherwise might be.

"Your mum mentioned you like having a big fry-up for breakfast." This morning, Rosie's voice carries some much-needed cheeriness to the narrow hallway.

A brief grin crosses Huan's face. The aroma of eggs, beans, and bacon were what had him running for the kitchen in the first place.

"You two talk about me now?" he asks Lin, a hint of hopefulness, of incredulity, creeping into his words.

130

"Only good things," Lin reassures him. "Now go get that bacon!"

"Consider it done."

Lin's satisfied that he's eaten his fill by the time he rushes out the door for school. She starts clearing the plates. "Go sit, relax," she says to Rosie.

"No, let me help you."

Lin motions towards the door to Huan's bedroom. "You already have. Thank you." Huan might be spending the next week at his father's, but he'd left on good terms, with a full belly and a plan to come back on Sunday afternoon. Lin isn't sure they'd parted on such good terms even once since Jian moved out.

With an understanding smile, Rosie acquiesces and heads to the couch. From the other room, she yells, "Hey, what are your favorite soaps? You a *Neighbours* kind of woman or H&A?"

Lin smiles as she scrubs the dishes, noting from Rosie's inflection of the word *Neighbours* that she most certainly prefers *Home and Away*. *Oh, I'll get her,* Lin thinks. Out loud, she calls back, "And what makes you think I'm into soaps at all?"

Rosie reappears at the edge of the kitchen. "You mean to tell me you're not?" She twists the remote back and forth playfully. "Even when all of your fancy smart TV's recommendations are new episodes of *Days of Our Lives* and *The Bold and the Beautiful*?"

"Fine, fine, you caught me. I just love *Neighbours* so much; I've been branching out into American soaps because I can't stand waiting for new episodes."

Rosie sticks out her tongue at her. "Ew, of course you do. *Neighbours* is so obviously inferior."

Lin pretends to be devastated, clutching at her heart. "Ohh, what judgment! And from a *Home and Away* girl, no less!" While Rosie is busy rolling her eyes, Lin takes a chance and splashes some suds in her direction.

"Hey now!" Rosie says with a laugh. "What was that for?"

"Cleaning up that filthy blasphemy you're spouting!" Lin laughs.

"Filthy, huh?" Rosie smirks. "Now that's the pot calling the kettle black." She waltzes up to Lin, swipes some bubbles from the sink, and dabs them on Lin's nose.

The two lock eyes and, before Lin can question whether it's a good idea or not, she stands on her tiptoes and kisses her, putting a soapy hand in Rosie's loose curls to pull her in close. The taller woman's hands press into the small of her back, run along her spine, find the curves of her ass.

Lin lets out a tiny moan. It's been a long time since she's felt so wanted. But then Rosie pulls back and puts a hand on one of hers gently. "This is a very, very bad idea," she whispers.

"Is it?" Lin whispers back.

"I wish it wasn't. But that doesn't change the fact that it is." She doesn't drop her gaze, instead drinking in every detail of Lin's face with an openness that defies shame. Rosie pulls Lin's hand from her hair and then holds it at her side.

"Yeah, you're probably right," Lin whispers, returning her gaze and putting gentle pressure on her hand. "Should we go put on some H&A reruns?"

"You bet." Neither one of them move.

"I'll just finish these up in here and I'll be right in." Lin gives a slight nod towards the sink.

"Wouldn't want to get in your way," Rosie says without so much as a twitch.

"You could never," Lin says, voice still barely a whisper. She dares to pull Rosie in for another kiss, but in doing so, she breaks the spell.

Rosie lets go of Lin's hand and picks the remote up off the counter. "I'll see you in there." Before she walks away, she wipes the last of the suds off Lin's nose.

#

Pania hadn't expected to roll from a sick day straight into bereavement leave, and so she tries to work on Monday. Robert had asked her years ago if she would help coordinate his funeral arrangements, so she knows she'll have to get things moving. But her appointment with the funeral home isn't until tomorrow, and it seems futile to sit alone with her grief all day. She'd spent most of the weekend doing exactly that as she went through his files, set out his funeral outfit, and looked for details on what he had previously arranged and what she would need to do. She also took a moment to place all the photos of him and Michael facedown out of respect, though the old bogan wouldn't have cared one way or the other.

Work is a welcome distraction, but she has to admit, it's not a particularly productive one. When Tom asks her how she's feeling, she avoids talking about Robert so she doesn't have to say his name, instead rolling with his assumption that she's still under the weather. Refusing to name a dead person would immediately call attention to herself as Aboriginal—the last thing she needs when she's asking the team for a little grace and her second Friday off in a row.

The next day, Pania isn't sure she wants to even bother with the TBI group, since she knows Sam will let the others know about Robert's passing and the funeral scheduled for Friday. But isolating herself when she's grieving feels wrong, and they're the people who knew Robert best.

Lin gives her a quizzical look when she takes the seat next to her, and that's when Pania pauses to think about how haggard she must look. "Rough day?" Lin asks.

"Rough week," Pania responds. Lin reaches over and pats her thigh reassuringly, and it's hard for Pania to keep her expression level.

The others file in and Sam gets through the dreaded announcement. Pania doesn't look, but she can feel the air change. She wants to bat away their sympathies like so many cobwebs crowding her face. Maybe isolation wouldn't have been such a bad option after all.

"To honor Robert, let's take a moment to think about some of our favorite memories with him. If anyone would like to share, please do." Sam's saccharine voice breaks through Pania's thoughts.

Instead of stopping at how irritated she is by the way Sam continues to say his name—an emotion she knows she's wearing on her face—Pania thinks back on some of her favorite small, everyday moments with her friend. How committed the old man was to growing past stereotypes, like in their conversations every week about Aboriginal Australian issues or his occasional goof-ups in group. They'd had quite the conversation about stereotypes after his comments about Lin's son and his interests. She also loves how his life was full of past loves and losses, but he still found new things to care about.

Like those goddamn milkshakes. She smiles softly at the thought.

The group stays quiet for several moments, but then Tim breaks the silence. "Man, that old guy sure did know how to hide a fart behind the noise of that oxygen tank." Lin giggles, which he takes as encouragement to continue. "I made the mistake of sharing an elevator with him once. *Once.* It was so awful, I left a special note about it in my phone and added a reminder tied to my calendar every week."

"Yeah, those protein shakes did him no favors, I'm not gonna lie," Pania says.

"Didn't do us any favors either!" Lin adds.

The group is hooting and it's not long until they're all sharing the elevator ride down to the lobby, still giggling about farts.

"Hey," Lin says softly, touching her arm lightly before the group filters out of the hospital. "Are you okay?"

Pania nods. "I will be. The old bogan wanted me to help with the funeral arrangements. I'm glad, because it's keeping me busy."

"Well, if you'd like to meet up for lunch once the busy-ness is done with, just text me, okay?"

"I'll do you one better. Let's plan on it. Sunday brunch? The Cooly Bistro?"

Lin's smile has a hint of mischief in it. "Best mimosas in town? I'm gonna have to warn you, that might cause some trouble."

"I'm gonna need a mimosa after this is all said and done." Her words are heavy, but her heart feels warm knowing Lin is looking out for her.

As they walk out the doors in separate directions, Pania realizes everyone had avoided saying his name after Sam's use of it so obviously bothered her. Her heart feels that much lighter as she makes her way back home.

Chapter 13: Edge of the Blade

Sleep has been a challenge for Lin for years. She used to hate lying alone in bed, twisting herself up in the sheets while trying to rest, or staring at their warm walnut-colored bedroom walls as she listened to Jian snore. But over the past few days, there has been comfort in the solitude, the silence of her bedroom. There are no expectations of her, no one to interpret or misinterpret her words or actions, no therapist pointing out her mistakes.

Instead, she finds herself thinking through what she actually wants out of her life and who she is, eyes glancing over Taurus's bright bull's eye in the patch of night sky that's visible outside of her window. Lin hasn't thought about astrology in ages. Jian always scoffed whenever he saw her going over her horoscope. She'd stopped reading it in the paper when she switched to a smartphone, and then deleted her astrology app when Jian criticized it after seeing the zodiac symbol on her home screen. She wonders what her current horoscope is, and resolves to check soon. Whatever it is, Lin's sure the "love" section will be like the ocean: still at the surface, but with undertows hiding, waiting to strand her out at sea.

What would her parents think if they knew she'd kissed a near-stranger—and a woman, at that—less than a week after appearing in divorce court? Perhaps it's time she worked on being a better mum and daughter, and figure out how on Earth an ex-wife ought to behave, anyway.

Ex-wife. What an awful term. Like she's been discarded as trash. After so many months of being afraid of her temper, it's empowering to let her anger about the divorce wash over her each night, when it can't hurt anyone. Makes the mornings run smoother too, at least from her perspective.

When the group learned of Robert's death, she immediately knew that Pania needed her support. In bed later that night, she reflects on how easily plans were suggested and then made—especially compared to their last trip, out to the museum.

Her mind wanders back to that trip, how her asking about the scar set Pania off. With so many triggers of her own to manage, Lin feels a rush of warmth and empathy towards her friend. What she wouldn't give to take back her question, to have said something light and pithy in its stead. All she'd been aiming for was to get closer to Pania, to connect with her on some deeper level than just being support group buddies.

Maybe she'd just needed an emotional outlet. Maybe now she could be there for her family and even for Pania... whatever that might look like.

There's no question in her heart that her life with Jian is over forever, though she knows that patching things up with him would bring her parents so much joy and relief. They worry she's going to end up alone, barely distinguishable from the dreaded "leftover women" back home.

But after so many months of despair and heartbreak, she finds herself considering her future with hope. Hope that there's someone out there who won't cringe over every reminder that her self-control isn't what it used to be and won't roll their eyes over things she enjoys, like soaps or astrology. Someone who isn't looking for the mild-mannered and submissive wife that she can no longer pretend to be. Someone who is, perhaps, a bit like Rosie.

When she finally drifts off to sleep that night, her dreams are hopeful and full of light.

#

"Whoah, hello gorgeous," Tim whispers when he opens his eyes the next morning and spots the woman in bed next to him. He quickly checks his phone. *Since when are Wednesdays starting off so damn well?* But his breath catches when he sees the calendar month casually displayed on the top of his lock screen. His heart rate begins to rise as he tries to figure out what the last thing he remembers is, and all he finds a mind full of fog. *Focus, Anderson!* The woman next to him stirs a bit, and he finds himself terrified of having to explain his poor memory to this straight-up hottie who's gonna write him off as a player when there's no way it was his fault this time.

Forget the girl, he orders himself. *Forget her so you can remember everything else. Anything else.*

Slowly, an image emerges: driving down the M1 in his mother's ancient Corolla, not knowing where to go. Hoping she felt guilty enough that she wouldn't report it stolen, since he still couldn't afford one of his own. Knowing he needed every penny he had for whatever was coming next.

He squints against the tears pricking his eyes as the memory becomes clearer. After Miriam's betrayal, he'd bolted out of their small town. From the brief glimpses of the suburban outdoors he can see from the window, he's guessing he hasn't looked back.

Well that explains that, at least, but what about all these missing months? The hell've I been doing?

He doublechecks his phone's date and time settings. This is just the kind of prank Brian would pull if he saw Tim having too much fun with a girl who's so clearly out of both of their leagues—though he doesn't remember now if Brian had left town with him. As he goes to close his settings, he sees he'd left his notes app open. The more he reads, the more everything falls into place and his panicked breathing starts to slow. When it feels like the world is no longer spinning completely out of his control, he puts down the phone and grabs the journal underneath the bed and documents how bits of his pre-accident memory scattered and resurfaced this time.

At some point, Jenny must have gotten up, because he's suddenly aware of the shower door closing and the door opening. *Okay, play it cool. Just because you don't remember seeing her naked, doesn't mean it hasn't happened. You've lived together for two goddamn years, Tim, get it together!*

She's wrapped in a towel, hair piled on top of her head and a toothbrush in her mouth. Around a gob of toothpaste, she asks, "What kinda day we having?"

He points to his phone. "I'm good. All good."

She shrugs. "Well yeah, but which notes did you need?"

His eyes narrow into slits. *Why should that matter?*

He must have spoken out loud, because Jenny replies, "I'm trying to manage your care, Tee." She walks back into the bathroom and spits before calling out, voice clearer, "You know, on top of everything else?"

"Still don't see why it matters," he retorts, an edge creeping into his voice.

"Ah, so you don't remember me, is that it?"

He stares at her, dumbfounded but trying not to let it show.

"Look, man, we've gone through this enough times for me to know when you feel I'm the love of your life, and when you feel I'm some hot stranger whose tits you wanna see for the first time."

His cheeks warm, but his voice sounds determined when he says, "And so what? I still don't see why it matters what I remember and what I don't. I'll just log it in my journal. Not like I have a doctor's appointment anytime soon in the calendar, so it doesn't matter."

She rolls her eyes. "Whatever, Tee. Listen, maybe stop reading the Miriam ones first thing in the morning. They always make you super testy."

"The Miriam ones?"

She flutters her hand towards the open journal and the phone he'd left on the bed. "The notes in your phone. Stuff only ever makes you irritable."

Now it's Tim's turn to shrug. "Well, you try having a horrible accident or months of abuse casually thrown at your face before you've even had your coffee."

"That's what I'm saying. Have your coffee first next time."

He rolls over, miffed that this is apparently so routine that she's down to lecturing him about it with her back half-turned. After she leaves for work and he snags some breakfast, it makes for the subject of that morning's journal entry.

When he's finally done, he heads out for the power walk listed for 10am, his favorite beats blasting. *No need to stay in a bad mood all day.* There must be more power to his walk than usual though, because he finds himself in front of his building again before his alarm to turn around goes off.

His mind is blissfully quiet as he walks up the steps to their flat, but he's brought back to the present when his Bluetooth headphones start dinging about low batteries. He turns off the music and heads into the bedroom to pop them on the charger, but when he opens the door, he startles Jenny.

"You sick or something?" he asks. Then, he sees his journal flat on the bed. In a split second, he takes in the razor blade on the bed, the loose pages, and the guilt on her face, and he understands.

Before she can respond, he snatches up the journal and the loose pages and walks right back out the door. There's no music for this particular walk, but his mind is louder than ever.

After finding his way to the park he found labeled in his notes as "great for journaling," he sits down and looks at the pages she had painstakingly cut out. It's the entry where he'd laid it all bare, told himself to think about breaking up. *Of course*. He takes a few deep breaths, and then tries to place them back where they belong in the journal. Luckily, he'd been dating each of his entries.

On a hunch, he looks back through the journal for any long gaps in the dates of the entries. Each time, when he pulls apart the binding, he can find the telltale edges where extra pages had once been. There are even a few pages missing between entries that are only a day apart. *How many times have I told myself to break up with her?*

The answer may elude him, but it's obvious he needs to take his own advice. *But how? Where am I gonna go? I'm not so stupid that I think I can live by myself right now.*

On an impulse, he dials Sam from support group. "I think I need your help?" His voice squeaks as he talks, and that's when he realizes how afraid he is. "I don't know what to do. And I don't think I can go home."

#

Pania doesn't have enough bereavement time to take the rest of the week off, so Wednesday morning she trudges to the computer and slogs through several meetings and the post-mortem from her team's latest sprint. By noon, everyone on the team makes it clear that they're not going to bother her until tomorrow, so she decides to take a late, extended lunch over at the community garden.

Despite having the best iced coffee in a ten-block radius, Pania tells herself she doesn't need anything from the coffee shop. Instead, she adds a guava leaf tea to her regular to-go order from the bistro on her way over. The enormous, house-made salad is delicious on its own, but Pania can never resist adding the sliced grilled chicken and candied pecans. By the time she reaches her usual lunch spot in the garden, the aromas are tantalizing her stomach and she can't wait to dig in.

The garden is often quiet during the mid-afternoon, being the hottest part of the day. Even with the nice autumnal breeze drifting in from the ocean, the benches in the sun are scorching hot. But today, the garden isn't as empty as Pania had hoped; there's a small group of Elders chatting next to the cotton candy blossoms of the Thyme Honey-Myrtle, and a familiar laugh erupting from its center.

When the sound first reaches her ears, Pania nearly chokes on a cherry tomato. Her hand trembles, and she presses her palm against her forehead to make sure she's not faint. A pinch reassures her she's not dreaming, but does nothing to quell the tightness in the back of her throat, the fear threatening to eject her lunch onto the scraggly, uncut grass.

The second time she hears the laugh, Pania's sure. The ghost of Sal is back. Only this time, she's not laughing at a goofy snapshot or a rewritten line of the Lord's Prayer. *Is this what it means to plan a funeral? To be haunted by the dead?* While she may not know for certain what Sal's fate had been, there's never been any doubt in Pania's mind that her betrayal of Sal killed her girlfriend. Whether that death happened immediately or took its time is a question Pania thrust far from her conscious mind long ago.

She resolves to go nowhere and do nothing until Robert is sent off on his final journey. *And we sure as hell aren't saying his name. Least, not his full name.* The last thing she needs is another ghost to haunt her. Careful not to attract the attention of the Elders, Pania scoops up her things and hobbles home as fast as her unsteady feet will take her.

#

Lin's finished her grocery list and is heading out the door when the phone rings. Not trusting herself to multitask in public, she puts her bag down with a sigh and shuts the door.

"Hello?" She can't help the annoyance in her voice. Luckily, it's Sam: pretty much the only person who doesn't take offense to her anger.

"I mean, I don't really have a spare bedroom right now..." she trails off, the edges in her voice softening.

144

"But if he just needs a couch, I've got one where he can crash."

#

Jenny hasn't stopped blowing up his phone, and Tim's worried it's gonna die before he gets to the address Sam had texted him. Of course, he hadn't remembered his wallet, so he doesn't have any cash to hail a cab. He speed-walks towards the coast and the ritzier neighborhoods that Google Maps indicates are his destination.

He doesn't recognize the woman's name, but Sam assures him the lady will know who he is. *Better hope none of these rich NIMBY neighbors decide to call the cops on me before I get there.* He's well aware that he's a strange sight, sweaty and breathing hard and clutching onto his journal for dear life. Hopefully the fact that he's holding a book will earn him some mercy.

When he finally sees the white two-story colonial on the corner, he nearly collapses in relief. The text message says to ask for Lin. His battery is at one percent.

Gathering his courage, Tim crosses the street and walks up the three steps to the bright red door. Sweaty palms get rubbed quickly against his basketball shorts and then he knocks gingerly on the door. Footsteps approach, and he takes a deep breath.

A short, thin woman with pitch black hair and a concerned look on her face opens the door. "Tim, are you okay?" she asks him. He shrugs. "Come in, come in," she urges, reaching up to put a hand on his shoulder and guiding him inside with surprising strength.

#

The boy at her door looks terrified, unmoored. Nothing like the cocky twenty-something who shows up to group every week in his on-trend clothes.

"Here, have a seat." She points to the couch, sensing he needs direction. "The remote is next to the lamp, so have a go at the TV if you'd like."

Obediently, Tim sits. The lost look in his eyes is breaking her heart. "What do you need?" she asks tenderly.

His eyes finally meet hers. He gulps. Hesitates. "I need a phone charger. And a pen."

An odd combination. "Of course, let me grab those for you. Remind me, Apple or Android?"

She bustles around, pulling out a spare cord and a pen. It doesn't seem like enough to give him, so she also pulls a cold Coke out of the fridge before heading back into the living room.

"You can stay here as long as you need," she says, indicating the couch. "I wish I had a guest bedroom to make you more comfortable, but I'm hosting someone whose home was destroyed by the bushfires in the south."

Tim nods, but Lin can tell from the glazed look in his eyes that his mind is elsewhere. She's not even sure he heard her. His movements are seemingly on autopilot.

"Alright, I'll let you get to it then," she says before heading upstairs to her bedroom. Sam hadn't given her much in the way of details, but the poor lad obviously needs some time to process whatever it is he's going through.

#

His body feels like it's been hit by a truck. And while his memory is less than reliable, he does remember everything that happened so far today. Now to write it down before it disappears and he goes crawling back to Jenny.

Great. One more woman whose phone calls are more dangerous than they seem. He recaps the morning's events in his journal while his phone attempts to charge. It can't be holding onto much battery life, the way Jenny keeps it buzzing.

When he's finally got all of the details down, he picks up the phone and texts Jenny exactly one time. *I'm safe. And I think you know we're over, so stop trying to contact me.*

Instead of slowing her messages down, his reply sends her into a frenzy. He tries not to read them, but it's hard not to take in the texts that keep pouring in. *I was only trying to help you. Please, come back. Let me explain.*

His resolve is faltering. Even if he hadn't remembered Jenny—or much else—this morning, it's clear that at one point not long ago, he loved her desperately. That, at one point, she was his home.

A voice breaks through his thoughts. Lin. "Are you okay, Tim?"

"Hold on." He looks up, confused. "Somehow, I just remembered your name when I didn't know it earlier. Have I been here before?"

She tilts her head to one side, like a confused puppy. "Well, you do have a lot of memory problems," she says, "but um, is that really what you're focusing on right now?"

He tries to hide his embarrassment behind a smile. "Uh... yes?"

"Well, this particular puzzle is easy to solve." She gestures to the wall next to the TV, and he realizes her name is painted elegantly on the side of a picture frame. "You've been staring in that direction pretty much ever since you sat down."

"Oh, heheh. Right."

There's a lengthy pause before Lin says, "So, uh, are you okay? You seem pretty upset, and, well, Sam didn't give me any details."

He blinks really fast. *You piss this lady off and you'll be living in the streets, man, so watch your words.* "You keep asking me that. Are you... are you prying? I walk in here with nothing—no home, no clothes, hell, I don't even have my wallet—and you just wanna have the scoop on the hot goss'?"

Lin's cheeks flush. "Sorry, I don't want to come off that way. I just want to know so I can help. I've gone through a lot in the past few months, and what helps me the most is when I can take care of other people. Kinda like a mom friend, you know?"

"Right..." He trails off, looking down at the pages of his journal and trying to sort through what happened once more. "I mean, what the hell, right?"

Chapter 14: Aftershock

Lin talks with Tim for most of the morning about everything that happened—in between coffee breaks, reruns of her favorite soaps, helping Tim block Jenny's number on his phone, making a list of what he'll need to start over, and updating Jian about her house guests per the terms of their divorce. With every story Tim tells, she feels more and more protective of the kid. His overconfident veneer is a shell hiding a damaged young guy, only a few years older than Huan, trying and failing to keep himself safe from abusers.

"I'm so sorry this happened to you," she says. She's sure she's repeating herself far too many times. But the kid needs to hear it, and remember it. She settles into the wingback next to the couch. "You two looked like such a cute couple when you went to the gardening thing a few weeks ago. I was definitely jealous."

"Jealous?" he asks incredulously from his spot on the couch.

She holds up her left hand and points at the indentation of her wedding ring. Her finger still bears the imprint of her ring. She'd finally taken it off after the divorce proceedings... and after kissing Rosie. "Jian and I were college sweethearts, and I'd really thought we were going to grow old together. Then, that stupid fucking accident came along and now I have nothing."

A cough lets her know she may have overexaggerated. "Imagine how I feel," he says softly.

She reaches over and gently pats his leg. "We'll take care of you. And no one in this house will ever snoop in your journal or your phone."

"Thanks. Who else even lives here?"

"Well, there's my son Huan about half the time, but he's with his father this week. And then there's Rosie in the guest room. She tends to disappear during the day. I'm not sure what for." Her eyes look downwards, over her blue plaid chinos and the wingback's pale floral fabric. Her boarder is probably avoiding the sexual tension that's been building again in the days after the kiss. Even if she's not, Lin's been grateful enough not to question it.

In the silence that follows, the boy's face hardens. His shell is returning. Bouncing toes betray his unease.

Lin smiles softly. "It's going to be okay. I promise." The bouncing slows.

"Maybe." He searches the room, as if trying to find a safe conversation to have. "Not to pry, but how did you get yours?" He taps his temple with his fingers. "Your injury, I mean."

Her cheeks warm with embarrassment. "Honestly? It was kind of my fault. Huan crashed a toy drone on the roof, and of course Jian wasn't home and I was too stubborn to wait for help."

"But what actually... yanno... happened?" He rests his chin on his knuckles, pondering.

She smiles a bit. "And you think I pry?"

"Sorry." Tim folds his hands together and looks so contrite, the laughter all but spills out of her.

"I went up the ladder to get it, but the damn thing was up too far on the roof for my short T-Rex arms to reach. Somehow, my foot slipped. When I woke up, there were poinciana flowers in my hair and a ladder on my back. Apparently, I hit a tree branch next to the house on my way down. With my forehead."

"Ouch. You don't even have any scars from it though!" He examines her head in amazement.

"Yeah, well, I'd take a couple of ugly scars over the TBI any day. At least then I wouldn't feel so responsible for destroying my family."

"Dude. That's still not your fault."

"What? Of course it is. I should've waited for someone to help me or thought through how to get it down on my own without risking my life."

"Might not've been the smartest thing to do but at the end of the day?" He shrugs. "You were just being a mom. The kind of mom I wish I'd had."

"Again, I am so sorry at everything you've been through."

"We've all gone through the ringer, seems like." His eyebrows wrinkle in thought. "Wait a minute. How did falling off a ladder destroy your family?"

She's not sure she wants to explain. But he's been so open with her about his troubles, the pressure to reciprocate is mounting. "You're a really good listener, kid."

"Thanks. You don't have to tell me if it's too personal. Like, if it messed with your sex life or something." He gives her a playful wink.

"No, no, nothing like that," Lin says quickly, dismissing the suggestion with a wave of her hand. "More that I can't stop hurting people now that my impulse control is fucked. And as I'm sure you know, it's the people you're closest to who you can hurt the most. And who can hurt you back the hardest."

"Doesn't your ex know that's not your fault?" He folds his legs underneath him on the couch as he makes himself more comfortable. "Like... duh?"

"I wish it were that simple." She sighs. "My behavior kept impacting Huan, to the point where my husband didn't trust me alone with my own child. Can you imagine that?"

"Uh... can you imagine leaving a kid alone with someone who's too disabled to be alone with a kid, and then getting mad because things aren't all rosy and perfect when they're left alone with a kid?"

"What?"

"He didn't even try to keep you within your limits. I mean, I know better than to think I can live alone. That's why I'm here and not in a hotel room or getting a new flat or something."

"Well yeah, but he works for an airline, so he takes a lot of work trips. Not like I could work after the accident."

"Why didn't you just get a nanny or something?"

Lin sighs. "We tried that. One coffee mug chucked at her and she was gone. We could never find another one after that, so she must've talked. My parents came in the meantime, but they couldn't stay forever."

"Okay, but like, there was really no other option for your husband? Cuz, I mean, who would think you can be alone with a kid when you can't even be alone with a kid and a nanny?"

Lin shrugged. "That's who I used to be. Dependable. Controlled. Quiet."

"Well, you're way cooler now, even if you crack the shits sometimes. But seriously, that guy does not sound like he paid enough attention to what you were going through. Real dick."

"Maybe, but I still have to live with the trauma I caused our son." She sighs deeply. Her gaze wanders to the photo capturing Huan's goofy kindergarten grin and the crack in the frame's glass. "When it comes to kids, it doesn't matter. Unintentional trauma is still trauma. And nobody should have to be afraid of their own mother."

"Least you didn't mean it."

"Would it matter if Miriam didn't mean to hurt you with what she did?"

The words tumble out rapid-fire. "That bitch knew it was going to hurt me, and she absolutely did not care. Pure selfishness. That's a lot different than being unable to think things through before just, yanno, doing them."

"In terms of intention, yes. But in terms of impact? I'm not so sure." If the disagreement continues, Lin knows she'll lash out, so she stands up and heads into the kitchen. Halfway there, she calls over her shoulder, "Want a sandwich? Figure we should eat before we head to the store."

"Oh, food! Good idea. I always forget to eat."

#

After they get in the Uber, the mood changes. "Now look," Lin starts. "We are going to need to get at least some of your things from your apartment. I'm assuming you take a shitload of meds, just like all the rest of the TBI group?"

Shit. "Can't it wait until tomorrow?"

"Can it? I worry about withdrawals and issues from missing all of your meds at once." She scowls at him like a disapproving mom. "And honestly, you should too."

"I can't... I can't face her." If the car weren't already in motion, he would've jumped out of it.

"Then don't. I'll do it. You'll just need to text her and tell her you want her to give me your stuff. If she's home, that is."

"Oh trust me, she's home. According to my journal, Jenny has had a bad habit of playing the martyr for a very long time. Doubt she'll be going to work the rest of the week."

"Great." Lin's voice is hard, like stone. "I've got the driver taking us to Tweed Heads. Should we reroute to your apartment? Is she gonna get destructive?"

He thinks about the journal. Wonders if she's heartless enough to flush his pills. When he realizes he doesn't know the answer, he tells the driver his address.

The car parks along the street opposite his building. Tim pushes his keys into Lin's cold fingers and tells her his flat number. "If she's there, just call me so I can tell her who you are."

"You think that's gonna help?" Lin asks.

"More than having a strange woman show up at the door?"

"Good point." She unbuckles, opens the car door. "Talk soon, I'm sure."

Her stride is strong and assertive as she heads across the street. *Miss Anger Mismanagement's going to do battle for me.* It's a comforting thought. *Let's just hope it doesn't backfire.* Last thing he needs is for Jenny to get the cops involved because Lin goes overboard. He thinks about the nanny and the coffee mug and practices his deep breathing and tries not to count the seconds Lin has been out of sight.

When his phone rings, it's a struggle to keep his voice even. "Hello?"

"Hi, it's Lin." Her voice is smooth, even. He hopes he can match her tone.

"Hi." Maybe if he keeps his answers short, Jenny won't

hear the terror, won't rush out of the flat and across the street to drag him back in there.

"You're on speaker. Can you tell Jenny who I am?"

He clears his throat. "Yeah. Uh, hi Jenny. This is Lin. She's part of my TBI support group. I'm gonna stay with her for a while. Can you—"

Jenny cuts him off. "How can you do this to me, Tee? To us?"

"We talked about this." Lin's voice is curt. "Your job right now is to listen. That's it." Tim wishes briefly they were on a video call, because whatever Lin is doing shuts Jenny right down with a sniffle and a trembly "okay."

"Go ahead, Tim," Lin says once Jenny quiets.

"OK, so this is Lin from my TBI support group. The one I go to on Tuesdays? I'm gonna stay with her for a while. She's safe. Can you just show her where my stuff is? I need my meds and my wallet an' stuff."

"How long are you going to be gone?" Jenny asks, and he can tell that she's crying. "I can't live without you."

He tries to sound as tough as Lin, but his voice falters. "You're gonna have to try, cuz I'm not coming back."

"You can't do this to me, Tim. You need me! No one else is going to support you the way I have, you ungrateful—"

The phone goes off of speaker, though he can hear chaos mounting in the background. Lin shouts, "Gotta go!" over the noise. He hears two dull beeps indicating the call is over.

The next-door neighbors are gonna be talking about this for weeks. *Just some young kids, you know how they get with their drama.* He can practically hear the old chooks and their heavy smokers' voices as they trade the latest gossip about the trouble over in 2C. He half-expects to see his belongings start flying out the door onto the lawn, but the street is unnerving in its peacefulness. Just a few passing cars, a maggie laughing its way through the trees, and the quiet hum of the Uber's AC, set to a chilly 23°C.

The wait is agonizing. By the time fifteen minutes have passed, he's sure that one or the both of the women are dead. "I'll be right back," he says to the driver before getting out of the car. "Please don't go anywhere."

"I'll wait," the driver says coolly. "Gotta see how this thing ends."

Great. Even the Uber driver thinks one of 'em's dead. But before he can reach the bottom of the staircase, Lin emerges with his duffle bag busting at the seams. "Back to the car, now," she hisses.

Behind her, Jenny's voice is high-pitched and desperate. "Timmy?!"

His eyes widen and he takes a step back, onto the street. A horn honks, then brakes screech.

He looks up to find himself face to face with a white-haired dude driving his mid-life crisis car. If he'd had more than a half of a second, he would have appreciated the slick red Corvette and its after-market front grille before it slammed into him.

Chapter 15: Fractured

"Man, less than 24 hours and we're back at the hospital," Lin remarks when they finally let her in Tim's room in the Emergency Department.

"I don't consider support group part of the hospital," Tim replies. "Doesn't hurt like this." He's got a cast on his left arm and a blanket over his body, but his color is good and there aren't too many monitors or lines hooked up to him. She takes these, at least, as good signs.

"Plus, this isn't nearly as fun as gossiping in group," Tim adds. "And I say that without even remembering any of it!" Without waiting for her response, he turns his phone around and she can see his list of notes.

From her vantage point across the room in the most uncomfortable chair she's ever touched, Lin can't make out any of the words, but he's talked about that particular coping strategy often enough that it doesn't matter. "Oh trust me, I know," she replies. A grin begins to form on her face. "I'm not the one with memory problems. Luckily for me, you also don't remember how many times I've bit your head off for being too sarcastic or saying the wrong thing at the wrong time or looking at me in a way I didn't like or even—" and here her cheeks warm at the memory— "just sitting in your chair the wrong way."

He rolls his eyes. "Come on. You've gotta be joking about that one."

She clears her throat. "I'm uh, definitely not, but it doesn't matter. How are you doing? You covered in casts underneath that blanket?"

He lifts it up to do a perfunctory check. "No—aaah!"

"What?"

"Ugh, that hurts like the dickens!" He drops the threadbare blanket.

"Did you not notice the cast on your arm, or..."

"Ha, ha," he deadpans. "I just didn't realize how much everything on my right side was gonna hurt from hitting the pavement. I thought I felt like I'd been hit by a truck when I got to your house, but dude, I had no idea. Not exactly having the best time over here, even with the hydrocodone."

"I hear you. How's your head?"

"Eh, it's been through worse. Just don't ask me to draw a clock, alright?"

She chuckles. "Some of us can't do that even on a good day, you know."

Tim's phone buzzes and he turns his attention to it. While he surfs the internet or texts or whatever it is he's doing, Lin's mind wanders. She'd had plenty of time while he was getting his broken arm set to alert security about Jenny. It was all Lin and the responding medics could do to keep the agitated, jilted woman out of the ambulance. Never mind the outburst after she realized he'd been hit, before there were any medics around to help keep her away.

Had Tim's terror that day and then her confrontation with Jenny only five minutes prior not been fresh in her mind, Lin would've been tempted to believe the woman's emotional outburst was sincere. Especially given how sweet the couple had seemed when they had shown up to the garden together last month.

But she knew better than to believe the tears, particularly when certain words and phrases started slipping out of Jenny's mouth. Like when she wailed about how dangerous the world was for Tim without her to keep him safe. Or when she blubbered on about how this kind of accident was why she tried to stop him from leaving. With what Lin knew about the razor blades to the journal—not to mention what else Jenny could have done to a boyfriend whose memory was so unreliable it required a medical diagnosis—the entire situation felt so manipulative that it left her stomach lurching.

One thing was and still is crystal clear: she has to help this boy escape. It's against her nature to see someone hurting and simply turn away. Particularly when that person, as irritating as he could be, did genuinely try to help with her own problems. Tim is always the person in the group who could step into Huan's perspective with ease, almost like he's still fifteen himself.

Of all the therapy techniques Lin has tried to smooth over her relationship with Huan, none were working so well as asking herself what Timmy would think of whatever she wants to do next with or around Huan. *Go to the beach and see all those hot, almost-naked girls while I'm with my* mom?! *That'd be a hard no—emphasis on the "hard."*

Of course, that doesn't stop her from saying stupid things or pissing Huan off at very regular intervals. But her son is on the edge of being sixteen. Getting mad at his mom is the most normal part of their relationship. At the least, that little voice keeps encouraging her to always apologize and always try again. And it saves her from many of the more avoidable missteps.

She looks up at the kid again, half-asleep from pain meds, phone slowly slipping from his hand. The nurse promises to come back quickly with Tim's discharge papers, but in case it's going to be a while, she figures she'd better go find a bathroom.

The movement must be just enough to wake him, because he mumbles, "Bye Momma Lin."

"Just stepping out for a second," Lin says quietly. "Anything I can get for you?"

He cracks his eyes open and gives her a droopy smile. "How 'bout a new arm?"

"Right. I'll also snag a yacht and ten billion dollars." Lin shakes her head and smiles. "Now get some sleep, ya big dreamer."

#

Why is death such hard work? Pania wonders as she emails the funeral director for the fourth time about what to use instead of Robert's photo for the funeral cards. "For the love of all things holy, what's so hard about 'find a stock photo of the ocean'?" she says to herself through gritted teeth.

She hits send, then tries to shift back into work mode. It has been a long couple of days, and now one of their biggest clients put a website development project on a rush timeline. The project she and her least-favorite team mate, Deedee, are working on together. The woman's overwhelming positivity and everlasting enthusiasm grate on Pania's nerves. If the sun disappeared tomorrow, Deedee could probably find the silver lining before she froze to death.

The icky sweetness drips through the team chat with too many emojis and exclamation points. *I know you can do this team, you're all superstars!* Her latest message is punctuated by glittering yellow star emojis before turning to the running to-do list.

Pania rolls her eyes. "Quit blowing smoke up everyone's asses," she grumbles at the woman's icon on her screen. With her fingers, she types out a quick reminder that she's on bereavement leave Friday. *I'll send over my bullet points for the client check-in before end of day tomorrow.*

Pania's been tasked with building an interactive map based on some of the client's internal data. Any other week, the map would already be drafted and in debugging, but Deedee doesn't need to know how far behind Pania is on their new timeline. By being vague, Pania's hoping to spare herself a pep talk. It works, but somehow that's even more irritating than the pep talk would have been.

She needs a walk. Deedee may normally be too much, but Pania knows she's overtired and far too irritable if the team's "Momma Dee" is annoying her even with her silence. An unhurried loop around her spacious apartment helps her center herself, and a chilled chocolate raspberry truffle puts her on the edge of a good mood. For good measure, she also marches in place for a few minutes before heading back to her chair.

A ding from her workstation as she sits down threatens to topple that good mood when she realizes it's another email from the funeral director. This time, he's attached a stock photo of the beach. *Close enough,* she thinks before sending back her approval.

The email is barely out of her outbox before Deedee messages her directly, outside of the team channel. *You okay? Seems like you're a little overwhelmed this week. If I can do anything to help, just say the word, superstar!*

Pania wants to be sarcastic but, for once, her witticisms desert her. After all, the woman has managed to sound almost sincere for once. But that's still not enough for Pania to accept her offer. Instead, she rests her chin on fingers steepled over her keyboard, and breathes deeply in and out.

It's certainly been a tough week, she finally types back, *but I'm fine.*

She won't allow herself not to be.

#

Before she heads back into Tim's hospital room, Lin calls Rosie and explains the situation.

"What do you mean, this is what the day has brought? Do your days often bring you people escaping from DV?"

"Well, I'm not about to let the kid go back into an abusive situation. His memory is awful, and he has no family. There's nowhere else for him to go."

They may not know each other all that well yet, but Lin can hear the tension rising in Rosie's responses. "How do I know he's not going to come in and assault me? Or you, for that matter? How do we know it's not some sort of ruse, or that he's a victim about to turn into a perpetrator?"

Her voice is as conciliatory as she can make it. "I'm sorry, this situation came as a surprise to me too. But I know this kid, and he's not a threat. A little clueless, but he's just a kid. He's got a great medical support team. They'll put him in touch with the right resources and get him sorted out, so he'll be outta my house in no time."

"Lots of abusive men are great at playing the victim when they get found out." Rosie's tone is harsh, like she's talking through gritted teeth. Lin wishes she was next to her, so she could hold her hand and let her know it will be okay.

"Trust me on this one, please? Like I trusted you when I took you in." She holds the phone up with her shoulder and taps the back of her hand with her fingertips. The beat calms her, and she hopes it's enough to keep the irritation out of her voice.

There's a huff on the other end of the line. "I went through a background check and submitted six references before they would list me on that site. There were no surprises for anyone by that point. Especially you."

"Look, can we not turn this into an argument? If you need a lock or something on your door, fine. We'll stop by Bunnings before we come home. But in the end, it's my house, and this is what I'm going to do."

"Oh." The woman's voice is quiet, defeated. "So that's how you wanna be?"

"It's the way it has to be," Lin replies before pressing the end button. Any more conversation will only end poorly. As it is, the muscles in her shoulders are taut, ready for a fight to come. A few deep breaths help return her equilibrium before she heads back into the room. The nurse is back, standing with his back to the door and giving Tim instructions about which orthopedic surgeon to follow up with in the morning. He circles the practice's phone number and then indicates several places in the discharge paperwork where Tim has to sign.

"You've got a few prescriptions waiting for you at your pharmacy," the nurse continues as he bustles around the room, turning off monitors and logging notes into the computer. "The antibiotics are standard because of the nature of your accident, but still, be sure to finish the full course. We don't want you getting an infection. Pain meds are as needed. You had your last dose only an hour ago, so don't take more until at least 18:00 hours."

"Thanks for being so quick with his care and discharge," Lin says, more to let the nurse know she was in the room than anything else.

"Of course," he replies without turning to her. "Most important thing is to follow up with ortho in the morning, so don't forget to do that."

"But you already did the cast. What are they gonna do, check your work?"

The man turns around and taps the hard plaster surface. "We did a temporary splint. The limb is stabilized for now, but he'll need ortho to do a cast. Besides being able to get it waterproofed so he can take showers without a plastic bag over his arm, it's designed for long-term use to give the arm stability throughout the healing process—not just for right now."

"Oh."

Tim speaks up. "Okay, signed. I've gotta go get meds at my pharmacy. Anything else before I go?"

The nurse shakes his head. "Nope, all set. Just remember, call ortho in the morning and look both ways before crossing the street."

"Ha, ha," Tim intones. "I'll do what I can."

#

Whenever Tim gets a little high—whether from accidental mixing of his prescriptions, or the more intentional but less legal means he enjoyed before the accident—his mind seeks out the most universal, most essential of human needs. Sex without kissing ("without intimacy," Jenny would scoff), or thick slices of homemade bread covered in slabs of butter that would've felt familiar to people anytime in history, anywhere in the world... it's a feeling he hasn't been able to relish in a long time. But in the aftermath of the Emergency Department visit, body still abuzz with painkillers, he can feel those essential desires floating around his body like so many particles of light.

There's already more than enough sexual tension in the house between the two women—or at least, that's what Lin told him on their way home from Bunnings. (Thank goodness he'd been sitting down because that definitely caught him off-guard.) And anyway, the thought of touching anyone at all (Jenny or Not Jenny) feels more dangerous than comforting right now.

So, he flops on the couch with the crumbliest piece of bread in the house and picks up his notepad and pen. Hums with the energy only oxy can give him. Taps out a drum beat rhythm with the pen that (together with his journal) saved his ass, finally, after so many weeks of trying. It's a little victory chant, *doo-de-doo-ba bat-a-bat!* But only with his right hand; the other is immobilized in its plaster shield. Still, the itch crawling up his fractured arm is basic enough. He gives the spot a tentative *tap-tap* with the pen before letting his mind explore what other essentials it deems important right now.

"Fuck, I love this butter," he mumbles around a mouthful before taking a swig of lukewarm water. Decides ice cold is more essential to the moment than the universality of the warm. Goes to the fridge and re-pours the glass, adds the brilliant cubes, crackling with potential and disaster. *Yes.* He smacks his lips in anticipation. Spots with delight a chair swing out back.

The slight tip back and whee forward are enough to keep him delighted for ages. Give him respite from the reality that knocked him on his ass. Help him forget that he's full of road rash and splints and pain meds and bad memories and sometimes no memories at all.

Whee.

\#

Lin watches the kid revert to a playful, unencumbered free spirit, his trademark overconfidence nowhere to be seen from her hallway window. She's not really sure she's ever seen any adult give in so fully to such a simple pleasure as a porch swing. *That's what a good dose of pain meds will do for you.* And yet, part of her wants to join in on the silliness, the primality and the innocence of this man-turned-back-to-boy. His squeals are what alerted her to his presence in the first place, filling the empty backyard as he rocks a few inches back and forth on the porch swing that Jian only deigned to sit on twice.

Disturbing Timmy, though, is out of the question. She has a job to do. Rosie had insisted on a separately locking bedroom door if there were going to be strangers (but really, strange men) in and out of the house. Like any dutiful house mother, she has to make sure everyone feels safe, whether they are swinging on the porch or hiding from what Lin suspects is some sort of horror in the past, as opposed to some harmless kid in the present.

Once the lock is installed, she texts Rosie. *New room key for you when you get back. Where did you go again?*

Lin strolls into her bedroom and sets the phone down on the bed with a sigh. No matter what she does, there is no happy family to be had or built in this house. Perhaps there never will be. *Maybe the house is cursed. Or maybe I am.*

To be fair, no one seems to be having a good go of it right now. The poor kid. She'd thought he and Jenny were such "#goals," as the kids would say. But turns out that was all artifice and lies... much like her marriage to Jian.

After all, why had he always insisted on a job that required so much travel? She hated being alone in a foreign country. Having Huan helped: women were usually eager to bond over their babies in the mom groups she tried. But behind everyone's loneliness was an anger and a desperation she dared not face. So, she stopped going. A few casual acquaintances survived, but they were left untended. Like the daisy from Huan's fourth grade project, they too, withered sooner than she expected.

And yet, despite voicing her unhappiness, Jian never changed a thing about their lifestyle. There were too many times she'd felt embarrassed at his work parties, like an accessory that didn't match the rest of his outfit.

He never attempted to change, like a stone wall or an ancient tree. At one point in her life, Lin had found that admirable. She can't remember why.

After all, maybe her accident had only dislodged the unhappiness they'd held onto for so long. Maybe it was the only way to get that burden off of her, so she could finally explore what else the world might have for her.

Like the support group, where all of her eccentricities only serve to help her fit in.

Like the myriad ways she's finding to fill her empty house. Perhaps not with happiness, but with people she can help. With a fresh start.

At the very least, no one's shackling her to misery like a ball and chain anymore. He's finally set her free.

\#

With most of the service details sorted, Pania has decided that Thursday is a day to rest ahead of the services tomorrow. Of course, that's only possible after a long day building the interactive map and letting Deedee know it's finally in debugging. Can't have that hanging over her head. By the time she logs out for the day, her stomach is complaining and her head is aching.

On a day like this, she'd normally order in. She pulls up the number for the bistro, but her fingers hover hesitantly over the call button. What if the spirit is waiting on the other side of the door for her? It's tempting to believe the ghost of Sal wouldn't just show up in her apartment. After all, it only seems to find her when she's out. But what if it starts getting bolder?

The very idea drives her to close curtains throughout the flat. *Don't find me today,* she thinks towards the spirit. *Not here. Not now.*

Dinner remains unordered. She doesn't have the energy to cook either. Her hands go on autopilot towards the stash of protein bars her doctor suggested she. keep in the pantry for days like this. Might not be the most exciting thing to eat, but at least she's eating. A large glass of tea is enough to wash down the white chocolate-encrusted junk. The wrapper falls from her fingers, landing next to the couch.

Pania wants to sleep, knows she needs to sleep, but her mind refuses to cooperate. Her feet mindlessly practice the few physical therapy maneuvers she can do sitting down while her thoughts tiptoe around her past. She doesn't even dare turn on the TV for fear of finding the spirit.

Why now? she wonders. *What could you possibly want with me now?*

When sleep does come, it does so in fits and starts. The spirit has no trouble finding her in her dreams.

#

It's a weird morning in Lin's house. Tim's still feeling sorta high with the pain meds and he's nervous he's gonna say something stupid (like usual) and stumble across a lit fuse.

"I'm gonna head out for a bit," he announces to the breakfast table. Lin and Rosie might be sitting across from him, but he's not addressing them. He's talking to his plate, hoping that will keep him out of trouble. "I'll set an alarm with the address so I don't forget to come back."

"Okay." Lin's words are muted, as though she, too, is unsure of what will make the sparks fly today. "What time should I expect you back?"

"Don't worry about me for at least two hours," he mumbles. "Got some thinking to do."

When he stands, Tim notices this weird look flitting across Lin's and Rosie's faces. Like they aren't sure if they should be relieved that he's leaving, or on edge because they'll be left alone with each other.

Whatever. I just gotta get outta here. Even aside from the tension in the house, he needs a walk to clear his head. Being closer to the ocean has left him aching to walk to the seaside, even if he can't get his arm wet yet.

Something about the thought of the ocean calms him. Perhaps it's because nothing about it could possibly remind him of his landlocked small-town home, which he knew he'd left on bad terms several years ago... though he can't remember the specifics of it today.

Lin had warned him it was all unpleasant stuff, so he'd decided to skip that part of the "mental download" this morning. Leave himself time to deal with the breakup of the only close relationship he remembers having. One problem at a time.

There's a patchy bit of shade on the edge of the sand, so he plunks down and gives in to his senses. The rush of wind against his hair, the laughter and screams of kids and vacationers filling his ears. His eyes focus on the wind surfers on the horizon, note the sunbathers in his peripheral. His lungs and nostrils fill with the salty, slightly fishy smelling air.

The nearly meditative state he puts himself into doesn't stop the heartache, but instead unlocks his emotions so that they flow down his cheeks. He thinks of the times he and Jenny spent on the beaches up in Coolly, by turns flirting and day-drinking and getting tanned. The rising sobs and sniffling nose are easily lost under the waves crashing against the beach and the sounds of the crowd.

Gotta let her go, man, he tells himself. *She's not good for you. Probably hasn't been for a long time.*

Still, Tim's grateful for Jenny. The beginnings of their relationship are blurry to him today, but he knows that when they met, he was still adrift. And he knows that Jenny helped him see what was possible, what could be next, if he just stopped running away.

But what comes next now? His shoulders rise and fall as he lets the tears continue to flow.

A guy's voice, one he knows he should recognize but doesn't, jolts him into suppressing his sobs. "You okay, dude?"

Tim swipes at his face with the palm of his hand. "I'm gettin' there..." he trails off, wondering who from his past this is.

The not-stranger's face softens, and he reaches down to give Tim some sort of complicated high-five. Like magic, his hand remembers the moves even though his brain doesn't. "I know I know you," Tim starts, "but, uh... I'm still recovering from an accident that messed with my memory."

"I know, man, I know," the guy says, his eyes downcast. He plops down next to Tim, and Tim notes the guy's cheeks are thin, like from too much drinking and not enough eating. His hair is that shaggy, sand-flecked style Tim suddenly knows he wanted desperately as a kid.

Tim's barely made the connections in his head when the man's name pops back into his head. "Brian?"

The guy's head hangs in shame. "Listen, man... are you okay? Because it's been messing with me that you're not okay."

Tim shakes his head. "Most definitely not. But that's not your fault." He remembers the journal entry he'd read this morning, the shock of realizing Jenny had blamed him for his own accident. "I was never good at turning down a dare."

"Right..." Brian trails off, looking at the water instead of looking at Tim. "I just feel like I'm looking at a ghost."

"Last I checked, I was still alive and breathing." Tim tries to crack a smile, but his face simply doesn't follow through.

"No thanks to me." Guilt is pouring off his former friend in waves, and Tim's not sure he has the strength to deal with it.

"Look. Forget about it, okay? It doesn't matter anymore. Is what it is, and all that."

"For real?" Brian turns and the light behind his eyes is sparkling, begging to be let off the hook.

Tim's struck by how self-absorbed, how weak, his supposed best friend really is. *But was I really that different before the accident?* Feeling as though he's releasing a weight from his own neck, Tim mutters, "For real, man. Forget about it." What he really means is: *forget about me. I'm too busy drowning to help you forgive yourself.*

Brian gives Tim's thigh a solid love tap, then pulls him in for a hug. "Glad you're doing okay, brother," he says, even though Tim had never said anything of the sort. He stands and grabs the surfboard leaning against one of the scraggly trees behind them. "See you around?"

Tim waves him on and mumbles something vaguely positive. *Just get outta here.*

Loneliness washes over him, but with it comes a kind of relief he hadn't expected. Like his old life is officially gone, and that maybe, just maybe, there will be room now for whatever is coming next.

An alarm labeled with an address goes off on his phone, and he pulls out his map app. Time to go... home? *Guess I'll find out when I get there.*

Chapter 16: Ghosts

A short message from Lin arrives the morning of the funeral. *Do you need any groceries? I want to make sure you're taking care of yourself.*

Pania thinks of all the years she did this for Robert. *Figured I'd have a bit more time before life came full circle.* She doesn't like to admit needing help but, then again, neither did Robert.

Appreciate that, she types back. *I could use a couple of mangos—Kent variety if you can still find them fresh. And two liters of vanilla ice cream. Going to make a killer milkshake tomorrow afternoon in honor of our old bogan friend.*

The reply comes quickly. *I got you.*

"Thank you," Pania whispers, mist settling over her eyes. Sleep comes before she remembers to text the words to her friend. An hour later, her alarm goes off with a reminder to get dressed for the service. The text is the first thing she takes care of after silencing her phone.

#

Huan is due back on Sunday afternoon, so Lin stops for some groceries before Robert's services. She packs Pania's milkshake ingredients in their own cooler bag, set apart from the Coke, beef jerky, Tim Tams, and chips that Huan loves so much. Rosie has her driver's license, so the old sedan, which has sat uselessly in the driveway since Jian left, is finally helpful to someone. The bags can stay in the backseat, where Tim is "pre-gaming" services by avoiding the two women and pretending to nap.

Before waking him from his faux snooze, she turns to Rosie. "You don't have to come in if you'd rather run errands or something. No need for you to attend a funeral for someone you've never even met."

"I'm not going for him," Rosie replies, her hand resting casually on the driver side door handle. "I'm going for you."

Lin shifts in her seat, unsure what this means. Her confusion must be written on her face, like her emotions always are, because Rosie quickly adds, "But only if you want me there. I just know how hard it can be to keep your composure at an event like this. Even if my impulse control is still more or less intact." She keeps talking, rambling about trying to repay Lin for hosting her in her home—a sentiment Lin hastily waves off—and being there for each other as friends, and—

Lin holds up her hand. "I get it," she says softly but firmly. "And I appreciate the gesture, really. I just don't want you to feel obligated."

Rosie's former sense of composure returns. In an overly formal tone, she replies, "And I, in turn, appreciate that." She motions towards the door. "Shall we?"

"Just one second." Lin turns to the back seat. "Quit pretending to be asleep and let's go."

Tim opens his eyes and brushes a hand through his hair. Mutters under his breath about how nothing gets by Lin.

"I have a teenager. I know how to spot fake sleep, especially when you're trying to stay out of trouble."

A faint blush creeps into his cheeks. "Alright, alright, let's gooo." He drags the word out with a nervous whine.

#

In her heart, Pania tells herself she's prepared for all of the spirits that will inevitably be congregated inside a funeral home. Even for her spirit, though she's done nothing but dread the possibility. Why her spirit would settle here is a mystery... unless it's been searching all this time for her. A shiver runs down her spine as she considers what the spirit might want from her. How it might try to get it.

Even so, seeing the spirit walk in with Lin and Tim takes her breath away. She falls into the chair she'd been sure to position just behind her and tries to focus on her breathing.

It doesn't approach, instead pushing Lin and Tim forward and then retreating to the back of the room. The spirit keeps as close of an eye on Lin as it does on Pania.

What are you doing here? Pania wonders. *And what do you want with Lin?*

Pania doesn't expect to get any answers, so she tries to focus on the mourners who have been trickling in all afternoon, including her support group friends.

But when Lin and Tim turn towards the door, she's surprised to see that they interact with the spirit.

It's only when Lin gingerly touches the spirit's arm and guides her towards the rest room, when the spirit itself gets goose bumps at Lin's touch, that she realizes.

That's no spirit.

#

Lin's quick side errand to the grocery store had been the perfect amount of time for Tim to refresh his memory on TBI group gossip and remind himself of who Robert was. *Old bogan, call him the old bogan in front of Pania,* he reminds himself before they walk in. He manages to keep the guy's name out of his mouth while they're talking to her.

Pania doesn't seem anything like his notes, or his fuzzy memories. His impression had been that she was strong, easily irritated, and didn't like him very much. The woman in front of him is sweaty and looks weaker than the draft from the open window. Her body sways back and forth and her eyes are bugging right out of her head, like she just realized she's being hunted. *I'm sorry,* he thinks while looking at her. *That's the second-worst feeling in the world.* He doesn't let himself dwell on the one thing that's worse.

"Hey, before we go, let's hit the ladies' room," Lin says to Rosie. Tim takes a deep breath when she dares to put her fingers on Rosie's arm and walk her into the rest room. *This is gonna be a long ride home.* Though he supposes if they go make out in the bathroom for a bit, that might make the atmosphere in the house more bearable. He hopes they aren't *talking* instead.

A movement in his peripheral vision catches his eye, and he turns just in time to see Pania collapse in front of her chair. *That's not good.*

Sam is just walking in the door. He waves her in and rushes over to Pania's side.

"What happened?" Sam asks, eyes on Pania.

"I dunno, but she hasn't seemed right the whole time we've been here."

She glances his way. "Where's Lin?"

"Rest room," he answers curtly. "Anyway, this just happened."

"Are you steady enough to help me get her into the chair?" She turns and spots an attendant. "Never mind, get that guy over here."

The guy was already walking over, so Tim motions him to come faster.

"Is everything all right?" the attendant whispers, his voice impossibly quiet.

"Obviously not," Sam replies. "I need help getting her in the chair. I'll get this shoulder, you get that one, and we'll lift on three. Got it?"

The man gets into position and, together, they get Pania into the wingback she'd been standing in front of. Tim wonders briefly if that was lucky or if she'd stuck herself there on purpose.

In his mind, he runs over what happened before she collapsed so that if anyone asks him any questions, he's able to answer them. It's hard to get past the scared look she'd had on her face. The fear in her eyes had reminded him of how it felt to be hunted. The only thing worse is realizing you've been caught.

#

"First thing you need to do to wow this... Sophie?... is super easy. Just close your eyes," Phil had said. When Tim hesitated, he added, "You have to trust me."

"Okay," Tim replied uneasily.

"Pay close attention. When your eyes are closed—" Phil stops mid-sentence to wag a finger in Tim's face, "fully closed, that is—your other senses work harder to fill in the gaps."

Tim sighed and closed his eyes all the way, but then jumped when he felt a finger slip inside his front pocket.

Phil laughed and stepped back. "See? Just remember that when you're taking Sophie home tonight, and you'll be fine."

Tim brushed off his pants to get rid of the lingering sensation. "Right. Got it. Thanks, Phil."

His date with Sophie had been a little awkward at first, but then he asked her to close her eyes and fed her a bit of bread he dipped in oil. A thread of oil dribbled down her chin, and he was quick to catch it with his napkin. When her eyes opened, they were dancing with mischief in the restaurant's soft lighting.

"Your turn," she said.

He dutifully closed his eyes, hoping that his breath still smelled okay. *Best. Advice. Ever!*

#

When Pania's faculties return, Sam is sitting next to her while Lin and Tim look on, worry built up in the lines of their faces. The spirit is nowhere to be found, and she doesn't dare ask about it.

Seeing that she's come to, Sam holds out a cold bottle of water. "Are you okay? You look like you've seen a ghost."

"I'm not sure I've stopped," Pania replies, eyes still searching for the spirit.

"Hey, look at me," Sam orders.

Reluctantly, Pania complies.

"This has been a very hard day for all of us, but especially for you. Let me drive you home." Pania murmurs her agreement. Much smarter than getting into an Uber with a stranger.

"Here, have a drink." Sam pushes the water bottle into Pania's hands. The freezing cold temperature and the condensation dripping over her fingers draw Pania back into the present.

The ghost—or hallucination? (Pania refuses to believe it could be anything else)—is long gone. She takes a deep breath in and slowly exhales, willing her pulse to slow down and the dizziness to subside. The small sip of water she dares to swallow sits like a rock in her belly.

"Can you stand?" comes Sam's concerned voice.

"If I'm gonna manage the rest of these calling hours, I'm gonna do it sitting right here."

"Pania." For once, Sam is the one who sounds irritated with her. "You've been overdoing it. He'll understand. You need to go home."

"But I need to—"

"Pania." Sam's voice is calm and steady. "Say your goodbyes. Then go home." Pania takes a breath to reply, but Sam interrupts her softly, the very tone of her voice a plea. "Please."

Her head starts pounding the moment she heaves herself off the couch, so Pania agrees. When it's time to shake off the energy of that place and go home, she settles heavily into the passenger seat of Sam's ancient Corolla. "Thank you, doc."

"You're welcome. He'd understand, you know."

"Still. He deserves better than to have me leave halfway through."

"I miss him too," the doctor says in reply.

The rest of the drive home is quiet and she's feeling much better when Sam parks in front of her building. The overly cautious young resident still insists on walking up the two flights of stairs and escorting her to her couch.

"I'm not keeping you company all night, so just head on home now," Pania says as the woman watches her pull off her sensible mauve flats.

"As long as you're safe," Sam replies. "Good night, Pania. Get some rest."

Pania nods and waves her silently out. Despite the turmoil in her heart, a deep, dreamless sleep descends almost as soon as her head hits the pillow.

#

When Tim stumbles off the couch the next morning, he leaves his phone untouched on the side table. The vibe of the house feels like the home he grew up in, and he doesn't pause to register the strange décor, the strangers' photos lining the walls. He expects to see Miriam cooking breakfast, so the empty kitchen disappoints him. Cupboards and snacks are in all of the places he'd expect, though some of the items themselves are unfamiliar.

A sense of dread fills his stomach when he bites into a stick of beef jerky. He turns around and, instead of seeing his mother, nearly bumps into a tiny Chinese woman with pin-straight black hair and an air of hesitation about her.

"Whoa, who the hell are you?" he asks in surprise.

"The woman who took you in when you had nowhere to go, and whose food you're eating," she replies without skipping a beat. "I'd suggest you find those notes in your phone to refresh your shitty memory."

"My shitty memory?"

"What's the last thing you remember before this morning? Because I'll bet it isn't going to bed on my couch."

The pit in his stomach intensifies as he tries to go back in his mind. Instead of last night, his mind serves up images of his mom's boyfriend making dirty jokes about beef jerky, and some of the many things he did after buying Tim's silence with a few embarrassing shared secrets.

The half-eaten stick of jerky turns to fire in his hands. All he can think about is escaping. So, he runs.

#

"You can have the jerky!" Lin calls after him as the kid bolts out the front door. "It's not a big deal!" She tries to keep her voice level, but fear is making her hands tremble. *Well, how on earth are you supposed to handle situations like this? This isn't my fault, this isn't my fault.*

Hopefully he won't go far; the boy hadn't taken his phone or even put on his shoes. "He'll be fine. Probably just walking around the block." He certainly won't want to cross the road in bare feet. Autumn may have begun according to the calendar, but the asphalt is still scorching in the late morning light.

When Lin dares open the front door, she's greeted by an empty street. The only sound is the tiny whimper falling from her own lips.

"Everything okay?" Rosie's voice floats in from the living room.

"No," Lin calls back, her voice hoarse. The thought crosses her mind that Rosie will probably be happy the kid is gone, but she pushes her annoyance away.

Rosie covers the distance between them in a few long strides, a bath towel still wrapped around her hair. "What's wrong?" Her finger grazes Lin's elbow, reassuring but cautious. After all, they've barely spoken since their chat—and stolen kiss—in the bathroom at Robert's funeral last night.

"Tim. I—I scared him, I think. I didn't mean to, I was just trying to be silly, but he didn't remember who I was and—I didn't mean to scare him, I swear, I was just trying to keep the mood light, but then he ran and—"

"Stop, stop right there," Rosie orders, putting a finger gently over Lin's lips. "Tim's a grown man. He might be young, but he's still an adult. He can take care of himself." Before Lin can protest, Rosie continues, "And you aren't responsible for his feelings. But if it would make you feel better, we can go look for him. Or maybe call Sam, the doctor from your support group? She might know what to do. What we aren't going to do, though, is panic. That doesn't help anybody."

Lin nods. "Right. Sam. I'll call Sam. Thanks." She flashes a grateful smile at Rosie and pulls her phone out of her pocket. When Sam's phone goes to voicemail, all of her willpower goes into explaining what happened as calmly and concisely as possible. "So, call me back please, okay? I... I could really use your guidance on this." Turning to Rosie, her voice trembles slightly as she asks, "What now?"

The two decide Rosie will stay at the house in case Tim returns, while Lin heads out to look for him on foot. His shoes, along with some beef jerky and a bottle of water, get slipped into a beach bag that she pulls over her shoulder on the way out the door. "Poor kid's feet are gonna be a mess," she mumbles. When she reaches the sidewalk, panic once again threatens to swallow her whole. *Not my fault, not my fault,* she repeats to herself over and over. *Now pick a direction and try to find this kid so you can fix the latest mess you've made.*

Chapter 17: Crossroads

His feet are starting to burn. The sensation draws Tim into the present. No one is on the street. A couple of kids kick a ball around the front yard of a beautiful two-story house. The mansion is nothing like the run-down farm he grew up on; its manicured lawn and paved turnaround driveway scream what he and Brian derisively labeled "suburbanite princess." Fake ass people who care about nothing except what their neighbors think.

But the lingering scent of beef jerky refuses to dissipate, and the smell carries the weight of shame and fear and it's everything he can do to stop spiraling again. He goes to wipe his face and is surprised to find he's still hanging onto the half-eaten stick of jerky. His fingers open reflexively and the snack drops onto the pavement. Those NIMBYS in the fancy house will definitely not like littering.

A ticket is the last thing he needs when he can barely remember where he woke up this morning. But he can't bring himself to pick it back up.

Before the kids up the street can clock what he's doing or what he looks like, Tim turns and heads back in the direction he came. The lady in the house this morning had said she'd taken him in when he had nowhere else to go, so best to go back before he forgets the way. Once the scent of gardenias crowds out the jerky, he takes a few shaky breaths and tries to figure out which houses look familiar. *Do I turn here, or should I keep going straight?*

A new kind of panic rises in his throat.

#

She circles the block twice before checking back in with Rosie, who hasn't seen hide nor hair of Tim. "Don't freak out on me, Meiling," she says from her spot on the couch.

"Too late?" Lin offers with a sheepish smile as she hangs the beach bag next to the door.

"Relax. I'm sure he'll turn up soon."

"I wish I could be so sure." Lin sighs. Her sneakers drop like lead weights from her fingers, her posture drooping as though her shoes are pulling her down with them.

"Eh, lighten up," Rosie says, patting the cushion next to hers. "Next time, put a tracker in his pocket."

"Rosie!" Lin scolds, even though the idea holds no small amount of appeal. *After all, the last time one of us went missing, it didn't end well.* "What if something happens to him, like Robert?"

Rosie sucks in her breath and Lin curses herself for forgetting Rosie is a First Nations woman. "Sorry, um, the old bogan. That's what Pania calls him."

Somehow, this makes Rosie even more agitated. Pushing herself off the couch, she starts pacing in tight circles and muttering unintelligibly.

"I'm sorry," Lin repeats. "I didn't mean to upset you." But Rosie doesn't seem to hear her. *Great, that's two people I've hurt today.* "Thank you for at least not running away and making me spiral," Lin adds with a nervous chuckle. "Though I might be starting to worry anyway."

Her pacing stops and she looks Lin in the eyes. "I'm not this upset because of you. I um..." She shakes her head, as if fighting with herself about whether or not to go on. "It's a—it's a personal thing." The pacing starts back up; Lin's not sure Rosie's aware she's doing it. "Something I thought I'd buried a long time ago. Nothing to do with you. Promise. I just—I don't—"

She's still trying to string words together when the front door slowly creaks open. "Oh, thank god, I've never been so happy to see you!" The boarder rushes over to give Tim a pat on the back. "Are your feet okay? Lin was worried about your feet."

"Thanks, I'll be fine," he mumbles.

Lin breaks out of her trance and cries, "Tim, I'm so sorry!" She rushes over but then stops. "Is it okay if I give you a hug? I didn't mean to scare you earlier. Really, I'm so, so sorry."

He doesn't meet her gaze, but his arms quickly envelope her in a hug. "Don't beat yourself up about it." His words are whispered in her ear. "It wasn't because of you. It was my past, coming back to get me. It always does. I just wasn't prepared for it this time."

She nods her understanding against his shoulder and lets go.

"One request though. Can you please put the beef jerky and the Tim Tams somewhere else? Like, I dunno, the trash?"

Lin smiles. "They're my son's favorites. If I throw them away, he'll hate me even more than usual, and we can't have that. But if I tell him they're in his room because they're his snacks..." she grins. "I think that should be just fine."

While she's reorganizing the snacks, it occurs to her that twice in the span of an hour, her house guests have done more to alleviate her worries than Jian did the last two years they were married. And yet neither one told me anything about what actually upset them. Curiosity is a much lighter emotion to carry than guilt, so she tries to feel grateful and push her questions out of her mind. The house is bursting with ghosts from the past: hers, Tim's, and Rosie's.

Instead of thinking about her house guests' problems, she tries to ready a few safe topics for tonight's video call with her parents. The list of things they can discuss without circling back to either how Lin's to blame for her failures or how much her parents want to take a pity trip to Australia once the travel bans are lifted seems to get shorter every time they speak.

Maybe I should just be too busy to chat this week. The thought gives her momentary satisfaction, even as she knows she could never do that to her parents. Not without a legitimate reason.

Her mind starts to wander, probing around for legitimate reasons not to talk to her parents. The search might come up empty, but it does give her an idea. Pulling out her phone, she taps a quick message to Pania. *Hey, if you want some company today, I could really go for a mango milkshake.*

It seems like ages before her friend responds. *Appreciate it, but I think I need a day alone. Wouldn't want the old bogan thinking I've replaced my milkshake buddy that fast. Rain check?*

Of course. To make sure she doesn't come across as cranky, she adds a heart emoji to her text. *Anyway, make sure you get your rest. Gotta be ready for brunch tomorrow!*

Safe topics to talk about with her parents be damned, Lin feels good knowing that at the least, she's still capable of being a decent friend. The thought buoys her for the rest of the night.

\#

Lin had asked Tim to check his journal and his phone notes to catch up on his life so he didn't risk another panic attack. While calling what happened earlier this morning a "panic attack" bothers him in ways he can't put to words, Tim doesn't resist. Instead, he settles onto the couch with his stuff and starts to read.

The entry he'd added to his journal last night leaves him feeling annoyed. Why would Rosie insist on coming into the funeral home to be there for Lin, but then head back out to the car when someone collapsed and there was an actual problem? It wouldn't surprise him if there was context missing from his journal entry given his terrible memory, but it's a struggle not to judge based on the information on the page. *Like, she literally deserted us for the car. What's not to understand?*

Next, he jots down what he can bear to relive about the morning's incident, as he refers to it. The memories that triggered the episode are simply too painful to document, and yet the past will keep ambushing him over and over if he doesn't know where it's hiding. So, he forces himself through a short, bulleted list labeled "Avoid At All Costs."

Mental exhaustion sets in, though it's barely 11 in the morning. He lays down for a snooze, praying to whatever might be out there that he doesn't forget again while he sleeps.

\#

The morning moves slowly for Pania, in part because—despite the work of the past week—she keeps forgetting that Robert is gone. She rolls out of bed wondering if there's anything special her old friend would like in this week's grocery run. But her phone shows only a text from Lin about milkshakes. Her face pinches as memory catches up to years of automatic routine.

After she's showered and dressed, the thought crosses her mind that she'll need to rush through the store so that she's not making the old bogan wait too long for lunch. But instead, she's the one people are grocery shopping for. *It's not like I ever minded doing it for him.* But the truth is, she hates that Lin offered to do it for her. She hates even more that she was too worn out, too unable to care for herself, to say no.

Her exhaustion has settled in too deeply to disappear in a single night, but it matters that she makes a milkshake in Robert's honor. Her balance is unsteady, so she sits at the table to prep the mango and scoop the ice cream into her blender.

"Cheers, my friend." She toasts the empty room. "I hope wherever you are, all of your favorite fruits are always in season. And may you never feel useless again."

The little milkshake ritual feels good, and she wants to formalize it, do it again next Saturday, and the Saturday after that, and the Saturday after that. A pen and pad of paper surface from the junk drawer so she can document it. To make it feel more real. She doesn't let herself even think it, but deep down, part of her wants to share that ritual with Lin.

Before she can write out the most essential steps, she must think of a good name for it. Every good tradition has a nice name. She starts by jotting down some potential names. None of them feel right though. She crosses them out, one after another, then decides to try freewriting about why the ritual felt good, then about

Robert more generally. Her energy flags before she stumbles onto anything resembling a suitable name for her ceremony. She tosses the sheet with the name ideas, but leaves the freewriting notes in case they prove useful when she's ready to try again.

I'll have to pick this up later. Her body aches, so she heads to the couch to watch a goofy sitcom. Ten minutes into the first episode, she drifts off. The sleep is exactly what her tired body and mind need.

#

The next morning, Lin's hands are jittery as they style her hair into its picture-perfect bob. Taking a hint from her last therapy session, she pauses. "What are you trying to tell me?" she asks her delicate, trembling fingers. "I'm listening."

Her fingers don't have an answer for her. "Stupid bullshit therapy," Lin mutters under her breath. But when she raises her eyes to the mirror, the sight of her perfect hair enrages her. Her hands tremble—not with fear, but with energy, with a desperate need for change. A slight grin curves its way onto her features. "Spoke too soon, I see," she replies to her face in the mirror.

Good thing there are no scissors in this bathroom. If there were, she would already have hacked up her hair. Jian had put all of the scissors in the house into a safe in the kitchen after a particularly heated fight. She knows the combination, but has decided she prefers to keep them difficult to access even now. *It's just safer... especially for my hair.* Already, the desire to hack it off herself has dissipated, but she makes a note to call her stylist tomorrow.

Her jitters slow, but her usual style still feels wrong. "Hey Rosie!" she calls.

The woman pops her head in the bathroom a moment later. "Yeah, what's up?"

"I want to do something different." She fluffs her hair. "I'm tired of trying so hard to be perfect with every little thing, you know? How do you do your hair?"

Rosie takes a half-step back. "Are you... are you insulting my hair?"

Lin's eyes widen. "No, no! It just feels so much more natural, where my hair is starting to feel..." Her index finger taps her chin as she thinks. "Sterile, maybe? Fake? I need something different, but I don't know what else to do."

Rosie winks. "I really had you going there, didn't I?"

Lin's mouth forms a tiny o. "You were messing with me?"

A laugh spills from her lips. "You're too serious sometimes. Now come on, let's play. What are you thinking? Up or down? Keep it straight, or maybe curl it?"

"I... I don't think I've ever curled my hair other than rolling under the bottom. Causes too much damage, you know?"

"Honey, that's exactly what the old you would say. And you're trying to do something different, right?"

"Well yeah, but—"

"It's never about your hair when it's about your hair," Rosie quips. "And if you want to let loose a little, then you're probably going to have to get used to causing a little damage sometimes."

"Hm." Lin frowns. "Just a little."

Rosie grins. "That's the spirit. Now let's get started. How much time do you have?"

When Lin finally heads out the door, she barely recognizes herself. The half-updo with bouncy curls that Rosie helped her create is light, relaxed, fun... *Not exactly that woman-of-the-apocalypse look I was hoping for, but maybe this is a better way to rebel against Old Lin. Just throw myself into enjoying New Lin.*

The mystery behind her sudden need for change remains, but Rosie's words ring true somewhere deep in her psyche: it's not really about her hair. Her therapist would simply tell her to focus on what feels right and stop trying to overanalyze everything. She rolls her eyes. *I'll give it a go for now, but I need to figure it out eventually.*

#

His phone alarm that morning is labeled "READ NOTES APP 1st". Since Tim doesn't remember what that means, he figures he might as well read them before he does... well, anything. The Miriam situation is quite fresh in his mind—too fresh—so he skips that one and the ones labeled with random days of the week. Then, he pulls out his journal and reads the last few entries.

By the time Lin rushes past him, hands wildly patting her hair as she runs out the door to catch an Uber, he's fairly confident he's caught up on everything. "Bye Lin!" he calls. Her movements are so fast that it's a wonder her delicate white flats stay on her feet.

Rosie doesn't come downstairs for another hour. Just as well. The way he'd written about her behavior at the funeral is fueling an anger he didn't realize he could feel towards anyone except Miriam. *Another woman who's great at saying one thing and doing the complete opposite,* he thinks. And yet somehow Lin has the hots for her! *Let's just hope that's over.* But Lin seems to have barely even noticed the way Rosie neglected her. That only makes Tim feel more indignant on his Momma Lin's behalf.

A scowl appears on his face when the boarder swooshes into the kitchen like she owns the place. "You all right?" she asks as she bustles around, pulling out pans and ingredients and god knows what else.

"I'm fine," he responds icily.

"You had Lin real worried yesterday," the woman adds, seemingly oblivious to his mood. "You know, she walked the neighborhood on her own for a solid half an hour."

His heart warms at her words, though he has no idea why Lin cares about him so much. But then he thinks about what Rosie said again. "Wait, what do you mean on her own? Lin hates being alone in public. You went with her, right?"

"Nah, figured you'd needed some space. Been there myself," she says casually. The thumps of a knife against cutting board reach his ears, but it may as well have been nails on a chalkboard.

"Damn, you abandoned her twice in two days?" His eyes practically hurt from how hard they are bugging out of his head.

The chopping stops. Rosie appears in the doorway to the kitchen, wiping her hands against her earthy brown skirt. "Abandoned her? What are you on about, *mate*?"

He guffaws. "Please. My memory's bad but my journal keeps a record. I know what happened on Friday." Her pursed lips and narrow eyes dare him to try her. "Or did you not tell Lin you wanted to be there for her, and then run and hide in the car the second something went wrong and she needed you?"

"You don't understand."

"Enlighten me," he challenges.

"Look, I don't have to explain myself to you." There's fire in her eyes now.

"No, but you should explain yourself to Lin." He crosses his arms, trying to look more intimidating while standing next to the couch he's called his bed for the last few days. "She deserves better."

"Trust me. I was just trying not to make things worse."

"And yesterday? Letting her run all over by herself while she was, what, freaking the hell out?"

"You mean freaking out over *you*?" She puts her hands on her hips. "You mean trying to help *you*? Besides, someone had to be here in case you came back. Or wandered by helplessly like a grown man child who can't even recognize where he lives."

"Are you shitting me?" Tim's voice cracks. "Does it look like I'm living here to you?" He gestures at the couch, at the single duffle bag Lin helped him rescue from Jenny. Despite himself, tears prick at his eyes. "I've been here what, three, maybe four days? I can't help that I'm fucked in the head. But you—" and here he pauses to point an accusing finger at Rosie— "you are more than capable of being there for Lin, and you keep choosing not to. She needed you, especially in that funeral home. Pania is a huge part of our support group, and she organized that whole service for the old guy by herself cuz the man had nobody. Lin cares about Pania way more than she cared about Robert, and when Pania passed out, you ran! What the hell?!"

"Don't talk to me about her!" Rosie shouts. Her hands are balled up into fists at her sides. "I don't owe her anything."

"Don't owe her anything?" he shouts back. "She's put you up for no other reason than the goodness of her heart. How dare you talk about Lin that way!"

Rosie starts. "I—I wasn't." Her defiant bearing falters. "Pania—I..." She leans against the doorway and takes a few deep breaths. "Can you go back to forgetting now?"

"The fuck is that supposed to mean? What is wrong with you?"

"I don't need to tell you anything, alright? Not now, not ever. For the record, I didn't even want you here."

"Of course not, that'd make it so much easier for you to take advantage of Lin when she's at her most vulnerable."

"That's—that's not what I'm doing, dude. I was trying to be there for her, and then I... I couldn't."

"That's some fair-weather friend bullshit if I've ever seen it. Oh, wait, that's not it either, cuz you also wanna snog."

"I didn't initiate that," Rosie protests, her hands up defensively. In a slightly apologetic tone, she adds, "I didn't mind, but I didn't initiate it. Are you crazy? My town is still unreachable thanks to the fire and then the flood. I have no one and nowhere else to go, same as you."

"Hang on." Rosie's comment about not owing Pania anything finally registers in his mind. "Do you know Pania?"

She gulps. "I don't wanna talk about it."

His eyes widen and he perches on the arm of the couch for support. "Oh my god, you do! How?"

"That is none of your business. None."

Tim knows he should leave it alone, but the curiosity is killing him. The question is out before he even realizes he's asking. "Is that why you came up here? So you could be near her?"

"First of all, I don't need to explain myself to you." Rosie crosses her arms, but then sighs. "But listen, I had no idea she was here, okay? I... we... we have a long history. I should have tracked her down a long time ago, but now it feels like it's too late, and I... I should stop talking." She turns to head back into the kitchen.

Feeling a sudden sense of loyalty to Pania, he snaps, "What, so you abandoned her too?"

"Don't be ridiculous." Her voice is testy. She keeps her back to him to reinforce that she's done with this conversation.

"No, that's exactly what it sounds like. You just run away the minute things get difficult, is that it?"

Rosie rushes back into the living room, spatula still dripping with runny egg as she waves it in his face. "Listen, you entitled prick, she abandoned *me*, ya hear? And then when I stumbled onto her family, I was still so angry, it didn't feel like it was worth the effort to track her back down. She should've been the one looking for me, not the other way 'round."

His jaw drops, and he has to make an effort to close his mouth. "Wait, you mean her birth family? Pania never talks about—" he cuts himself off as he puts the pieces together. His first thought is that Pania isn't old enough to have been part of the Stolen Generation, but he's not about to let Rosie off the hook by asking after technicalities. "Wait, and you've been keeping this to yourself?"

The woman's face crumples in shame. "Look, I know how bad that sounds. It's—I wasn't keeping it from her, I just didn't know where she was, you know? And a funeral didn't seem like the right place to get into it."

Tim's eyes narrow. He hopes he looks fierce and not like a twenty-four-year-old invalid with worse memory than most dementia patients. "Well, you know where she is now. Tell her, and soon. I don't care what she did to you, you don't keep something like that a secret."

Rosie huffs. "Relax, I was always going to tell her. You think Lin would help me get in touch with her?"

"Probly. Or you can just crash one of our support group meetings. Pania's always there."

"Right. I don't need anyone else judging me based on half the story, so just, keep your trap shut until I can talk to Pania, alright?"

Tim rolls his eyes. "Fine. But you'd better act fast—she deserves to know."

Rosie heads back into the kitchen to finish up her sizzling omelet. Just as soon as she's finished cleaning up after herself, she retreats to her room with her plate and not so much as a glance in Tim's direction.

Tim pulls out his journal. His pen hovers over the blank paper. It might be his private journal, but Jenny had violated it enough times that even writing about the encounter feels like a betrayal of Rosie's secret. *At the very least, I need to make sure I don't forget. So I can make sure Rosie follows through on her promise, and make good with Pania if she doesn't.*

#

When Pania spots Lin walking into the Cooly Bistro, she barely even recognizes her. Worry lines may still edge her face, but her hair. *Her hair!*

"Well alright," Pania says in greeting. Lin turns and smiles, taking a seat on the bench where Pania is sitting, waiting for their table. "I didn't even know you owned a curling iron!"

"Oh, I have plenty of things I don't use," Lin says. Her cheeks are a little pink, and Pania's not sure if it's from wind or walking or... *Could that be a blush?* Pania's intrigued.

"Well, if you don't use 'em, you run the risk of losing 'em," Pania replies. "Though you certainly didn't forget what to do with that curling iron."

"Oh, no, if I did this myself, I'd have burn marks all over." She rubs the soft, pale skin on her neck self-consciously. "My boarder helped me with my hair. I listed the guest bedroom on one of those find-a-bed sites after the bushfires."

Pania leans in a bit closer, wondering if the boarder has anything to do with Sal's ghost coming to town. "Now see, this is the kind of thing that shows who you are. What a wonderful thing to do," she says warmly, hoping that will encourage her friend to go on.

"Rosie thinks I'm the one doing her a favor too, but she's wrong. Huan loves her, she cooked a meal from my childhood on divorce day... and on top of that, she curled my hair like a fuckin' pro!"

"Sounds like a real win for both of you," Pania remarks.

Lin's hesitation is controlled within an instant, but Pania knows that look. The woman is hiding something. "What is it?"

"Well... we might have... kissed?" Lin's tone rises at the end as though the kiss is a question, not a statement.

Indeed, the revelation's caught Pania off-guard. But before she can ask any questions, or identify any of the emotions swirling in her head, the server announces their table is ready.

After they settle and order their drinks (mimosa for Lin, cold tea for Pania), Pania finally manages, "So about what you said earlier... I didn't realize you weren't straight."

"Neither did I until several years into being married." She shrugs, as though it's no biggie. "It's not something many people know about me, mostly because they assume things based on, yanno, all the years I spent married to a man and the fact I've never dated a woman."

"If you want to dish on any more of the details, I'm listening," Pania responds. "I mean, about the kiss. Great distraction from the rollercoaster I've been on this week. You know, I even saw—" she stops herself. No need to talk about ghosts.

"You saw what?" Lin lays a reassuring hand on hers.

"Never mind," Pania says under her breath. Lin's touch is electric, and that's more than enough distraction from the ghost of Sal. "So, about this kiss..."

Lin grins. "Okay, but it's not like it's a thing." There's a twinkle in her eyes that defies her words. She takes her hand off Pania's and rests her chin in her palm.

"Then how come you're smiling like that?"

She takes a sip of her mimosa. "It was a hell of a kiss. But we agreed not to do anything else until she's done living in my guest room. Not a healthy power dynamic."

"Very mature of you... but good luck!" Pania laughs, flipping through her menu to avoid looking Lin in the eyes.

"I mean, we only agreed after a second make out sesh."

"*Sesh?!* What, are you seventeen?"

Now there's definitely a blush in Lin's cheeks. "Everything was so awkward and tense... it just kind of, helped us put a pin in it, you know?"

"Next thing you'll tell me is you were making out in the middle of the movie theater like a couple of kids."

Lin groans. "I wish it would've been a movie theater." She immediately sucks in her breath, like she wishes she hadn't said anything.

Pania remembers how Lin let her own accidental slip of the tongue go a moment ago, so she tries not to pry too hard. "Did you want to share where it was?" She grins slyly, trying to share in the forbidden moment with her.

"No, no I do not," Lin replies. "It was inappropriate and wrong."

"Oh, now I'm really curious," Pania says. "If you were just making out, it couldn't have been that bad."

Lin looks like she might cry. "It was bad, okay? Now let's just drop it, please."

"No problem. But if you do start doing things you shouldn't with this... Rosie... you're gonna have to start letting go of all of this shame about every single thing you do. Just let go, have your fun, and move on, you know?"

"Let's just forget about it, okay?" With that, Lin downs the rest of her mimosa and sets the empty glass down on the table. "Where is that server? I want another drink. Oh, maybe I'll get a pitcher, that'll make life easier."

Pania clears her throat. "Will it?"

Through the mist in her eyes, Lin manages a wink. "Well, you are distracted, aren't you?"

Now it's Pania's turn to place a comforting hand on Lin's. "Hey now, no need to spiral just to get my attention. You've got it."

The server reappears. The women place their brunch orders and Lin gets another mimosa. "I suppose I don't really need a pitcher." Lin pushes a stray curl out of her face. "Even if I would enjoy a pitcher. But Huan's coming home this afternoon, and I've gotta be in a better state of mind so I don't fuck up again." She huffs. "Like being sober will stop me."

"Why are you so hard on yourself all of the time?" Pania asks. "I've never understood that."

"I mean, aside from my kid hating me because I've been a shit mom for four straight years with no end in sight? I've been officially divorced for nine days. NINE! And I've already kissed someone else... twice."

"But you're not a thing, so don't worry about it. And you're single anyway, so it wouldn't matter even if you were."

"Just doesn't seem right, not spending more time mourning what was."

"You can wallow in the past, or you can build your future. Up to you, but don't blame yourself for choosing the second option." Pania takes a swig from her iced tea.

"What if I'm only attracted to Rosie because she was in the right place at the right time?"

"Then it'll be fun for a while, and after that you'll let it go," Pania replies. "Some things aren't meant to last forever. That doesn't have to be a bad thing."

"For someone who's perpetually single, you sure have plenty of relationship advice." Lin smirks, the twinkle returning to her eyes.

"Hey now!" Pania smiles at the jab. "Once you've made as many mistakes as I have, you figure out what you did wrong along the way. Don't wallow, don't panic over little mistakes, and give yourself some grace—the opposite of what I did after my accident." The words are out before Pania even realizes she's saying them, but the admission doesn't feel like the big, dangerous moment she'd always assumed it would be. Lin's nodding, lost in her own thoughts. Her finger traces the condensation on the glass of ice water she'd requested along with her second mimosa.

"I suppose that's fair," she replies blandly. "Were you with someone when you had your accident, or are you talking more generally about like, Huan and stuff?"

"I mean, it applies to all kinds of relationships because I've messed up just about every kind there is. But to answer your question, I very much was with someone. We probably wouldn't have lasted even without the accident tearing us apart, but you never really get over your first love, do you?"

"That's what Jian was. My first love." Lin's lips sink into a frown. "Though sometimes I wonder if I even know what love is."

"You'll figure it out... with the right help."

This remark snaps Lin out of her trance, like she's seeing Pania for the first time. "Who better to help than the woman who's been single since she was sixteen, right?" Her smile is playful.

"I dated after her!" Pania exclaims. "Just, you know, not much. Or long. They all complained I was still stuck on her."

"Were you?"

"Well, obviously." Pania rolls her eyes. She's relaxed with Lin, but this doesn't feel like the time to mention that she's been on exactly three dates since Sal. Every single one gave her a panic attack at the idea of letting another person get too close. At the idea of getting hurt like she'd hurt Sal or being in a position where the only real option is to inflict that kind of pain again. "I like to think I've finally put that chapter of my life behind me, but it took a long time. I have a lot of regrets about the way things ended." In her mind, Pania's no longer sure if she's talking about Sal or about dating in general.

"You were just a kid. And, well..." Lin shrugs. "Kids are stupid. Silly to regret things you can't change, anyway."

"You'll get no arguments from me on that one!" Pania replies. "Luckily, I learn from my mistakes." She giggles, attempting to keep a tight lid on her discomfort. "Well, eventually."

Just then, the server arrives with their food. "And how can you be so sure you've learned, hmm?" Lin asks after the man leaves them.

"Guess I'll have to try again." She gives Lin what she hopes is a meaningful look before delicately spearing one of the strawberries on top of her waffle.

"I'd love to know how that goes," Lin says. "You'll have to give me all the juicy details." She *mm*s and *hmm*s over a forkful of her acai bowl.

"Ha! First, I have to get somebody to agree to go out with me..." *And not freak me out by agreeing,* she mentally adds. She turns her attention to her plate.

A few moments later, Lin's words break through her reverie. "How about you and I go on a practice run? You know, get you back in the game."

Pania's cheeks warm. "I wouldn't want to make your boarder not-girlfriend jealous," she says by way of deflection.

"Oh, that won't be a problem. It's just two friends, having a night out."

"Mm, that doesn't sound so bad," Pania agrees. Her muscles are still relaxed, calm; maybe this can work.

"Lay down some ground rules?" Lin suggests. "Hard to practice without knowing where the boundaries are."

"Makes sense," Pania replies around a bite of waffle. "What'd you have in mind?"

"Meet me at the venue."

She purses her lips. "Given your... situation... makes sense. Kinda silly for me to pick you up when neither of us drive, anyway. What else?"

"Keep the practice date to the date night itself. We're still friends, let's not make it awkward. And don't go too hard on the sweet talk during the date, please."

"Is this even a practice date at that point?" Pania bursts out. "I just figured you didn't want me to kiss you."

Lin shrugs. "Fine. I'll be flexible there, that way we can still call it a practice date."

"That's not what I was after." Pania points her loaded fork at Lin before taking another bite.

"I know. And that's why I'm leaving it on the table."

"And are you going to spiral into a guilt trip if I take you up on it?" Fork down, she crosses her arms and tries to look stern. A kiss will not do; her nerves are bristling at the very idea.

Now it's Lin's turn to blush. "I deserved that." She shakes her head. "But hey, maybe I can practice just letting go and having some fun, hmm? We can both get some practice out of it. We're adults, a goodnight kiss doesn't have to mean anything."

Pania pushes aside her fears with a grin that she hopes comes across as carefree. "If that's what you want. Where to and when?"

Chapter 18: The Best-Laid Plans

Over dessert at the bistro, a plan had come together for a night at the movies on Friday. At first, Lin thought the practice date was one of her more reckless suggestions, but as they discuss it, she realizes she's genuinely looking forward to it. She tries to tell herself it's just because she wants to help Pania—and not because of the tiny thrill she felt in her bones when she realized Pania might be flirting with her.

"In case you want to drop me off at home, I should probably bring you by the house, show you where I live," Lin says playfully when the server brings back their cards.

Pania laughs. "I'm not giving you more than a goodnight kiss. You know that, right?"

"Of course I know that!" Lin rolls her eyes. "Forget I said anything."

"Oh, don't be like that," Pania says as she slips her purse over her shoulder. "I don't want to start off on the wrong foot." She taps her cane on the floor next to Lin's shoe for emphasis. "I'll go with you back to your house today and Friday too. That way, you don't have to worry about issues with jerks on the bus or anything."

"Oh no, can't have you coming to my house, can we? Might give you the wrong impression about what kind of woman I am."

"Good lord! Maybe I'm just curious about this house guest you've got yourself all worked up about."

"I am not all worked up about her! ... Am I?"

"'The lady doth protest too much, methinks,'" Pania quotes with a wink.

"You are ridiculous," Lin replies as they shuffle towards the door. "But also, maybe." The banter makes the way back home seem shorter than usual.

"This is so cute!" Pania exclaims when they reach Lin's house. "Very classic suburbia. No wonder no one thinks you're gay."

"I'm not gay," Lin snaps back. "Bi erasure's not cool."

"Sorry. But still. No wonder people think you're straight."

Lin shrugs. "Anyway, what about you? You live far from here?"

"I'm over near the hospital."

"Oh, so you really came out of your way to meet Rosie, did you?" She turns to open the door and grins to herself.

Pania's response falls on deaf ears, though. Something is wrong. Lin has always been an expert at picking up on tension. It's a skill that's only aggravated her post-accident, since she's unable to stop creating it. But the atmosphere in the house has absolutely nothing to do with her this time.

"What happened here?" she asks Tim.

He's sitting on the couch looking glum, lost in his journal. On spotting her, he slams the book shut. "Nothing." But his eyes register surprise when Pania walks in behind him.

"Thought I'd introduce Rosie to Pania properly," Lin explains. "She home?"

"Uuhh..."

"You two fought, didn't you?" Her hands are on her hips before she even manages to take off her shoes. *Maybe it's not me who's cursed after all. Maybe it's this damn house.*

"Look, I—" he falters. "I don't know what to say. Yes? I don't think Rosie's ready for visitors."

"Boo," Pania says lightly. "Well, maybe next time." She turns to Lin. "Looks like you've got your hands full, so I'll just head back to the bus stop."

"You sure?" Lin asks. "You can stay for a few, have a drink."

"What, and miss all of this?" She gestures with her free hand, and that's when Lin takes in what's become of her living room. Tim's belongings may be neat, but his entire life won't fit in this space, and it shows. Whatever fight her two house guests had gotten into has put Tim in a bad mood and Rosie—wherever she is—in an even worse one.

"Right." Lin manages not to say it out loud, but inside she's pleading, *Take me with you?* "You going to be okay walking back on your own? Wouldn't want you to get lost." Before she can stop herself, more words tumble out. "Can't have that on my conscience twice in one weekend."

"What now?" Pania asks.

"Never mind," Lin and Tim say in unison. Quietly, she adds, "We had a rough day yesterday, is all."

"I'll be fine," Pania reassures her. "See you both Tuesday."

"Right, Tuesday," she echoes. The support group had nearly slipped her mind in her excitement about movie night.

"Don't get tunnel vision on me, friend," Pania jokes on her way out the door. "Tuesday!"

The door closes, leaving her and Tim alone. "I have something I think I need to tell you," he starts.

"You think?" Lin snaps sarcastically. "What in hell happened? I was gone barely two hours! I'm not your mother. Don't expect me to babysit the two of you and referee when you can't get along." Tim's eyes fall to his lap. "Sorry," Lin adds. "I don't mean to be hard on you. You okay?"

"Yeah, yeah," he replies. "It's not really about the fight so much as it is about something I found out during the fight."

Before he can continue, Huan bursts in the front door. "Hey Mum, what's good?" His backpack is draped carelessly across his shoulder. When he gives her that awkward side hug he's begun to favor, the bag knocks into her side. Instead of annoyance, it relieves her with how normal the exchange feels.

"I hope you don't mind, but I had to go in your room while you were at your dad's," Lin says. "Left some things on your desk for you."

Her son grunts. "Where's Rosie?"

"Upstairs. Oh, and this is Tim. Dad may have mentioned, he's staying on the couch while he's figuring out a new living situation. We met in my support group. You might need to be a little patient with him, because he has problems with his memory. Tim, this is my son Huan."

The two look each other over and trade "hey"s. "Do you game?" Huan asks.

Tim nods. "I loved my 3DS when I was in high school. Not sure what I've played more recently though."

"Wanna try some *Call of Duty*? It's a first-person shooter. We can play in the basement game room."

"Sure."

"Sweet. Lemme just drop my stuff in my room first."

After Huan heads to his room, Lin tries to get back to the conversation Huan had interrupted. Either Tim's genuinely forgotten, or he's pretending he has as a way to avoid talking about his and Rosie's fight.

"Sweet!" Huan yells from his room. "Thanks Mum!"

Ah, so he found the snacks. She heads over to his room and knocks on the doorframe. "Hey, just so you know, Tim has some weird anxiety thing that gets triggered by the beef jerky and the Tim Tams. You're welcome to eat them whenever and wherever, obviously, but figured I'd give you a head's up so he doesn't freak on you while you're gaming."

"Oh." Her son's face falls. "And here I thought you were just being nice by sticking these in my room."

"No, no, I'm trying, I really am!" she replies quickly, hoping to reassure him. "Tim would've preferred it if I tossed them. I told him no." Huan's defeated posture hurts her heart, so she adds, "I told him no fuckin' way."

"Wait, really?"

Lin smiles. "Not in so many words, but yeah. You're my son. You'll always come first." Skepticism glances over Huan's face, but he's quick to replace it with a plastered-on smile.

"Thanks Mum," he manages as he slides a can of Coke in each pocket and grabs a few mini bags of chips for each hand. "S'cuse me." He heads back to the living room. "Let's go dude." The boys' footsteps echo down the hall and thump into the finished basement.

"So much for whatever Tim had to tell me," Lin mutters to herself.

Her house may be filled to bursting, but she still manages to end up alone. The two boys are bonding, shooting zombies in the basement. Her boarder is holed up in the guest bedroom, sulking over heaven knows what argument she had with Tim. It doesn't seem like a good idea to disturb her. *I wonder what Pania is up to.*

Lin folds her legs underneath her and perches on the wingback. Even though she knows better, it's tempting to pick up her cell and text Pania. To distract herself, she puts her phone on an end table and then looks around her living room as if seeing it for the first time, like Pania had earlier.

The small space reminds her of when she'd first left the hospital after her accident; Jian had rearranged the living room to feel more like a bedroom so she didn't feel like she had to climb the stairs. Though her balance issues were temporary, those early days after the accident were filled with uncertainty.

With one misguided exception, she thinks. She'd been certain Jian would be by her side forever. Absent-mindedly, she picks at a loose thread on the arm of the chair and wonders just how Pania's accident had caused her breakup. The thought crosses her mind that the two of them wouldn't have problems like that, but she brushes it aside as quickly as it surfaces.

Even knowing how her own relationship ended, she still has to give her ex-husband credit for how present, how caring he'd been those first weeks of her recovery. From the moment he showed up in the hospital, Jian had his eyes completely, fully on her. His attention hadn't been that dedicated to her since they were dating, flirting over homework between classes and spending furtive weekends in each other's dorms.

If only she'd known how quickly it would end. She would have savored his devotion more. It was hard to pinpoint exactly when, but as weeks and months turned into years, he'd lost patience with her recovery. The amount of attention she and Huan both needed from him simply didn't fit into how he lived, how he wanted to live. *And he was never much for change,* Lin muses. Their planned international move had been postponed and avoided until his superiors warned him his position was being eliminated domestically. The thought of changing companies, changing jobs, was much harder for her husband to stomach than the thought of packing his bags to do the same job somewhere new.

A thud from upstairs calls her attention back to the present, to Rosie. The people she's invited into her home may not be perfect, but at least they don't expect her to magically turn back into the woman she used to be. Old Lin isn't coming back. At this point, she doesn't even want to go back to her pre-accident self. After all, what did her obsession with being the most accommodating wife and perfect mother give her? A husband with lukewarm affections and an injury that made it impossible for her to be a decent mom. Time for something new. What that something new is, though, she doesn't know.

She and Huan cook dinner together that night. They whip up Tu Dou Si shredded potatoes and lamb kebabs that remind her of so many happy moments over the years with both her parents and her son. Those memories must be crossing Huan's mind too. "Gotta add another dash of peppercorns for Lao Lao."

A smile sneaks its way onto Lin's features. Her mother does tend to overdo the peppercorns. "You'll have to let our guests know what those do for the potatoes. I'm not sure either of them has had Sichuan peppercorns before."

"Oh, good point. Don't want to catch them off-guard," he says with a laugh. When the table is set and he warns their guests that the peppercorns are "basically Pop Rocks that make the spicy stuff taste better," Lin can't help but beam. It's such a normal and wonderful start to dinner, even if Rosie only manages a few polite bites before heading back to her room.

At least Lin and Huan have managed not to argue so far this afternoon. Mother and son are still trying to find their footing, but she dares to hope that at least he doesn't hate her. *Figures, now that Huan and I are getting along a bit better, the other two people in the house are fighting. Their problems best not bleed into Huan's and mine. Not when we're finally making progress.*

Guilt zings through her brain as she thinks back over the day. Between brunch this morning and Huan coming home and then her extended trip down memory lane while the boys gamed in the basement, Rosie has barely even crossed her mind. Tim better not have done something stupid.

She corners him by the kitchen sink as he takes care of his plate. "What in the hell did you and Rosie fight about?" When he starts to sputter, she adds, "I need to know. And if you've forgotten, then go read your journal or check your phone notes and when you figure it out, come find me. Huan doesn't deserve to go back to walking on eggshells around here because of the two of you, you understand?"

The boy refuses to meet her eyes. His shoulders slump in defeat. "She has a secret," he says, so quietly Lin isn't even sure she heard him properly. "I feel like I shouldn't tell you. I stumbled onto it while we were arguing, but that's not really why we were arguing."

Lin sighs. "Keep her secrets, then. But why were you fighting?"

Tim gulps. "I was mad at her."

"For what?" she presses. She manages to keep her suspicions unspoken, but her tone is still more aggressive than she intends.

"She's been real shitty to you, you know that?" His voice takes on a hint of defiance. "You don't seem to care, but she's all happy to make out with you and then just desert you the second you need her."

"Wait, what?" There's a prick of shock as she realizes Tim was defending her. Rather than addressing his accusations against Rosie, she says, "You mean you were meddling in my personal life?"

"Oh, uh, it was bothering me." He scratches the back of his neck and stares at the floor. "Sorry. Thought we were looking out for each other after what you did for me with Jenny."

"I appreciate that, but please don't. Jenny was manipulating your injury to keep you trapped, which is straight-up abusive. You needed help to get out, so I offered it when you were out of options. Rosie..." She sighs. "Just, apologize to her, okay?" Lin nudges him aside so she can do dishes. "And next time you're concerned about my affairs, either tell me in private or sort it out in your journal."

He murmurs in agreement and then slinks off to the couch.

Kids. She rolls her eyes. Cleaning up by herself gives her plenty of time to think. *Not as if Rosie owes me anything just because I made a move.* But the circumstances do make her question if she owes Rosie anything. *Maybe I should give her a quick head's up about Friday.* Even as she thinks it, she knows she won't. It would only confuse her. And Lin's already feeling confused enough for both of them.

#

"You coming back down, bro?" Huan asks, popping his head into the living room.

Tim sets his notebook back in its place in the front of his duffle bag and sets a reminder to write about the fight before bed. "Yeah, be right there." Huan's footsteps thunk back down the carpeted stairs. The video game theme music drifts upward. He must have played a lot of video games before the accident, because the controls had come back to him like muscle memory. Ask him how he was doing it though, and he would have had no words.

After his chat with Lin, he's too distracted to enjoy his newly discovered ability to kill on-screen zombies. *How does she not care?* He'd thought the two women really liked each other, but maybe he'd misjudged how serious they intended to be. The idea that Lin might just be after a fling challenges Tim's image of her as this prudish suburbanite mom whose only issues stem from an injury. Tim's sure that Huan would rather not talk about his mom's edginess, so he keeps his mouth shut as they proceed through the levels.

"Ah man, thought you were watching that door!" Huan groans as a gaggle of zombies sneaks up behind them.

"Whoops, sorry. Got distracted."

"I'll say," the teen grumbles. Their characters both die, and Huan opens one of the bags of chips while the loading screen takes them back to the list of available maps.

They munch. Tim hopes keeping his mouth full will stop the questions from coming, but Huan doesn't care. "What's up, man? We were on such a roll before dinner."

Tim shrugs. "Just getting tired, maybe, I dunno."

"My mom mean to you?"

"What?"

"She gets mean sometimes. It's not on purpose, just happens." Huan shrugs like it's no big deal. "Sucks though."

"Nah, she was fine," Tim replies. Before the teen can ask him anything else, he tries to come up with an excuse of sorts. "It's still weird living here, you know? Didn't exactly plan to uproot my whole life on a moment's notice."

Huan makes a half-hearted attempt at a laugh. "Been there before. When my dad got a flat, I went with him at first. Didn't wanna be here when Mom figured out what was going on in case she decided to start throwing things again."

"Again?" Tim's eyebrows inch upward.

"Might not be her fault, but that doesn't mean I wanna stick around and get hit by one of her missiles. You know, once she chucked a coffee mug so hard across the room, it left a dent in the cupboard?"

This sounds vaguely familiar, but Tim can't place it. "Yikes."

Huan nods. "Yikes on bikes."

"Least she doesn't mean it. She's sweet on the inside."

"Right," Huan says skeptically. "Cuz everyone who throws things when they're mad is just an absolute saint."

"I mean, she's letting me crash here so I don't end up homeless. That's gotta count for something."

"Yeah, but try having her as a mother. Nightmare city."

"My mom's a piece of work too, but she's mean on the outside and the inside." He grabs a can of Coke to wash down the chips. "And it's not because of some freak accident either."

"Sorry dude."

"Not your fault. Just hers." He steels his face. "Now let's kill some more zombies."

Chapter 19: Veneer of Normalcy

Lin manages to catch Rosie alone before she heads out the door in the morning. "Hey," she says, moving closer and touching her lightly on the arm. "Tim told me a bit about your disagreement yesterday. Sorry he butted in—just know that he doesn't speak for me." Lin searches the other woman's eyes, trying to determine how best to smooth things over. "I hope you're okay."

"I'm fine," Rosie replies, a little too quickly. "Now if you'll excuse me, I'm running late."

"Late?" Lin asks. Her curiosity gets the best of her. "For what?"

"Just because I've been displaced by bushfires doesn't mean I'm not working," Rosie snaps back. "I came up here because my job has me on a project that I can handle better in person here than sitting in a cramped hotel room a hundred kilometers away with shitty internet. And right now, I'm late for a meeting."

"Sorry, didn't mean to pry. Just surprised, that's all. You know I can't always control what comes out of my mouth."

Rosie's scowl softens. "Right. Anyway, I'm fine. Just, call off the attack dogs, wouldja?"

Lin shakes her head and smiles. "I talked to him last night. You shouldn't have any more issues. Promise."

"Thanks love." As if on autopilot, Rosie leans over and gives Lin a quick peck on the lips. "See you later."

The door closes and Rosie's footsteps fade before the realization hits. *Did she just... and then...?*

#

Now that the old bogan is safely in the ground, Pania prays that Sal's spirit will have moved on. Brunch and the visit to Lin's—which were both devoid of the supernatural—give her extra reassurance that things are, in fact, back to normal.

The weight is off of her shoulders, and Pania flies through her workday on Monday. "You haven't been this chilled out in ages," Tom jokes after their morning standup. "What, you got a date or something?"

Pania smiles to herself and types back, "Or something." Finally, the past has really and truly let her go.

Even Elaine notices the change in her mood at dinner that night. "What's got you all perky?" she asks over a hefty plate of steak and veggies.

"Last week was long and tough, Auntie," she replies around a mouthful of pepper and onion. "Think I'm just grateful I survived, and that it's over."

"Mhm." Elaine's tone suggests she doesn't believe her. "Most people don't bounce back quite that fast without something else going on. Especially not you, and especially not after what you told me happened at the calling hours. So, care to share what's really going on?"

"And if I don't?"

"Then I'll keep my neenish tarts to myself," Elaine jokes.

Pania groans. "This is coercion."

"I care about what's going on in your life," the older woman replies. "Isn't that allowed?"

"You mean you're *nosy* about what's going on in my life," Pania retorts. "But for one of your neenish tarts, I suppose you've earned a story." Talking about Sal in any way is out of the question. So, as evenly as possible, she outlines her Friday night plans instead.

"You are playing with fire, girl," Elaine says when she's finished. "A new divorcee and a practice date? The hell even is a practice date?"

"We're just friends going for a night out, Auntie," Pania replies. It's the same line she's been repeating to herself to keep her nerves at bay. "Besides, need I remind you that I'm not sixteen anymore? I'll play with fire if I so please."

"A mother never stops looking out for her child." Elaine holds up a finger to shush Pania before she can object. "Same goes for an auntie."

"It will be fine," Pania says. "It's time for a tart, not all this fussing. Are you hiding them in the fridge?"

#

"I know I should have called you earlier, but honestly? I had a lot going on." Tim sighs into the phone, preparing himself for a Monday morning lecture. *Maybe I should've left the house for this call.* His support coordinator, an older man whose name he constantly forgets, is there to help him access services related to being disabled, which usually doesn't cover flats. The agency had recently done a huge fundraiser and created a domestic violence escape fund to fill that gap, but it was only eligible to women and children. "It's not like you were going to do anything to help me."

The man on the other end of the line gives a political response (likely the only kind allowed on the recorded line) and then starts asking assessment questions to determine the level of support Tim will need to live on his own. "Is there someone living with you now who I can talk to about your needs? It can be helpful to have more than one perspective. That's particularly true in your case, where memory is an issue."

"What, you think I'm lying to get out of working or something?" Tim huffs, shifting in position on Lin's couch. "Listen, I may have learned a lot of ways to compensate for my memory, but at the end of the day, we both know my brain is still a war zone. Just look at my medical records, man."

"You misunderstand; it's not about whether I suspect fraud—which, for the record, I don't. We're just trying to set you up to be as successful as possible. Wouldn't want to overlook or forget anything you need."

Tim rolls his eyes, then taps the phone's mute button. "Momma Lin!" he yells. "You around?" Unmuting his cell, he says, "Yeah, alright, I'll try to get someone. But I haven't even been here a week, so I dunno how helpful this is really gonna be."

A few moments later, Lin plods into the living room. She's looking dazed, in her own world. "Did you call me?" she asks.

He doesn't bother muting the phone this time. "Yeah, can you talk to this bonehead for a few minutes? It's my support coordinator. He's got some questions about what I need to live alone."

"Bonehead, huh?" She shakes her head and smirks. "Don't worry, I feel the same way about mine too sometimes."

She takes the phone when he offers it. While he can only imagine what questions the guy is asking her, some of the things she says still catch Tim off-guard. "I've been really afraid of him wandering off without his phone and getting lost, or going back to his old flat and taking his abusive girlfriend back."

The reply on the other end of the phone makes Lin bristle. Her next words are acidic. "If we thought the cops would do something besides laugh, we would have called them. But we both know they don't take abuse accusations seriously from men, regardless of the circumstance... As long as he has his phone with him, I know he's safe because he has so many notes and reminders, but without it..." Lin chews on her lip instead of finishing her sentence.

The conversation continues for a few minutes longer before she hands the phone back to Tim. *Good luck,* she mouths before heading back upstairs.

"Got what you need?" he asks the coordinator.

"Yes, thank you. Now let's chat about the kinds of supports that best suit your needs and how we can make this work with the funding you have available, okay?"

By the time Tim gets off the phone, his brain feels like it's fried. He wanders into the kitchen and grabs a soda from the fridge. He chugs it. *Caffeine, sugar, time to work your magic!*

The coordinator wants him to try getting a part-time job so he can afford a better flat than his disability pension will allow. But the mere idea's making him drowsy. His notes about the accident have had him out of work since June. Almost nine months. Trying to find work again seems to have crossed his mind a thousand times since the accident. There are four different notes dedicated to new career ideas in his list. But having to start right now, when his brain is still so unpredictable? Even going for an interview feels overwhelming.

He heads back to the couch and holds his head in his hands. One thing at a time. *Let's get off of Lin's couch full-time and then we'll deal with the job thing.* It might not be the timeline Josh would prefer (*I knew I'd remember the guy's name eventually,* Tim thinks triumphantly), but it's what he's going to get. He shoots the coordinator a quick email before he forgets, making sure to sound as professional as he can manage. *Let me know when you expect the services that we agreed I need to become available for me so I can plan a move-out date, with a list of which supports have a waitlist (if any). For obvious reasons, I need everything from our call in writing so I can look back on it, but those are the most important pieces to me so please bold them or something. I need to get settled into my new place before I start looking for work. It's just too much to do all at once, especially while living on someone's couch.*

He sends the email, then realizes he forgot to sign off with his name. *Oh well. It's obvious it was me.* He hides under a thin blanket the rest of the afternoon, watching reruns and waiting for his email to ding. But his phone stays stubbornly silent.

#

Lin is supposed to check in with her own support coordinator every quarter according to their agreed-upon plan. After talking with Tim's and helping with his independent living assessment, the thought strikes her that she's ignored the last three calls from him. *Pick a better time to call, dude!* Then she giggles. *Dude?!* Tim must be rubbing off on her.

Before she can come up with a good reason not to, she picks up the phone and heads to her room, punching the redial button on the last missed call from his number. "Hi Matt," she greets him, trying to sound cheerful. "It's Lin! Sorry I've missed your last few calls." She closes her door as gently as possible, remembering the times she'd slammed a door within Matt's earshot. And that time she slammed one in his face.

The surprise in his voice makes her wonder if she's caught him at a bad time. "I can call back later if you're busy right now," she offers. But after the way she's avoided him lately, he's intent on keeping her on the phone.

"Why don't you tell me how you're doing?" he asks. The shuffling of papers in the background settles. She's sure her file has worked its way to the bottom of whichever stack he's looking through.

"Well..." She swallows hard, remembering why she's been avoiding this call. "It's been a rollercoaster. Jian divorced me, but don't worry, I'm not living alone. I have a boarder affected by the bushfires staying with me and I took in someone from my TBI support group who needed a couch to crash on short-term."

"Wait, wait, you got divorced?" The paper shuffling starts up again. "And you have long-term guests? You know you're supposed to touch base with me whenever anything big happens in your life."

She bites her tongue to swallow the snapback she wants so desperately to deliver. After a deep breath, she manages, "Not exactly a situation I've been eager to talk about. But the divorce was only final like two weeks ago, so it's still pretty fresh. It's not been super long, you know, but it's been a long time in the making—I'm trying to say it's fine." She takes another deep breath. *Keep it together, Lee.* "I'm sorry I didn't get in touch before."

"And I'm sorry about the divorce," he says in a softer tone. "How do you feel about your support needs? You've got the funding if you'd like someone to drop in a couple of times a week to help you adjust to living alone. I take it you're still seeing the anger management therapist, right?"

"I'm still seeing him, yes. I'm not living alone though, not technically. Boarder from the south and the guy from my support group are staying here, remember? And of course Huan, but only about half the time. Anyway, I had a different request in mind. I think I'm ready to get a job."

"A job?"

"It's not about money. My husband made sure I wouldn't have to work because, well, he thinks I'll never be capable of working again."

"You'd like to prove him wrong?"

Lin smirks. "As much as I do, that's not why I want a job." She outlines her goals and they carve out the beginnings of a plan. "You think it sounds doable?"

"We'll never know unless we try." They make plans for an in-person evaluation of Lin's interests and skills.

"Thanks, Matt," she says. "I'm really looking forward to giving this a go."

"You'll be great," he replies. "Talk soon."

A smile forms on her lips as the realization hits her. *I can do this.*

Lying in bed later that night, the elation from leaning into New Lin with a new job has all but vanished. It's been replaced by nerves. When Rosie came back from her work meeting, she acted as if nothing out of the ordinary had happened that morning. Her lips kept a platonic distance from Lin's for the evening.

There had been no word on when the boarder would be able to go back home; at least, none that she had shared with Lin. The fire in Richmond Valley that Rosie was escaping from had been extinguished a week or so before she'd even arrived on Lin's doorstep.

Lin knew a lot of flooding had followed on the heels of the rainstorm that put out the fire. Presumably, roads were still blocked, and it was likely that any hotels in the area were full, so traveling back without knowing if her home was standing had its risks. Then again, why should she have to stay at a hotel? Doesn't she have friends, coworkers nearby that could put her up for a few days?

It strikes her as odd that the woman hasn't spoken about going back, even just to check whether her house has been spared or not. If work isn't an issue, maybe she just doesn't want to go back. Lin's heart skips a beat at the possibility.

And then there's Pania. Her feelings shouldn't be complicated, but they are, all the same. She knows she should talk to Rosie about Friday night, but the delicate balance of the household could be thrown into chaos if she doesn't handle the topic perfectly. And, well, she doesn't trust herself to be sensitive or perfect.

Her body language would give too much away; likely more than even Lin herself wants to admit. The heat in her bones (and quite possibly her cheeks) over having any kind of a date, even a fake one, with someone whose company she enjoys as much as Pania's, will only create problems between her and Rosie. Like playing with fire.

Lin rolls over in bed, tangling herself up in the top sheet. She sighs and kicks it off so she can unravel the tangled mess. The room is in darkness but for a pale moonbeam. She glances through the bedroom window and notes the moon is in Leo tonight. *My moon sign.*

Rather than dwelling on how problems with her and Rosie could spiral into conflicts that encapsulate everyone in her home, Lin decides it's time to check her horoscope. A few moments on Google give her plenty to think about. *You're likely going through emotional storms. Explore where your curiosity leads you and remember: what will be, will be. The path you are meant to walk will reveal itself when the time is right.*

Lin purses her lips in thought. If only it were so easy to calm the chaos in her heart. No, she will have to make a choice, sooner or later. It's not even a real choice. Pania might or might not have been flirting with her, but either way, they aren't planning a real date. *What will be, will be.* The words echo in her mind, and she takes a deep breath to soak them in. With Pania, there is only friendship. At least, that's what her mind wills her to believe.

She resolves to keep her Friday night social calendar under wraps in the name of preserving household peace. It's just two friends, helping each other out. No need to create drama where there is none.

Still, her sleep that night is fitful.

Chapter 20: Lean on Me

Maybe it's the tarts that Elaine sent her home with, or her conviction that Sal's ghost has moved on, or the fact that she's going to see Lin tonight at group. Whatever the reason, Pania breezes through her work day as though she's walking on air. The interactive map design she'd been working on has already been approved by the client, and now it's simply a matter of swapping out placeholder data for internal data they haven't provided yet.

"The client is still waiting on a few departments to submit data for the map," Deedee notes during their afternoon video meeting. "They're hoping to have it to us this week. I'm pushing for tomorrow so we have more time for testing. Even though you guys are rock stars and don't need it, I want to give it to you anyway." She makes finger guns, then moves on to bullet point-style updates on the other aspects of the app and website they're working on.

Pania tunes out as much of the meeting as she can to avoid Deedee's little pep talk zingers. But when she minimizes the window, she only goes from seeing Deedee's face to reading her and Deedee's private message thread. *You should take the rest of the afternoon,* she had written a few minutes ago. *I know it's been a hard couple of weeks for you, and the client's dragging their feet on this spreadsheet. Probably going to end up a mess we need to fix later, so I'd rather have you rested up and ready to go when they finally get their act together. Sound good, rock star?*

Forgetting she's on camera, Pania lets a smile cross her face. *Thanks,* she types back. *Think I'll take you up on that.* She resists the urge to add something sarcastic to the chat or the video meeting, instead trying to decide whether she needs another tart or a mid-day nap.

Eh, screw it, I deserve both, she thinks on the short walk to the fridge once the meeting ends. Deedee was right about how much she needs a rest, and the woman didn't even know the half of it.

"Mm, Auntie, you really outdid yourself." Elaine is always generous with the jam and the mock cream, piling the fillings until they rise slightly above the tart shell. Pania licks a bit of the messy jam off her finger and settles onto the couch with a yawn. An alarm gets set for an hour so she has time to cook a light dinner before group, then she pulls up some rain sounds on her phone. The rest of the delightful little tart goes down in a single bite and then she attempts to drift off.

But her happy mood vanishes like a mirage in the desert as her mind wanders towards Lin. Practice run or not, the idea of going on a date again is unnerving. *Why did I even pretend I want to date again?* Pania had given up on dating well over a decade ago, and for good reason. The dangers of romance were all too clear, and the benefits all too murky. She can't even trust herself, much less someone else.

And yet, Lin feels different. Sure, the dangers are still there, but Lin's injury makes it difficult if not outright impossible for her to lie. Brutal honesty commands Pania's respect, and then there's how much Lin still manages to surprise her, even several years after joining the support group. Pania's intrigued. The more she thinks about what happened at brunch, the less she knows about what she wants out of their little Friday night practice run. By the time she's finishing up the dishes and getting ready to leave, Pania comes to the conclusion that she's ignored her heart for so long she doesn't have the faintest idea what it wants. The realization chills her very bones.

#

Tim walks into group with Lin, and he sits between Lin and Sam. There's an empty chair between Sam and Pania. "Thought there were only three of us now," he whispers to Lin.

Without skipping a beat, Lin pipes up. "Expecting someone new today, Sam?"

The resident blushes, the color an intense contrast to her white lab coat. "Um, no, I don't think so, although I probably should get a few more folks in. It's hard to gauge how many is a good number for a support group like this, you know?" She stammers on, but Tim loses interest. He notices Pania's hand resting gently on the empty seat and then he understands.

"It's for him, isn't it?" Tim interrupts.

"Didn't seem right not to leave a seat here for him, one more time." Sam's eyes glisten in the harsh cafeteria lighting. For a second, Tim thinks she's going to cry, but instead she clears her throat and turns to her laptop. Her straight back and reserved tone convey nothing but professionalism when she asks, "So, how is everyone adjusting at your house, Lin?"

Tim watches Lin's face carefully, but her expression's placid. The exact opposite of her messily curled hair, which Lin had insisted was her way of embracing joy and accepting the inevitable chaos life has thrown her way. "It's been an interesting transition, but it's been good for me. Good for Huan." She glances at Tim. "I don't want to speak for you. How do you think it's going?"

Startled by the group's focus shifting to him, he stumbles through a vague answer while looking around the empty cafeteria and evading eye contact. "I mean it's not easy. But I'm out of danger, out of that relationship. Don't like being controlled or manipulated by people I'm supposed to be able to trust."

"You can tell me to mind my own business, but I think I'm missing a piece of the conversation," Pania interjects. She leans forward, a hand on one knee. "What happened with you and your girl? I thought the two of you were pretty serious."

"Uh, well..." He runs a hand through his hair to calm his nerves. "She was going through my journal and cutting out pages that were critical of her. Entries where I told myself to break up with her."

"Oh." An artery in her neck starts to pulse, and it strikes him that Pania might actually care about him, despite her tough exterior. After an awkward silence, she adds, "I'm sorry that happened to you. Given your memory problems, that's tantamount to entrapment, isn't it?"

"That's why I had to run the minute I caught her doing it. I didn't even have my wallet on me when I left. Thank goodness for Sam and Momma Lin." He shoots a grateful look towards both of them.

The tension in Pania's shoulders seems to relax under her lavender-colored grandma cardigan. "I'm glad you're in a better place now."

"Yeah. Except I've gotta figure out how to live on my own, and fast. It's hard, ain't it? What kinds of things do you do, yanno, to make it easier?"

Pania looks off into the middle distance before she answers. "It's changed a lot over the years. I wasn't stable enough on my feet and had too many migraines to function on my own for a long time. When I moved out on my own a year or two after finishing uni, I had someone come by at least twice a day to help with day-to-day stuff like carrying laundry baskets. And I needed someone to supervise my PT exercises. Tried to reduce my risk of falling when no one was around, you know?"

Tim murmurs in agreement, hoping she'll go on, but she doesn't. He asks Sam, "What about people who have issues with their memory? Any of them able to live on their own?"

"Of course, Tim." She makes a point of setting her laptop on the floor and looking him in the eyes. "Every disability comes with a range, and your brain is still healing from the accident. I'm not sure if you realize this, but when you first came in here four months ago, you could barely even carry on a conversation because of your memory problems. I hardly ever have to remind you of what the group is talking about anymore."

"Really?" He tries not to get his hopes up too high.

"Oh really," Lin interjects. "You gave your opinion about Jenny's pajama choices three times in a row on your first night here."

Tim cracks an embarrassed smile and gives a little shrug. To Sam, he says, "You think I'll be able to live on my own like, in a few weeks or a few months?"

"I won't lie to you. It'll be very difficult at first, but there are a lot of supports and strategies you can use to compensate for poor memory. I think once you get into the right rhythm, you'll be okay."

He bobs his head, trying to absorb her faith in him. His mind comes up empty when he tries to remember what supports he and Josh had agreed he needed. All he knows about the conversation came from his phone's notes, which were woefully inadequate. Perhaps rehashing the topic will jog his memory. "What kind of stuff d'you think will be helpful, doc? I already use my phone to within an inch of its life. It's got my daily schedule, appointment reminders, notes about ongoing stuff like this group, important addresses, and warnings about how dangerous my mom and ex are. Not to mention it's also got my text messages and emails and social media and, you know, normal phone stuff."

Instead of letting Sam answer, Lin speaks up. "Right, but what happens when you forget your phone, or don't look at it first thing because you don't remember you need to?"

He looks down. He takes in his scuffed low-tops and the spotless tiles underneath his feet. "Guess I'll have to think about going old school too, huh?"

"Sticky notes are a wonderful thing," Sam agrees. At some point, she picked her laptop back up, and now her fingers are typing a mile a minute. "What about a dry erase board on the back of your apartment door, or maybe on the fridge or bathroom mirror? Somewhere you know you'll look either first thing in the morning or before you leave the house."

"I like that," he replies. Though he'd woken up that morning without remembering anything after getting on the highway in Miriam's Corolla, he suddenly has a flashback of pitching something to someone—his ex-girlfriend, perhaps. "I could set up a chart on like, an art easel maybe, and put it in front of my bedroom door. Figure the old school way only works if I'm forced to pay attention to it, yanno? And it's not exactly easy to ignore something huge in the middle of my doorway."

"Oh lord, just don't go tripping yourself when you forget it's there," Pania pipes up. "Last thing you need is to give yourself another good knock on the noggin."

"Yeah, I know what you mean," Tim replies. "Maybe I'll put it in the middle of whatever room is next to the bedroom, not the doorway."

"If you think that will work for you and you want to try it, I'd encourage you to test it out now, in Lin's house—if that's okay with Lin," Sam says. "Build out what you want it to say and see how it helps and where it falls short over the course of a few days. That way, when you're on your own, you aren't starting at zero."

"Preparation is the mother of success," Tim says wryly. "So yeah, let's prep for this shit. Sound good, Momma Lin?"

When she nods, the motion makes her curls dance. "I want to help, any way I can. Pop by Bunnings on the way home?"

#

Lin's grateful to have a reason to bolt out of group that evening. She and Pania may have agreed to keep the practice date to Friday night, but it keeps surfacing in her mind. The last thing she needs is to blurt something inappropriate out at the wrong time.

But Tim holds her up, chatting afterwards with Sam about some suggestions for living alone that she wrote out for him.

Pania catches her eye and gestures for her to walk towards the cafeteria doors with her. Reluctantly, Lin follows.

"What's good, Pania?" Lin tries her best to sound casual, but it's hard for her to look her friend in the face.

Pania swallows. Hesitates.

"Whatever it is, just spit it out. You know I would."

"I'm not sure about the practice run thing," she finally replies. "Kinda freaking me out a little bit."

"It's not stepping outside of your comfort zone if you're still comfortable, right?" Lin tries to keep the mood light, but she's sure her face is betraying her.

"I may not have been totally honest about how much I've dated since... her," Pania goes on. "Truth is, I've barely tried at all."

"Then why don't we change up the plan, hm?" She twists a curl around her finger. "How about just dinner? No date. We can chat about her, about why it's been so hard for you to move on? Might help to process it all with a friend." Pania still looks squeamish, so Lin adds, "If Friday night dinner still feels too date-ish, we can do a different night."

"How about tonight? Just coffee... unless you still need to eat. I don't think my stomach can handle food with that particular conversation."

Lin glances back at Tim. He's still deep in conversation with Sam, taking notes and looking at things on her laptop. "Let me just text him first," she says. Tim prefers having a written record of everything, just in case his memory fails him. She waits until his phone dings and he sends a thumbs up emoji back before following Pania out of the hospital.

When the two women reach the café at the edge of the hospital grounds, it's closed. "Well, where to?" Lin asks.

"Nothing much within a short walk," Pania replies. "You okay with just finding a bench to sit and chat?"

"Sure." She doesn't want to spook her friend, who's looking jittery and unnerved.

"Actually, no, I don't want to sit outside. Let's take a bus to Tugun Beach—there's bound to be a few things open over there."

"Okay." Despite her curiosity, Lin tries her best not to ask for details before they're settled into a cozy booth fifteen minutes later, with waters on the table and Lin's order on its way to the kitchen.

Chapter 21: Letting Go

Pania's fiddling with a napkin, folding and unfolding it almost compulsively. Her eyes stay focused on the task, as though she's afraid to look anywhere else.

"Hey." Lin waits until she has Pania's attention. "You're safe, okay? Whatever it is, you can tell me. I know I'm blunt, but I also care about you." She clears her throat, realizing that might make matters worse. "You know, because that's what friends do."

"I've—I've never told anyone about this before."

"Whatever it is, it must have been eating you up, keeping it inside like that for so long. You deserve to let it out. Set yourself free."

"Right." Instead of telling her story, the woman continues playing with her napkin.

"You can trust me." Lin rests her hands on Pania's hands. "Start at the beginning. What happened?"

"I need you to understand. This part of my life does not show me at my best."

Lin throws her hands up and laughs bitterly. "Have you not heard how bad of a mom, of a person, I've been these past few years? You know plenty about me at my worst. How could I point fingers at you?"

This seems to reassure her friend a bit. "Still. You sure this is going to help?"

"Nothing's going to help until you process what happened. Obviously, holding it in has not done the trick."

"What the hell, right?" Pania sighs. "Okay, let me tell you about Sal. We met when we were just teenagers, goofing around and getting into trouble. We were both foster kids—my fosters didn't care about me one way or the other, but her foster dad was nasty."

#

After the Lord's prayer game that ended with two canings, Sal's foster dad had been brutal. He'd never left a mark where anyone could see before, but the black eye she was sporting that Saturday defied even the heaviest of makeup.

They decided to run that very night over wine Sal snatched from her foster mom's stash. "Okay, but how are we going to get out of here?" Sal asked, words a bit slurred. She was stretched across Pania's bed, hugging the half-empty bottle. "We'll just get found and taken back if we try to walk it. And money? What about money?"

Pania was sitting in the curve of Sal's legs, stroking her girlfriend's thigh tenderly. "Mallory's dad keeps a spare key for the Mustang in their garage. If we ride it to the coast, bet we could sell it pretty easy once we get there."

"Two birds, one stone. Nice." Sal took another swig of wine and offered the bottle to Pania, but she refused. "But what about Mallory? Her foster dad's pretty shitty."

"What, you think she'll wanna come too?" Her hand stopped at Sal's knee.

"I don't wanna leave her to that dude's wrath." Sal touched her bruise gingerly. "Been there, done that, and I don't wish it on anybody."

"Fine. We'll bring her along."

Sal shook her head. "I don't think she'll go."

"What? Why?"

"She's crushing on Bobby."

Pania had to make an effort not to laugh. "The kid covered in pimples and acne that works at the hardware shop?"

Sal smiled. "The one and only. And he ain't gonna leave."

"He doesn't have the imagination to even think it." Pania rolled her eyes. "What a catch."

"Still. Best to let her know what's coming, don't you think? Wouldn't wanna leave her high and dry." Sal shifted uneasily until she was sitting up and facing Pania. Her fingers went again to her bruised face. "I know all too well what that's like."

"Wouldn't it be better in that case if she doesn't know anything?"

Sal considered this. "Suppose there are benefits to that. Especially since she'll never come with us. I just hate seeing her get left behind—if her foster dad's anything like mine, she'll end up the punching bag for his anger whether she deserves it or not."

"Hey—" Pania waits until Sal meets her eyes. "No one ever deserves that."

The girls decided to walk down to Mallory's house. "Best make sure that key is where Mal said it is, you know?"

Pania took one last swallow of the wine and grabbed her purse. "Let's go then."

Sal was a little too tipsy and rolled off the bed in a fit of giggles.

Pania started to say that they didn't have to go down there tonight, but her breath caught in her throat when Sal's shirt slid up her back. *No wonder she never wants me to touch her.* There were crisscrossed scars along with a few new bruises, so that Sal's back looked like a patchwork quilt. *No. We are leaving. Tonight.*

Luckily Mallory only lived a few houses away. It hadn't been hard to find the key, to convince a still-tipsy Sal to get in the car. Their fates were sealed the moment the engine fired up and Pania gunned it out of the garage, down the street, and into the night, away from Mallory's screaming foster dad. Just a few miles out of town under the weak light of a waning moon, an enormous roo was waiting for the right time to jump the quiet hinterland road.

#

Silence overwhelms the table. A server drops by with Lin's burger.

"Thanks for trusting me with that," Lin responds quietly when they're alone again. "Are you doing okay?"

Pania sips her water, hoping the action will be enough to loosen the tightness in her throat. "I... I think so."

"For what it's worth, I don't think you have anything to feel guilty about."

Pania stares at the wedge of lemon in her glass. "Don't patronize me." Her words carry a bitter edge. "Intent never matters as much as impact. You've said as much a thousand times when talking about your son."

"It's a little different in your case. You were young, and trying to help Sal, and you just didn't have the tools to deal with things going sideways."

The two lock eyes briefly. "You really think you have the tools you need, Lin? Cuz I think if you did, you wouldn't be divorced and your kid would adore you as much as any sixteen-year-old is capable of adoring a parent."

"What's your point?" Lin's eyes are alive with passion. Instead of getting snippy, she takes a bite of her burger.

"You don't need to hold me to a lesser standard out of pity or condescension or whatever it is you think you're doing," Pania says defensively. "All that does is piss me off. Sounds like Sam."

"If it helps, I wouldn't hold any teenager to the same standard I hold for an adult. That's just ridiculous." Lin snorts. More somberly, she continues, "You can't seem to give your past self any grace, but that doesn't mean you didn't deserve it. Teenagers make all sorts of crazy mistakes. It's part of growing up."

"That night went so badly, it's literally followed me my entire life." She points at her cane propped against the table. "Can't imagine what it did to poor Sal, and it's all because of my meddling. I left her in that car, you know—abandoned her to the cops, her foster dad, Mallory's family... I didn't even have the decency to wrap her bleeding head." Pania leaves out that she was in shock, that she walked for over an hour before realizing the car's shifter knob was somehow, inexplicably, in her hand.

"What a weight you've been carrying all these years." Lin's voice is soft, gentle. "Not to sound like your therapist, but I think you should try to forgive yourself. Bet Sal already did."

"If she lived long enough." This whole conversation is making her want to run. Lin seems to know that, because she *tsk*s until Pania meets her eyes. "What?"

"All this guilt is going to sink you if you don't just let it go."

#

"But how?"

The pain in her friend's eyes is killing her. "Again. Not a therapist. But I have an idea."

"I'm listening."

"It's a weird visualization exercise my therapist has me do with my anger. Sounds outrageous but bear with me, because it helps."

"Oh, just spit it out."

"Now you sound like me." Nerves make Lin giggle. "Okay, so imagine your guilt, your anger at yourself, whatever negative feelings that are holding you back, are right here. A physical object." Lin cups her empty hands and motions for Pania to do the same.

Her expression is amused, but she copies Lin's movements. "Now what, hm?"

"Now put it down. On the table, on the floor, into the trash can. Put it somewhere you can leave it behind. Where it won't follow you." Lin throws her hands over her shoulder. Pania rolls her eyes and then makes a show of putting her handful of feelings onto the gleaming wooden tabletop.

"That's it?" she asks, skepticism bleeding through her words.

"Not quite." Lin drops a few bills on the table and then stands, motions to the door. "Now we leave it behind."

"You're serious?"

"Like I said, it sounds bonkers... but it really helps. Come on." She holds out her hand. "Let's go for a walk."

The women head out onto the street. Though night has already fallen, the heat of the day still emanates from the pavement. A breeze off the ocean cools their faces as they amble away from the restaurant.

"Nice night for a walk," Pania remarks. "Good idea."

"It is, isn't it?" Lin replies. She doesn't dare ask how her friend is doing, because she doesn't want to put Pania in an awkward position if the exercise didn't help. It certainly didn't help the first time Lin used it. A sigh escapes her lips. *What a mess my life has been.* She tells herself things are finally turning around, but whether that's true or not is anybody's guess.

Pania breaks the silence again. "Thanks for listening back there. It helps, getting it off my chest, you know? Didn't expect it to, but it did." Her friend chuckles. "You always find ways to surprise me."

"I'm glad it helped," Lin replies blandly. She feigns interest in the illuminated shop windows so she doesn't have to meet Pania's eyes. To wonder what her friend meant by that comment.

The two meander a bit longer, past closed shops and dimly lit restaurants and the mottled trunks of streetside ivory curl trees. The warm night air carries with it the scents of eucalyptus and car exhaust. A plane whines overhead as it makes its descent into the nearby airport.

"You know," Pania says, "I ended up here more or less by accident, but I've never regretted staying here. Couldn't have picked a better place to live if I tried." She takes a deep breath and exhales slowly. "Fantastic weather, the beach, solid public transportation... and plenty of great people."

"I ended up here because of my husband—may not have been my intention, but it most certainly was his. Anything to avoid upending his career. Life here had its ups and downs for me, and more than a fair share of loneliness, but... it's growing on me, now that I've found my people."

"And who are your people, exactly?"

Lin stammers. "Well, you know, the uh, the support group and of course I'm enjoying the boarder though she's not from around here. I'm even working on getting a job."

This makes Pania holler. "You go, girl! What field?"

Lin shrugs, trying to play it cool. "I've found I like caring for other people. So I'm looking for something that will let me do that."

"Let me know if you need any help with cover letters and stuff," Pania replies. "I do a bit of mentoring on the side. It's usually just for Aboriginal folks, but I don't mind making an exception for you." She grins.

"Oh, cool." Lin tries to keep her replies short and non-committal so Pania doesn't ask too many questions. She doesn't want Tim to find out, in case she isn't able to get a job providing the services he needs. In case she isn't able to save him from the otherwise inevitable waiting list by being his support person. No one, not even Pania, can know.

#

He may have given Lin the thumbs up when she said she planned to leave with Pania, but Tim is still nervous about making his way back to Lin's alone. He procrastinates by chatting with Sam for as long as he can string the conversation along. It isn't nearly long enough.

His phone's battery is running low. Tim scribbles the directions from the map app on his forearm in case his phone dies before he reaches Lin's. In case he forgets where he's going. Or why. In case, in case, in case.

So this is what it'll be like, going home alone to an empty house. He hates it.

The depths of evening twilight unsettle him: the rustling of rodents in the shadows, a car slowing down on the street behind him. Several times he's startled by the silhouette of a man in the doorway of a bar, the edge of an alley. *Stop it,* he orders himself. *You came home alone from group all the time when you lived with Jenny. You can do this.* He walks on, putting all the effort he can into feigned confidence and swagger.

But then a couple spills out of a restaurant and he swears it's Miriam's laughter he hears. The man next to her looks like what he'd imagine an older, washed-up version of Phil would. His entire body commands him to flee. He listens.

When his feet finally deliver him up the steps at Lin's, he's breathing hard but the panic has left him. Tim hasn't felt this exhausted since he escaped Jenny's without a plan or a prayer. His breath doesn't slow until he's fast asleep on the couch he calls home.

Chapter 22: Peopled by the Past

While Pania thought she'd exaggerated how much Lin's little exercise had helped, the truth is she wakes up feeling a bit lighter the next morning. And the morning after that, and the morning after that. During her lunch on Friday, she texts Lin. *Glad we canceled the practice date and chatted instead. Next time you see 'em, thank your therapist for me, would you?*

When her phone buzzes, she can't help but smile as she reaches for it. But instead of a reply from Lin, it's a message from Elaine. *I know you said you were doing that not-date thing tonight, but if you can squeeze us in, the Elders have some exciting news to share. We would love to have you there. Meet me at the community center at 17:00?*

Seems the week is going to end on a high note. *You bet, Auntie.* The afternoon slips easily by and soon, Pania is on her way to the center. A few gracious clouds keep her from burning up under the early autumn sun.

"Hey Auntie!" Pania gives Elaine a quick hug after she steps into the coolness of the old community center. This is the very place where Pania first felt she belonged to the Clan who had so eagerly welcomed her as one of their own as a teenager. In recent years, she's favored the community garden over the center—the fragrant native shrubbery offers a connection to Country that she desperately needs after so many hours each week cooped up in her apartment writing code. But the center, which is always filled with easily accessible Elders and neatly cordoned-off Minyangbal artifacts, is where she learned what Country was all about.

"How long until you disappear for your little flirting with fire experiment?" Elaine asked, lips slipping into either a smirk or scowl—Pania couldn't tell which.

"Actually, I decided to cancel." She shrugs. "I haven't needed to date for this long. Why start now, eh?"

"I thought it wasn't a date, hmm?" Elaine's lips settle into a smirk.

Pania rolls her eyes in response. "The idea was to practice so I could try dating again, but you knew that. So anyway, what's this big news, Auntie?"

"You'll see," the older woman responds. "Now let's go have a seat. Did you want me to grab you some punch?"

"I'm fine, thanks."

The chairs are the standard folding metal variety, and within minutes, Pania's back is complaining.

But then she catches sight of Sal's spirit hanging back in the corner... dressed in a business suit of all things.

Pania gasps. Her fingers grip either edge of her seat so she doesn't fall out of it. "What kind of news is this?" she asks Elaine through tight lips.

"Are you okay?" Elaine's voice is edged with concern, and it takes Pania back to the beach where she'd met Elaine all those years ago.

All of the years since that moment have taught Pania that here is a person she can tell the truth to, safely. So, voice in a whisper, she responds, "No."

Before they can leave their seats, Elder Charlie walks over to the microphone set up in front of the rows of chairs. "We are so happy to be here tonight, and thank you to everyone who helped get the word out on such short notice. There's been an exciting development for our people, and it's all thanks to our friend Rosaline from the Aboriginal Legacy Institute. Rosaline?"

Sal's spirit steps out of the shadows and takes the mic. Pania doesn't hear anything the woman says, just feels the weight of the past come barreling down on her after decades of hiding from her guilt. She isn't dead after all. But based on the way Sal is glancing over her, either she doesn't recognize Pania or she's determined not to let it show.

The few tattered things she does absorb from Sal's speech are about Yugambeh language classes and grant funding and teachers. It makes Pania wonder if she's just dreaming. She points at relevant figures on the projector screen, and talks about how many speakers of the language there are; how many there could be in the future. *Sal not only isn't dead, but she's doing the exact kind of idealistic shit she was talking about when we were kids? Ain't no way.* But based on the excited applause and the worried looks Elaine keeps throwing her way (and the notable lack of disturbing non sequiturs that her dreams serve up whenever Sal is involved), Pania is certainly wide awake. If she and Lin hadn't canceled for tonight, she would have been texting her right this minute to either reschedule or cancel. Definitely cancel. After all, if Sal isn't a ghost... *has she been following me?*

#

Lin's scheduled appointment with Matt at the support coordinator's office in Tweed Heads is running late, and she's grateful that she isn't on a time crunch to go out with Pania. They'd started a full hour late. Lin finds herself trying to meditate to quash the anger rising within her. It's not perfect, but the practice does keep her from tossing magazines at Matt's closed door. *Take that, intrusive thoughts,* she thinks triumphantly.

When they do finally get started, Matt gives her a questionnaire about her career interests. Unsurprisingly, caring for other people is at the top of her list. *Maybe because it's the only thing that really matters.* Still, it's nice to have that confirmation that it matters to her, spelled out unambiguously on the computer screen.

"Now comes the tough part," Matt says softly after they've gone over her results. "We have to make sure you can handle your own emotions, Lin. We can't have you taking things out on your clients."

He braces as if for impact, but Lin only sighs and looks down at the fresh manicure on her fingers. "You think I don't know that? I feel like I'm ready for this, but I'm not exactly surprised I have to prove myself. My track record's no secret. Not a big deal if I mess up at home with an acquaintance who's crashing on my couch; bigger deal if he's paying me for support services."

He folds his hands on the cluttered wooden desk. "Glad you understand. I hope you're aware of how much progress you've made since even the last time you sat in this office."

Lin smiles at the recognition. "To be honest, I think the divorce has been good for me. I was always worried about setting Jian off—I couldn't be the perfect wife he'd had before my accident. Everything I did seemed to be too much, too emotional. I'm just not the person I was before the accident."

"And now?" He looks closely at her face as he speaks and leans ever so slightly forward in his chair, as if he's listening for her response with his full body, not just his ears.

"I'm much more relaxed without having to live up to his standards. Like I'm able to meet myself where I am, you know?" She giggles and adds, "Of course, it doesn't hurt that at night, I spend at least ten minutes before bed just cussing out the darkness. I let the anger from everything that's pissed me off all day wash over me and respond to it then." She purses her lips and pinches her eyes shut. *Matt did not need to know that!*

He makes a quick note on his clipboard. "I'm glad you're finding coping mechanisms that work for you."

"Wait, what?" Her disbelief must be showing on her face. She'd expected a scolding.

"Your goal doesn't have to be to never feel angry, Lin," he replies. He adjusts his glasses before adding, "It's okay to find safe ways to feel your emotions. In fact, I'd say it's critical. You sat in my waiting room for an entire hour and not once yelled or pounded at the door. Not one thing thrown. I'd say keep doing what you're doing."

She bites her lip to keep from tearing into him. *Of course he kept me waiting on purpose. What an absolute bonehead.* "Will do." Her voice may be terse, but her hands are still. "Guess that means my evaluation started on time after all."

He lets out a pleased *heh* and holds his palms up. "Got me."

Somehow, this makes Lin feel less annoyed. Maybe because the wait wasn't wasted time. "So, what's next?"

\#

The moment it's polite to, Pania bolts from the room with Elaine struggling to catch up. Pania's not exactly sure what revenge or retribution her ex is planning—if that's really what following her has been about—but guilt has her brain tripping over all of the punishment she deserves.

"Do you wanna tell me what's going on, my dear?" Elaine asks, hand gently touching her shoulder.

"No, but I don't think I have a choice, do I?" Pania tries to lighten the mood with a little half-smile, but her hands are trembling.

"Do I need to get a doctor?" Pania shakes her head vigorously. "What is it then?"

Pania points back into the room, where Sal is still mucking it up with the Elders, shaking hands and exchanging pleasantries. "That's my ex-girlfriend."

"I'm sorry, who?"

Pania clears her throat, then leans in close. "The one in the power suit. She's, you know, the reason I don't date."

"Oh. OH." Elaine's deep brown eyes widen with shock or perhaps something else, but then she tamps it down. "Well," she says evenly, "she seems nice."

"Auntie." The tone of her voice snaps Elaine to attention. "I left her in a stolen car with a head wound. It... it was awful. I was awful." The words spill out before Pania can stop to think, before she can temper the past to avoid Elaine's judgment.

The older woman's smile falls away and she gestures towards the door. "Let's not talk here." They head outside and Elaine points at a nearby bench. "Can you make it that far?"

"I want to run forever," Pania replies without thinking, eliciting a stern look from Elaine. "But relax, I'm only going to the bench. With you."

They settle in next to each other, and Elaine pats Pania's leg. "You know, you can let it eat you up forever, or you can just go back there and apologize to her. Seems like the universe is giving you a gift, an opportunity here. One that you need a hell of a lot more than a practice date."

"I can't face her—she must hate me." Pania sighs. "I certainly do."

"Does she look like she's suffering?"

"Maybe not on the outside, but—"

"But what? You're still punishing yourself, and you hope it's for a good reason?"

"Auntie—"

"You know, that woman didn't even have a scar on her head."

"It's been thirty years!"

Elaine's hand grips her thigh tightly. "And that, my dear, is my point."

"Just because she looks fine, doesn't mean she is fine. Or that she's forgiven me for the way I treated her."

"That's exactly why an apology is in order." Pania squirms, feeling like a teenager in Auntie Elaine's house all over again. "Come on. Let's go." Elaine hoists herself up and clucks her tongue. "No time to waste."

They amble back towards the community center. The crowd has largely moved to the refreshments table, but Sal isn't there. "I need to do this on my own," Pania says. She walks back into the room with the projector, still set to the final slide of Sal's presentation.

Her ex-girlfriend is kneeling on the ground near the podium, fiddling with some papers that don't want to fit in an overstuffed binder. "Um. Hi." Their eyes meet.

Sal clears her throat. Doesn't look up from her papers. "Hi."

And just like that, Pania feels sixteen again. All of the awkwardness and defensiveness and nerves are clogging up her throat and making it impossible to speak or even think. "Look, um, Sal—"

"I don't go by Sal anymore," she responds curtly, eyes turned downwards. "But I guess you wouldn't know that."

"Right... listen, I'm really—it's—it's good to see you," Pania finishes lamely. "You've obviously done really well for yourself, in spite of everything."

"Yup."

"Look, about when we were kids. If I could only go back to that night, I'd do so much differently."

Sal shoves the binder into her briefcase and stands. She swipes invisible lint off her golden-brown pantsuit and tucks a single stray hair back into place. Her gaze is intense, her voice cold. "Are we really doing this now?"

Pania's heart is beating so fast and yet she's still breathless. "Well, it's just this huge weight I've been carrying all these years, and I—"

"I'm working, okay? I need to go network, get an idea of who might be benefiting from these language classes. So unless you're signing up, I need to go." She brushes by her, the soft silky fabric of her sleeve brushing against Pania's bare arm and sending goose bumps across her skin.

"When you're ready—how will I be able to find you again?"

"Talk to Lin." And with that, she's gone.

After she leaves the room, Pania smacks her forehead. *Shoulda signed up for one of those classes.* But the moment is gone. She could easily follow her into the other room and sign up, but the conversation they need to have can't happen tonight.

Still, it lightens her heart knowing that Sal isn't dead. That she's managed some amazing things after all these years. *And hey, she doesn't even have a scar!*

She makes a bowl with her hands and sets it down on the podium before leaving the room. "I'm going for a walk. I'll text you when I get home," she tells Elaine before heading onto the street. The dying light throws its warmth over her shoulders like a blanket as she meanders through the streets, towards the ocean she and Sal used to dream of back in high school. She settles on a bench and texts Lin: *I need to see you. Can we meet tonight, the place over at Tugun Beach?*

\#

Lin sees the text from Pania when she finally finishes up with Matt. *Is everything okay?* she texts back.

She shoots Tim a quick message to let him know she'll be home late. "I guess it's time to go to the beach," she says to herself. The bus she needs is just pulling up on the corner, so she hurries across the street. It's full of rush hour commuters. There may be room, but she's nervous about the crush. "You've made so much progress—you can do this," she tells herself. Then, she boards the bus.

Her stop is over twenty minutes away. She needs all of her willpower to keep from causing a scene as she's jostled and elbowed in the crowd. Every stop, more people seem to get on than get off. A young guy in a suit manages to spread his legs all the way across the aisle to where she's standing. "Listen mate, quit the manspreading, and quick," she barks at him. He looks like he's going to argue, but murmurs of agreement among the other passengers nearby shame him into bending the knee.

"Sorry ladies," he mutters. "Just a tall guy."

Lin rolls her eyes and refrains from answering. It feels good knowing that the other women on the bus have her back, at least.

After what seems like an eternity, she's on the sidewalk at Tugun Beach. She opens her phone: nothing from Pania. That's odd. She wanders towards the restaurant they'd stopped at just a few days ago, but her friend is nowhere to be found. She calls Pania's number, but it goes straight to voicemail. *Hmm.*

Rather than jump to conclusions, she decides to grab a sandwich and wait. But by the time she's halfway through her meal and there's still no word from Pania, Lin starts to feel like she needs to do something.

It doesn't feel like the kind of thing to bother Sam with, and it strikes her they don't really have other acquaintances in common. *Wait, the carer at the garden!* Building up her courage requires several deep breaths and several minutes practicing a script of what to say. She thanks her stars Sam had made her take down Elaine's number a few weeks ago. Her finger is shaking when she presses the call button.

The older woman picks up on the first ring. "Pania?" she asks breathlessly.

"Hi, is this Elaine?"

"Sorry, forgot to check the caller ID." The emotion bleeds out from the woman's voice. "Yes, this is Elaine. Who's this?"

"My name is Lin; I'm a friend of Pania's. By any chance, have you heard from her tonight?"

The woman on the other end of the line sighs heavily into the phone. "You can't get in touch with her either?"

Lin sits up straighter, sensing something off. "She wanted to meet up with me, but she never showed. Her phone's going straight to voicemail."

"I had the same problem. She told me she'd check in when she got home. Now, knowing her, she's probably taking the long way home after what happened, but her phone being off is very out of character. I don't like it."

"What happened, exactly?"

"Shit," the woman whispers. "I don't think I was supposed to say anything. And anyway, it's irrelevant. She went for a walk and now neither of us can get a hold of her. That's what matters."

The two women compare details on where Pania had been and where she'd intended to go. Knowing her medical history, they agree it's too risky to wait for her to surface again so they divide up where they need to look. Lin pays the check and heads into the night, heading down the street towards the community center where Pania was last seen.

#

Huan is back at his dad's for the weekend. Tim's not sure where Lin or Rosie are; they'd both left separately more than two hours ago. Lin, at least, isn't planning on coming back anytime soon.

His stomach is starting to growl and he's debating on whether it's safe to attempt cooking by himself. Not something he was confident at doing even when his brain was normal. "Listen, if you're gonna live by yourself, you're gonna need to figure this out. Stop being such a wuss." He tries to give himself a pep talk but it feels wrong to go through Lin's cupboards—even if she has repeatedly told him she doesn't care.

He hasn't left the house since coming home alone from the support group on Tuesday. Even power walks feel out of reach right now. The idea of running into someone who knows him—who he may or may not recognize on any given day—has his nervous system up in arms.

Still, hunger is a powerful driver, and he knows the nearest grocery store is just a few blocks away. So, he gathers up his courage and a short list of things he needs and heads down to the market. The cramped aisles make him feel claustrophobic; his shoulders tense into knots as he looks for some noodles and marinara.

"I can do this, I can do this," he mumbles under his breath. "How the hell can I work if I can't even buy groceries? Can't even feed myself?" An older woman with what he thinks of as a "pensioner's perm" gives him a wide berth as he walks the aisles and he realizes what he must look like.

He's just walking out the automatic doors with his haul when he hears it again. Miriam's laugh. The plastic bag falls out of his hands and he hears the glass jar of sauce break. "I'm sorry," he says to no one in particular. He grabs the box of spaghetti and dashes out, leaving the marinara-splattered bag behind on the sidewalk.

His phone rings halfway back to Lin's house. When he goes to answer it, the battery dies. *Fuck.* He walks faster and doesn't look back until he's safely back in Lin's house with the door deadbolted behind him.

Just go through the cupboards next time. And give Lin the twenty bucks for groceries.

It takes fifteen minutes before his hands stop shaking. It's another half an hour before his stomach is settled enough to actually eat the meager dinner he's pulled together.

When he opens his phone after dinner, there's a missed call and a text from a random number. He clicks on the message. *Thought you might need some more after what happened earlier!* It's a photo of the same kind of marinara sauce he'd dropped at the store. The oxygen leaves the room when he sees who's holding it.

Miriam.

Chapter 23: Found Family

Elaine calls much quicker than Lin had expected. "You find her?" Lin asks.

"Not exactly." Her voice is tense.

"What's wrong?"

"There's this pad of paper on her kitchen table—it's full of these really strange notes, I think it's related to a friend she just buried."

"Robert?" Lin guesses.

"Ah, so you're from the support group," Elaine responds. "Then you know what happened to him."

Lin gulps. "What do the notes say, exactly?"

"It's hard to follow, but there's some notes about being useless, being worse than useless..." The other woman's voice fades.

"What else?" Lin presses.

"I'm sorry, I just—I thought she was doing better, but I should have known she was just hiding her pain." Elaine coughs. "Anyway, I'm not sure there's more that makes any sense."

"Fine. Does it look like she's been home since you saw her earlier?"

There's a pause and then some rustling on the other end of the line. "It's hard to say. Same pair of shoes is missing from the front entry if that counts for anything."

"Alright. Do you..." Lin trails off, unsure if she wants to set the older woman into a panic. But it must be said. "Do you think I should go down by Snapper Rocks?"

"You don't think—no, she would never..."

"Even if she didn't, maybe that's where she went on her walk."

"That's way too far for Pania to walk," Elaine responds. "But the beach near the center might be a good place to check."

"Okay, I'll head there next." Lin hangs up the phone, nerves building in her gut. She has a missed call and several messages from Tim, but she can't even bring herself to read them. After all, he's at home—he'd probably just forgotten that he'd called and then texted her out of habit. First things first.

#

Against her better judgement, Pania had let the calming, soothing rhythm of the waves lull her into a light snooze. When she wakes up, the sun has disappeared and so has her purse. "Ah, shit," she mumbles. She hefts herself off of the bench. Her bones ache and her feet sink into the cool sand.

She heads over to a young couple looking at the stars. "Can I borrow your phone? Someone snatched my purse and I need to make a call."

The woman is already digging through her bag, but her boyfriend says skeptically, "And how do we know you're not just going to take her phone? I know those tricks."

"Look mate," Pania says with a huff, "I'd go ask somebody else but I'm disabled and it's hard for me to walk on the sand. I just need my auntie to drive me home."

"Relax, George," the woman says as she holds out her phone to Pania. "She needs help."

"Thanks," she says to the woman. She dials Elaine's number but the woman doesn't answer. "If that number returns the call, can you just tell her Pania is hoofing it back home from the beach?"

George starts to protest, but the woman cuts him off with a fierce *shh*. "Yeah, of course," the woman replies. "You need a hand getting to the sidewalk?"

The streetlights at the edge of the sidewalks are maybe fifteen meters away. "I'll be fine, thanks. Just pass the message along if she calls back." Slowly, Pania turns and walks towards the street.

#

Lin's not answering her phone. Tim's trying his best not to panic, but this is different than Miriam calling from home. She'd gotten a new number. She'd stalked him. She'd found him, and just a few blocks away from home.

After furtive glances outside, he pulls the curtains closed. Haphazardly, he turns the couch so that he can lay down in front of it and not be seen from the glass inset in the front door. Even though darkness has fallen, the lights stay off.

He pulls a blanket over his head and dares another look at the picture she'd sent. It wasn't a selfie; someone else was holding the phone. Terror truly takes hold in him when he notices the rock on her left hand. The necklace with the letter P hanging from her neck.

Code Red, Momma Lin. Code Red. They're here. They're both here.

It had taken him months to break free from Jenny, and only with help from both Sam and Lin. But the kinds of things Phil could divulge about him... would Lin kick him out to keep Huan safe from Phil? Would the two of them manage to twist the truth until Lin blames Tim for the abuse, the way Tim still finds himself doing despite years of therapy? He shivers. They could take everything away from him, and then what?

With thoughts like these racing through his head, the locked door does little to stop the panic rising in his belly. Neither does Lin's silence, though he's pretty sure if she calls him, he'll be too afraid to speak.

There's a knock at the door.

"We can make this right, Timmy—I know you're in there!" His mother's voice is muffled but unmistakable. "We just want to be a family again!"

He shakes his head. This can't be happening. But it is.

#

Lin hurries towards the beach and nearly runs straight into Pania. "Hey! Are you okay?" She checks her friend up and down under the streetlight.

"Sort of," Pania admits. "I'm not hurt, but I need to get home ASAP. Someone took my purse and I'm sure they're headed on a shopping spree as we speak—I need to get those accounts frozen before they make off with too much."

"Oh goodness, I'm sorry to hear that. Should I call an Uber? Maybe the cops?"

"I don't want to wait that long. And please. What are the cops going to do? If you'll let me borrow your phone, I'll just get Elaine to bring me home."

"Oh, good idea!" Lin pulls out her phone and hits Elaine's name in her recent calls. Pania raises an eyebrow but doesn't say anything, just takes the proffered phone.

They take a seat on a nearby bench to wait for Elaine. "You scared us," Lin says. "You um, said you needed to see me. What's going on?"

Pania huffs. "I just have one question. How the fuck do you know Sal Mina?"

Of course, Lin recognizes her boarder's last name, but the first name throws her for a loop. "Wait, I'm not sure I do."

"Oh yes you do. You absolutely know Rosaline fuckin' Mina. My question is, how?"

"Oh, you mean Rosie?"

It's as though she's punched Pania right in the diaphragm. She doubles over and yells into her lap. "She's your *boarder*?"

"What is going on with you? Yes, she's my boarder. Is she in trouble?"

Pania sits back up and pulls her hair back into a thick ponytail. Her voice is restrained. "That's... that's Sal. My Sal."

Lin's insides twist into knots. Of course she manages to crush on two women who also happen to have dated at one of the most pivotal times in their lives. Pania, at least, is still stuck on Sal—she's still calling her "my Sal," for heaven's sake, even though they haven't dated in what, three decades?

And now they reconnect because of me.

Elaine pulls up in a tiny blue sedan. Lin searches Pania's eyes, hoping her friend doesn't automatically hate her for snogging her ex. "We cannot be done with this conversation."

"Later, though, please. Tomorrow?"

"Fine." She opens the passenger door for Pania. Together, the three women head back to Pania's flat. The ride may be short, but Lin is incredibly grateful for Elaine's chattiness. It gives her time to organize some of her thoughts—Pania seems to be doing the same, although of course she could also be tallying up credit cards and accounts to freeze once they get her back home.

"Thank you both for coming to my rescue," Pania says. She gives each of them a quick hug.

"I hope you're okay," Lin whispers as they embrace.

"Me too," Pania whispers back. After they break apart, she adds loudly and almost playfully, "Now, I've got work to do cancelling these cards. Shoo!" Pania waves them towards the door. "I'll talk to both of you tomorrow, I promise."

#

Tim hopes his silence will buy him safety. But they must know, somehow, that he's inside, and the knocking only gets more insistent.

"We brought you some more of that sauce you like!" Phil's voice is muffled by the thick wooden door, which Tim notices is nearly the same color as the marinara he'd dropped. A little more blood-like though. He shudders at the comparison.

His brain is running a thousand miles a minute; it's paralyzing him. Time doesn't slow down, but his thoughts scurry so fast that it's tempting to feel like it does. Instead, the seconds tick by far too fast, and there are so many decisions to make and things to consider and he still hasn't moved and now the taps are on the glass window instead of the wooden door. A whimper escapes his lips. He doesn't even realize he's made a sound until his mother's voice returns.

"Timmy, my dear Timmy, are you hurt in there? Tell me you're okay, just tell me that you're okay." The faux concern isn't for him, he knows that; it's for any neighbors worried about the strangers on Momma Lin's doorstep. Still, his heart longs to believe it's real.

The taps come more forcefully now. "Can you answer me?"

"Son, answer your mother," Phil adds gruffly.

Hearing his abuser call him "son" enrages him, fills his mouth with bile, makes him want to vomit. Tim doesn't dare open his mouth, but dials 000 all the same with trembling hands.

"You're leaving us with no choice—we need to make sure you're safe," Miriam cries, her voice a metallic, piercing shriek. When the glass cracks, Tim screams and runs for the bathroom in the hall. He fumbles with the lock, the darkness broken only by the dim light of the phone he'd dropped in the sink.

When he picks it back up, a woman's voice asks calmly, "Police, fire, or ambulance?"

"Police, police please." He answers the dispatcher's seemingly endless questions in a shaky whisper.

The sound of breaking glass stuns him into silence. "Are you still there?"

He nods, afraid to speak, forgetting that the dispatcher can't see him.

"Sir?"

"I locked myself in the bathroom," he whispers. Two sets of footsteps fall on Lin's living room carpet. "There's—there's nowhere else for me to go."

"Timmy?" his mother's voice echoes through the house. "Where are you hiding, dear? We just want to make good, my boy."

He stays silent. They have to know where he is, but now that they're inside, they seem to be taking their time.

"We aren't going anywhere," Phil says. "Not until we solve this."

Tim settles his weight against the back of the bathroom door. He's thankful for the flimsy lock and for being tall enough to brace his legs against the vanity on the opposite wall. He can hear the sound of Phil's breathing when he walks up to the bathroom and tests the door.

"We have news to share!" Miriam croons. "Why don't you come on out and we can have a little chat?"

Eternity couldn't be nearly as long as the next twenty minutes, which is how long it takes before the sirens approach. The two bolt through the house, looking for the back door. It isn't until the police officer in the hall has reassured Tim twice that they've both been handcuffed and taken out of the house that Tim dares re-open the door.

#

Elaine offers Lin a ride home. "Are you sure it's not too much of an imposition?" Lin asks.

Her laugh is genuine and puts Lin at ease in an instant. "Consider it my thank you for finding Pania. Tonight could have gone so much worse without you here."

The two women chat comfortably on the ride home—mostly about Pania and her stubborn independence. Elaine recounted stories of when Pania first came to live with her. "Couldn't even manage a flight of stairs but boy, you'd regret it if you brought that up to her."

"I didn't realize you raised Pania," Lin says. "I didn't think you were old enough for that."

"Oh, you flatter me." Elaine's smile is warm, her grip on the wheel relaxed. "Or maybe you just insult Pania."

"Oh goodness, I'd never hear the end of it if she thought that!" Lin says with a laugh. *So, this is what it's like to get along with strangers. I'd almost forgotten.* In the moment her heart is happy, despite the fallout sure to come from the fiasco with her house guest.

Her comfort turns to consternation when Elaine turns onto her street. Several cop cars are parked up ahead, lights flashing.

"Which house is yours, honey?" Elaine asks. "I don't want to get too close to whatever they're doing up there."

Lin gulps. Sees her own tiny front porch and feng shui-approved red door illuminated by the flashing lights. "You'll have to if you want to take me home." That's when she remembers those messages she'd ignored from Tim earlier. She whips out her phone and calls him. No answer.

"Do you want me to wait here for a minute?" Elaine asks.

"No, you go on. Don't want you to get wrapped up in whatever shitshow's waiting for me." She doesn't say goodbye, just bolts for the door as soon as the car comes to a stop.

#

"Are you the homeowner?" the officer standing guard on her porch asks.

"Yes, I'm Meiling Lee."

He checks her ID then grunts. "Please follow me." He opens the door and walks inside, shoes crunching over broken glass.

Tim's holding a blanket over his shoulders, standing next to another cop. The poor kid looks terrified. When he spots Lin, he crosses the room and practically jumps into her arms. "Momma Lin!"

"Hey, what on earth is going on?" She pushes him out of the hug and looks into his face. "You're safe now, okay? You're safe here."

He shakes his head. "Not anymore. They found me."

The officer who'd walked her in clears his throat. "So, I take it you know this man?"

"Yes, yes, of course. This is Tim Anderson. He's been staying on my couch for the past couple of weeks—I helped him out of an abusive relationship." A light bulb goes off in her brain. "Oh my god, is Jenny out there in that car?"

Tim's face is unreadable. "Worse. It's Miriam and... and him."

Before Lin can respond, the cop asks, "Ma'am, do you know a man by the name of Phil Murray?"

"No, not at all. Were these people trespassing?" She turns to Tim. "Did they hurt you?"

"Appears to be an attempted break-in," the cop responds.

"Oh heavens!" Her hand flies to her mouth. "Tim, are you okay?"

"That guy is the one who... he's—he's the reason I don't talk to my mother," Tim manages. "I've got a no-contact order against Miriam, but I—I guess I thought no contact was already in place for him. I thought that was enough to keep them away."

"Is that the guy who..." Lin trails off, unwilling to say it out loud.

"Yep." Tim's eyes are red. "That's the guy."

She pulls Tim back into a hug. "Oh Tim, I'm so sorry I didn't answer earlier. I'm so sorry."

"Don't worry, we'll get them out of here," the cop says loudly. Tim breaks out of the hug and takes a few steps back. The cop adds, "They're both in violation of no-contact orders as well by being here, so that will be considered an aggravating factor."

"Good! Now please, get them far away from here."

The officer takes a short statement from Lin and then the cars are off, lights fading into the night.

#

Now that Lin's home and Miriam and Phil are gone—without even having a chance to speak to Lin—Tim finds it impossible to hold himself together. He heads up to the shower and uses the sound of the water and some music from his phone to drown out his sobs. The stress leaves his body as the tears flow. His body feels empty once the tension is gone. The look on Momma Lin's face suggests the music wasn't quite loud enough to cover the noise he'd been making.

"Do you want to talk about it?" she asks. Her feet sink into the lush pink carpet lining the upstairs hallway that leads from the bathroom to the stairway. "You don't have to, but it might help."

He shrugs. "I actually feel a lot better now. Just had to make some space to feel everything that's been pent up for so long, you know? I've been dreading this night since I stole Miriam's ancient sedan and booked it out of town. Literally could feel my stress levels rising as the miles passed on the M1." Something in Lin's face changes. "Sorry, I know, you hang out with a bunch of car thieves," he jokes.

"A bunch?" Lin questions. Then she shakes her head. "No, never mind that. You told me you didn't remember anything before the accident today—when we were having lunch. Do you remember?"

He thinks back. Turkey sandwich, lots of potato chips, and... *That's right. I couldn't remember Miriam's shit, but at least I'd left myself the hint to avoid the Tim Tams.*

"What changed?" Lin asks. "Did you have a nap and like, your brain switched gears or something?"

"Hmm, no..." His mind turns over the events of the afternoon. "When I was at the grocery store getting some stuff for dinner, I heard her laugh and I—it was just all there. Like it had always been there. Everything Phil did to me, how she read the letters he sent from prison, our fight when she decided to let him stay on the couch after he got out... even the way she excused taking him back a few months later. She said he was a changed man. Can you believe that shit? After everything he did to me, she still wanted to sleep with him." He looks down at his feet. There are a few splotches of marinara sauce on his socks. It makes his skin crawl, remembering how close he'd been to them, how vulnerable he'd been. He pulls off the socks and drops them like they're on fire.

"I'm sorry," Lin whispers.

"Don't be. I've got a new family." He meets her eyes with a smile. "And, somehow, I remember all of that too."

"Your neurologist is going to be thrilled."

He shrugs again. "If it lasts. I could just as well wake up tomorrow and not know you from God."

"Well, if you don't know who I am, I'll be sure to remind you," Lin promises.

"Thanks, Momma Lin." He steps closer and gives her a tight hug. "Now if you don't mind, I'm going to bed. I'm exhausted."

"Night, Tim." She moves to the side so he can head downstairs. "And hey. Take Huan's bed, will you? I want you to feel safe. Somehow, I don't think the living room's going to do that for you right now."

"Are you sure?" He runs a hand through his hair. "Wouldn't want to intrude."

"I'll just wash the sheets tomorrow. Or would you rather I set up a futon in the game room?"

His smile is hesitant. "Yes?"

"I have to warn you, it's monstrously uncomfortable, or I would've offered it to you before making you stay on the couch."

"I'm so tired, I could sleep on pavement. I don't care. You sure it's not too late for you? I feel like I've already caused enough trouble for one night."

"First of all, none of this is your fault." Her no-nonsense tone is convincing; he really wants to believe her. "And no, you want the futon, so the futon is the game plan. You may be exhausted, but I'm not. It's still early—barely 22:00 hours."

"Wait, really?" It feels like it's the middle of the night.

"Really."

She follows him downstairs and rustles around in some closets while he grabs his phone charger, his journal, and a pen. When he meets her in the game room, she's already got the bed folded out. They put the fitted sheet on and then Tim waves her off. "I literally don't care if I have a blanket. It's plenty warm down here."

"No problem." She points to the recliners he and Huan sit in to game; there's a top sheet and several blankets folded in a neat pile on the chair closest to him. "In case you change your mind."

"Thanks. Night Momma Lin."

She smiles and turns to go up the stairs. "Night Tim."

He'd intended to write about everything that happened before going to bed, but he's out of it before he even manages to write out the date.

#

Rosie had come home while Tim was bawling in the shower. Her face was drawn and her breath smelled like whiskey. "What happened here?" she'd asked, but then she held up her hands. "Actually, you know what, I've had enough unexpected bullshit for one day."

"You can say that again!" Lin agreed.

"You can hit me with whatever this is tomorrow. Long as we're safe?" She pointed to the trash bag covering up the empty window pane in the front door.

"Safe enough. The people behind the damage are long gone, and I made the cop promise to send someone to drive by in the night a few times, make sure we aren't going to have any new problems."

"Great. Then I'm turning in." And with that, she'd disappeared up the stairs.

Now that Tim's safely in bed, Lin finds herself wondering what happened. How Pania was involved. When Rosie left the house early that afternoon, it was for a work presentation that she was excited about— enough so that she mentioned it to Lin. *Oh no.* What if she has to leave soon? While the two women agreed they aren't going to pursue anything while Rosie is living under Lin's roof, Lin also knows that going back home would mean being at least an hour's drive apart, maybe more. Being unable to drive makes that distance feel insurmountable... maybe it feels that way to Rosie too.

She heads upstairs and raps lightly on Rosie's door. "You in the mood for a chat?"

The door creaks open. "Not really. Come in anyway?"

Lin crosses the threshold and eases the door closed behind her. The bedside lamp gives off a warm yellow glow, but it's not soft enough to hide the turmoil in Rosie's eyes. "Can we just hold each other? As in, cuddle, with no expectations of anything else?"

She nods. They wrap their arms around each other and Rosie nuzzles into Lin's shoulder. They stay that way until dawn bleeds through the rattan bamboo blinds.

Chapter 24: Room for Living

When there's a knock on the door the next morning, Lin hopes Tim's mom and abuser are still in custody. She checks her phone and sees a message from Pania. *Didn't want you to think I was avoiding you. Breakfast, on me?* She heads downstairs, glad she'd already done her hair, and opens the door. Pania is wearing a loose yellow cardigan over a white blouse and a pair of dark blue jeans that flatter her curves.

"What happened here?" Pania asks, pointing at the wrecked door.

"You know, it was a long night. Also, I don't think I've ever seen you in jeans before."

Pania looks down as if noticing her outfit for the first time. "Hm. Yeah, not my favorite. Laundry day."

"Well, they suit you." Lin motions for her to come in. "I do feel like I should warn you, Rosie is upstairs. She usually comes down around this time."

Pania's shoulders tense, and she takes a deep breath. "Right. Thanks for that."

"Did you have somewhere in mind to grab breakfast? There's a quiet little café at the end of the street that serves a great fry-up."

"Yeah, we can go there if you want to." They stand awkwardly around the living room.

"Do you want to?" Lin asks.

Pania shrugs. "I just wanted to make sure we were okay."

"We?" Lin echoes.

"You know, after last night." Pania's eyes are trained on her hands.

"Yeah, I wanted to make sure of that too." Lin catches her eye and smiles. "You uh, don't hate me for snogging your ex, do you?"

Pania laughs. "Please. After thirty years, I'm pretty sure the statute of limitations has passed." She takes a finger and moves a stray curl behind Lin's ear.

"What's going on here?" The two women turn and see Rosie standing at the bottom of the stairs, eyebrows knit in confusion. She's still wearing her pajamas.

Lin takes a step back and stammers. "Uh, nothing. This isn't—um. Good morning. Pania's here."

"I see that." She crosses her arms and stares at Pania. "So, it's not enough for you to have ruined my faith in humanity, now you have to try and steal my girl, too?"

Lin's cheeks warm at being called Rosie's girl but the feeling fades fast. Before the situation devolves into a fight, Lin speaks up. "I thought we agreed nothing could happen right now. But it sounds like you've decided all sorts of things for us without consulting me."

"Really?" Rosie's voice is thick with emotion. "We hit the pause button, not the stop button. Was that not clear?"

"No," Lin whispers. She's aware of Pania's gaze burning into her very soul and she uses all of her willpower to keep her voice and expression level. "That was not clear."

"I'm not stealing anyone. Just making good with Lin."

"Yeah? And when were you gonna make good with me, huh?"

"I tried last night, and you told me, 'Not now'—or did you forget about that bit?" Pania sets her cane against the couch, which is still out of place from last night, and crosses her own arms. "I've wanted to apologize ever since I left you there. I was literally in shock—it took me an hour or more before I even realized I had the stupid shifter knob in my hand. But you think that decision didn't kill me? Hasn't been killing me every day since?" Her eyes fill with tears. "All this time, I thought you were dead. That it was my fault."

"How are you making this apology about you right now? If I died that night, it would have been your fault."

The words strike Pania like a blow, and she grabs onto the back of the couch. "I—I was just trying to save you. I'm so, so sorry."

#

Tim wakes up to an enormous knot in his shoulder and yelling in the living room above him. He freezes, thinking Miriam and Phil have returned. But then he hears the women's voices and realizes something else is happening. Something that, despite his initial relief, still doesn't sound good.

He's not sure how Lin got in the middle of everything, though he can take a guess. He decides to wait it out on the basement stairs so that he doesn't get dragged in too. Whatever Pania did sounds really messed up. *Wait, I haven't heard about that before, have I?* Luckily, he'd thought to grab his journal before sneaking up the carpeted steps, so he thumbs through the entries while the women work through their weird love triangle bullshit. But no, his memory hasn't failed him this time. In fact, all of his memories are still intact—from yesterday all the way back to boyhood. He takes a moment to feel grateful, but only a moment.

Pania's sobbing out an emotional apology, and Rosie still hasn't said a word about her own secret. *Come on*

Rosie, don't hold out on her. Don't make me get involved. The yelling stops, and he can no longer follow the conversation from behind the closed door. *Well, here goes nothing.*

\#

The tears she's been holding in for decades all decide to spill out at once. She's aware that Sal—err, Rosie—is unimpressed, that she thinks this is all some sort of self-indulgent show, but there's nothing Pania can do to stem the tide.

"I think about how much I would differently if I could go back every damn day. I'm sorry that I was so impulsive, that I put you in danger, that I wasn't—" she stifles a nervous giggle—"that I wasn't a better unlicensed, tipsy teenage driver. I just... you rolled off the bed and I saw all the scars Kevin gave you, and I couldn't bear to let you live like that anymore."

Sal's stern stance is undercut by her wobbling lip. Her voice trembles as she speaks. "But that's what I don't understand. You *did* leave me to live like that. Only, you know, with a nasty concussion and minus the girl who made all those days bearable."

"You don't have to forgive me," she says, looking into Sal's eyes and begging her silently to do just that anyway. "I haven't, so why should you? I just—I need you to know that the way I treated you is my life's biggest regret. I'd give anything to make things right between us, but—" she stops to sniffle— "but I understand. It's impossible."

Sal nods and rubs at her wet eyes with a closed fist. "Yeah. Sure feels that way."

A door creaks open behind Sal. Tim clears his throat and stares her down.

"What?" Sal snaps. "Can't you see we're in the middle of something?"

"Oh, I can see, Rosie," he replies. "And I want to make sure you tell Pania what she deserves to know."

Rosie bites down on her lip. *Is he going to bully her into accepting my apology?* Tim may not be her favorite person in the world, but she appreciates the way he's trying to stand up for her now... even if it's a bit juvenile.

"You don't have to forgive me, even if Timmy insists."

Rosie snaps her head towards Pania. "I know." But the anger has seeped out of her posture. She uncrosses her arms and clasps her hands, almost like she's the one who needs forgiveness.

"Well?" Tim pushes. When she's silent, he turns to Pania. "She's acting so injured and blameless, but she's hiding things from you. Things you need to know."

Rosie blinks away her tears and says the one thing Pania never expected. "He makes it sound so horrible." Uneasy laughter tumbles from her lips. "It wasn't intentional or anything. You uh, remember all those photos I made you take with me when we were a new thing?"

"Of course," Pania responds. *Where is this going?*

"I burned most of them after that night, but I did keep one." She swallows hard. "At first, just because I missed you, you know? But then, I started to miss the happiness we had. It was so fleeting, but it was the highlight of my time in that wretched town. Later, I told myself I didn't want to forget, to fall into the mistake of either idealizing the good times or demonizing what we had.

"Over the years, I've compared every relationship I've ever had against the litmus test of the happiness in that photo... I've used it to remind myself to never, ever put myself in a position where someone could hurt me the way you did." Sal leans against the bottom edge of the railing and sighs heavily. "Anyway, the point is, I kept it because it mattered to me. We were holding our hands up—the ones Miss Altro caned—and sticking out our tongues at the camera. It was the ultimate act of defiance. But more importantly, it also showed your birthmark."

"My birthmark," Pania says flatly.

"Yeah, the bird-shaped one on your right arm."

"I know what my birthmark looks like, thank you very much. What does it matter though?"

Sal looks up at the ceiling, exposing the slender lines of her neck. "I'm getting to that. Um, so, in the last few years, I've been working with different Aboriginal peoples on getting funding for language classes, yeah? With so many folks spread out and in remote areas, I've been relying on video calls to get to know people, screen applicants for their ability to meet grant requirements, that kind of thing.

"One call, the guy on the other end of the call was obsessed with that picture of us—I had it on the wall in my office. I thought he was creeping, so when I talked to him again, I hid the photo. But he kept asking about it. About you." Sal rubs her forearms with the palms of her hands, as though warding off a sudden chill. "Pania, that guy recognized your birthmark."

The words don't make sense in Pania's brain. "What do you mean, he recognized my birthmark?"

"I found your family. Your birth family." Pania is dumbstruck. Rosie adds, "You belong to Bigambul Country."

She blinks rapidly. Her brain is moving so fast, she can't think straight, much less speak. Her elation is tainted by fury and complicated by what that might mean for her identity, for her place within the Minyangbal. She's still processing Rosie's words when Tim speaks up and demands Rosie to keep going. "There's more?" Pania's heart is pounding against her chest. How could there be more?

"This um, this wasn't a recent discovery. I didn't know where you were—" Tim interrupts her with an aggressive cough, and her face reddens. "I just—I was still so angry. I'm sorry, Pania."

Her brain finally has a single angle to fixate on, and the focus unlocks her ability to speak. "Wait, wait. How long ago was this?"

"Just a couple of years. Three, maybe? Five?"

Pania doesn't remember standing—which is unusual for a woman with balance issues, but the shock and the anger within are overwhelming her in ways she didn't even know emotions could. The room is closing in and she has to get out. After mumbling something (*probably utter gibberish*), she hobbles towards the door.

Maybe intent matters after all, she thinks as she settles on the front steps. A lone magpie skitters along the edge of the sidewalk across the street, stopping to investigate some leaf litter and then cocking an ear towards the ground. It must not hear anything good; soon, it's hopping on top of a mailbox and canvasing the street. Pania focuses on the bird's movements instead of facing the overwhelming chaos swirling in her mind.

The door behind her cracks open and Lin pops onto the front porch, alone. "I can't imagine how you're feeling right now. Mind if I sit?" She points to the other side of the step.

Pania motions for her to go ahead, but keeps her eyes trained on the maggie. Lin must notice. "Glad to see the little bugger being quiet. Must get all its screeching and laughing out of its system while it's sitting in front of my window every morning."

"And how can you know it's that magpie tormenting you, hm?"

"How can you know it isn't that magpie?" Lin asks in return. The two women fall silent. After a few minutes, Lin pats Pania's knee and heads back inside with a mention of needing breakfast. Her jumbled emotions return to the surface once she's alone again, but they feel a hair less overwhelming than before. It's not much, but it's a start.

Chapter 25: Four Months Later

Tim's memory is becoming more reliable as the weeks pass, but living alone doesn't just scare him. The idea of an empty flat utterly repulses him, even as he's afraid of becoming dependent on anyone the way he'd been dependent on Jenny. "I'd hate not seeing you every day, Momma Lin," he says before every viewing he attends with his support coordinator Josh. His waffling is quickly compounded by a pandemic-accelerated housing crisis. Now, he's not sure he can afford to get off of Lin's couch. At the least, he managed to move into the guest room after Rosie was finally ready and able to move back home.

His despondence over moving out of Lin's lightens when she gets licensed as a direct care worker; she promises to follow him wherever he goes. "But, you know, let's go somewhere over the border—I've gotta sell this house and get into Queensland." Huan's school and Jian's flat are both over the border, which has caused no small amount of inconvenience between hours-long lines, frequent confusion over how she can cross the border without driving herself, and the battle to make sure her son still has both of his parents in his life.

Weeks drift into months. Tim feels like they're at a housing stalemate. "It's so stupid," he complains at breakfast one morning. "Pandemic? They should just cut out the extra letters and call it a panic."

"Very funny, but it's still dangerous—just be glad we aren't dealing with thousands of deaths, like Hubei, China or the entire country of Italy."

"I know you're right, but ugh. What a buzz kill. We don't have TBI group anymore, I can't go out to the club, can't even take a girl out to dinner. Stinks." *Not like I'm ready to start dating, but still,* he mentally adds. *I do miss that stupid support group.*

Lin rolls her eyes and walks out of the kitchen. Tim starts to clean up breakfast, a chore he was eager to take on regularly so he could tell himself he's not just a bum. A few minutes later, Lin rushes back with her phone on speaker. "Can you repeat that for Tim?"

"Sure," Pania's voice comes through the speaker loud and clear. "The executor of the old bogan's estate called me. Apparently, there's a small plot of land that he very vaguely willed to the 'good of the TBI group'. Now, there's nothing on the land and it's a bit off the beaten path, so don't get your hopes up. I think he and Michael used to go camping there. It'll need a couple of tiny houses or maybe an RV to make it habitable. But—I figured it should be offered to either or both of the two of you and Sam agreed. If neither of you want it, it'll be sold and the money donated to TBI research at GCUH."

Lin's eyes are bright. "Text me the location so we can take a peek at it on the internet. We'll talk about it and get back to you. Okay if we have a decision by the end of the week?"

"The property's sat there this long," Pania replies. "It can wait until you decide what to do."

Tim knows before Pania hangs up that as long as the property's across the border, then he wants to make the leap. If not for the light in Lin's eyes, then for the faint stirring of hope in his own heart.

#

The coronavirus pandemic may have slowed down Pania's physical reunion with her family, but they've begun a nightly video call ritual that she cherishes deeply. And today's the day they can finally meet in person. Elaine's agreed to drive her out to Bigambul Country. "I only wish we could have more of the family there," Pania had said on the video call with her parents the night before. Thanks to pandemic-related restrictions on gatherings, Pania will only be able to see her parents, a cousin living in their household, and another aunt, uncle, and cousin who live on the Queensland side of the border that cuts through Bigambul Country. Interstate travel restrictions block the rest of the family from coming, despite being less than five kilometers away on the other side of the Macintyre River. Recreational stops in the Outback are also out of the question for travelers from the coast, so she and Elaine had packed lunches they could eat in the car.

Her and Rosie's relationship may still be a bumpy, hesitant one, but they text a few times a week and are at least starting to feel like friends again. Pania spots a sign on the highway announcing a turnoff towards the town where they met. Instinctively, Pania raises her scarred hand and sticks out her tongue at the sign. She snaps a selfie and sends it to Rosie. *Glad we both got out of there.*

Rosie texted back a photo of herself in the same pose. She's standing in front of the burnt-out shell of her house back in Richmond Valley, which she'd avoided going back to until just a few weeks ago. Pania tries not to dwell on why she waited so long to leave Lin's house and go back home. Rosie claimed it was still easier to work at Lin's than in a hotel room back home, that her boss preferred having her close to the Queensland border for checking in with the Yugambeh. Never mind that the border's a proper nightmare she hasn't crossed even once in the last quarter.

A couple of hours later, the car is pulling into a dusty dirt driveway and all thoughts of Rosie vanish. Pania's breath catches in her throat at the sight of the worn front porch from her few scattered memories of home.

Her family is there as promised, dutifully spaced 1.5 meters apart, waiting for her. She's finally home.

#

Other than the paperwork she fills out for Tim's supports, Lin's day-to-day life hasn't changed much since Matt helped her get into direct care work. Until she manages to cross the border to live in Queensland (or the pandemic restrictions ease), she's not going to take on any more clients. Just Tim.

The situation suits her; it gives her time to process Rosie's departure and to figure out where they are headed... if, indeed, they are headed anywhere. Though the three women didn't make a habit of being in the same room at the same time, Lin couldn't help but notice the way Pania and Rosie looked at each other on the few occasions it did happen. She doesn't want to get in the way of a romance three decades in the making.

Even aside from feeling like a third wheel, she's discovered joy in being single. No one complains when she paints her room the most outrageous shade of yellow she could find to honor her moon sign, or when she hand-paints her sun and moon signs in black paint on the ceiling. Even if it will need to be painted again ahead of a sale, the joy it brings her every night makes the time invested worthwhile.

She and Tim spend the days after Pania's call figuring out where they can find tiny homes. "Look at this layout! Plenty of room for landscaping. Plus, we have enough of a footprint to place two tiny homes so we each have our own space," Lin gushes. Tim's face falls at the suggestion, so she adds, "And, there should be plenty of money left over from the eventual sale of the house, plus yours and my savings. We should hire a contractor to come in and build a little covered veranda to connect them. You know, so we have bug-free outdoor space and an airy breakfast nook to share."

Tim grins. "Now that's what I'm talking about!"

#

Pania's crying before she even gets out of the car. Her parents come down to greet her. Her dad is wearing a stained baseball cap; bushy gray hair escapes from the edges and his dark eyes are shining with tears. Her mother moves like a dancer, swooshing towards her in an earth-toned ankle-length skirt, bare arms and calloused hands outstretched towards her.

Together, they envelope Pania in a tight hug that begins to heal her deepest wounds. She cries harder. When she can finally speak, her words are muffled by her mother's shoulder. *My mother!* It still feels so unreal. "You never gave up on me," Pania says. "Thank you."

"Giving up—that was never an option," her dad whispers in her ear. Her hair, her cheeks are wet with his tears.

"We're so proud of you, Pania," her mother sniffles. She pulls out of the hug long enough to motion for Elaine to join them. "You must be Elaine. Thank you for looking out for my baby when I couldn't—your ancestors and ours are all smiling down on you."

There are many more happy tears that day, rivaled only by the laughter and joy their reunion has sparked. When she and Elaine get back in the car to go home, Pania feels a dozen years younger. The soul-rending loneliness that she's always disguised as a need for independence is simply gone. In its wake is a growing sense of belonging and interconnectedness. The shape of her soul has long been hidden in darkness, but now it's brilliantly lit up for her and anyone else she lets in to see.

#

It takes time, but by the end of October, Tim and Lin are safely settled in their own tiny homes, an airy covered veranda separating their two homes.

Huan isn't so sure about the setup at first, but a few weekends spent camping with five of his buddies in the back of the lot convince him it's not all bad. Lin's not sure, but she suspects Tim slipped the guys a case of Great Northern lager to help with their first impressions.

The bus route's a bit far, so Lin buys a couple of bikes with baskets to make grocery shopping less of a hassle. But she would have walked ten kilometers uphill through a tropical cyclone for groceries if it meant being in the same state as Huan; she makes a silent pact never to complain out loud about the inconveniences of tiny home life.

The black paint and the thin brush resurface. It takes her over a month, but she paints the entire Zodiac on the ceiling above her bed. The night after she finally finishes, her dreams are as full of light as the galaxy itself.

#

The gift of having her family and her cultural identity restored changes Pania's outlook fundamentally. After several visits to her parents' ranch, she decides to let go of her lingering bitterness about the past. *I'm done being mad at you Sal,* she texts.

There's no reply for hours. When her phone finally dings, she finds a simple, yet powerful, response: *Me too.* Pania smiles at her phone, then turns back to the novel she's reading. A few minutes later, though, she gets another text. *My boss wants us to have a presence in every state to eliminate all the issues we've been having with border crossings. Guess who's moving to the Gold Coast?*

You might have a tough time finding housing right now, Pania texts back, her fingers typing a mile a minute. *But you have a place to stay with me, if you want.* She holds her breath after hitting send, but Rosie's reply is almost instant.

Yes please.

When she arrives a few weeks later, the two women embrace for the first time since they were starstruck teenagers.

Pania makes sure to hang their high school photo right next to the bed.

Acknowledgements

Self-publishing is not for the weak. I'm so grateful to everyone in my life who has given me strength as I continue on my writing journey.

To Gary, for being an amazing partner and such a dedicated dad. To Audrey, for reminding me of the importance of books and stories.

To Abigail, for being my cover magician. To Mom, for workshopping large-scale plot problems with me and for all of your support with iHeart Oswego. To Devin, for your incredible attention to detail and your sharp editorial eye. To Carol, Nicole, and the Wandering Wordsmiths for offering community and friendship in what can otherwise be an isolating field.

I'm also eternally grateful to you, dear reader. Thank you for going on this journey with me.

About the Author

Bekkah Frisch believes in the power of bravery and authenticity to make the world a better place. Her writing invites readers on a journey to discover radical empathy and tragic optimism.

Bekkah holds a Bachelor of Arts in English from Wells College, where she graduated magna cum laude.

Her debut novel, The Great Quiet, earned the 2024 Silver IPPY Award for Aotearoa/Pacific Rim Regional Fiction and was hailed by Kirkus Reviews as an "ambitious, moving saga." She has been profiled by LA Weekly, among other publications.

She lives in Fulton, NY with her husband, daughter, and their two lovable, untrainable dogs. Bekkah also owns and operates iHeart Oswego, a media corporation based in Central New York.

For updates, visit:

bekkahfrisch.com
Instagram / Facebook / Threads: @authorbekkah
Bluesky: @authorbekkah.bsky.social

Did you love this book? Please leave a review!

GoodReads | Amazon | StoryGraph

Book Club Guide – Sample Questions

Note: questions 8 through 10 include spoilers for the final third of the book.

1. The Yugambeh people use multiple names for their nation, including Minyangbal and Nganduwal. They believe using only one name would oversimplify their people's complex identity. Discuss your own name and its variations. Consider the implications of someone using a nickname for you instead of your legal name, and the ever-evolving role of name changes in marriages. How do all of these variations impact your own personal identity in various social contexts?

2. While Pania is not part of the Stolen Generation of Aboriginal Australians who grew up on missions, she is still effectively separated from her family and culture by the foster care system. Discuss the pros and cons of the foster system in your own locale. What kinds of harm can come from the foster system? How can we work to mitigate those harms?

3. In Australia, Aboriginal children are placed in foster care at disproportionately higher rates than those of white European heritage, even today. In part, this is due to culturally different expectations of parenting and resulting misunderstandings with care workers: Aboriginal children often spend extended amounts of time with aunts, uncles, and other family members outside of their parents' home because of differing perspectives on nuclear family and stability. The differing rates are also partially due to higher levels of poverty and generational trauma among Aboriginal

Australians, which can impact the level of care that children receive at home. In what ways does the Australian foster system improve the lives of Aboriginal people? In what ways does it make their lives worse?

4. Tim says a few hurtful things about Pania in Chapter 4, calling her an "angry Abo lady". Have you ever said something hurtful or racist without intending to, or perhaps heard someone else making hurtful remarks about a third person? How did you make it right? Would you do anything different if you were in a similar situation today?

5. Lin is an immigrant to Australia and faces racism during the COVID-19 pandemic due to her ethnicity. How does your community treat immigrants? In what way does fear impact their reception?

6. In the scene on the beach at the end of Chapter 15, Tim tells his buddy Brian to "just forget" about his role in Tim's four-wheeler accident. What was Tim's motivation? Have you ever felt burdened by someone who wronged you? How did you react?

7. What does the title mean to you? Have you ever gone through an experience—whether an injury or not—that fundamentally changed your personality or outlook on life?

8. When Tim discovers Jenny's betrayal, he becomes homeless, even though he does not sleep in the street. Discuss how real-world victims of abuse cope with the risks of leaving an abuser. In what ways can

people in their lives support them? How can the economic and emotional impacts of abuse follow survivors, even long after they leave?

9. Tim finds himself in a cycle of abusive relationships. He escapes his mother and Phil, only to end up with Jenny, who is more manipulative and subtle in her abuse. Many survivors of abuse find themselves in similar situations. Why do you think this happens? How can survivors break the cycle?

10. Towards the end of the novel, a love triangle emerges. Who did you want to end up together, and why? Did you agree with the pairing that emerged?

A Note on Type

The text has been set in Atkinson Hyperlegible, a font developed in 2019 in a collaboration between the Braille Institute of America and Applied Design Works. The font is designed for those with visual impairments, with each letter maximally distinguishable from every other letter.

This font was chosen to enhance the visibility for people with low vision and other visual processing disorders.